On His Terms

Book 1

Anastasia Hill

Dedication

*To all the ladies out there, if he doesn't call you 'baby girl'
while you're on your knees sucking his dick,
find yourself another boyfriend.
Preferably, a billionaire.*

Trigger warnings

Dear Reader,

This book will have some intense themes, I'd like you to be aware of before you jump into this story. If you need any clarification about this list, please feel free to contact me at anastasiahillauthor.com or via my social media platforms.

Triggers

Anal stimulation

BDSM (dominance and submission)

Bondage

Clamping

Degradation

Flogging

Forced proximity

Humiliation

Orgasm denial

Praise kink

Sex toys

Spanking

Unprotected sex (no condom)

Prologue

"Don't you want to hear my terms?"

"I do."

"You know what slaves are, don't you?"

"I-I do," Maria said quietly.

"Then it won't be hard for you to behave and obey my orders, will it, Maria?" Sam purred. He was so amused that he couldn't hold back a smile. An unkind smile.

Maria was silent. She looked at Sam with wide-open eyes and nodded gently. The mask of calmness was still on her face, but her heart was pounding very fast. The girl threw all her strength into listening.

She tried to catch every word because even one phrase could play a cruel joke on her. But it couldn't get much worse than that. Or could it?

Slaves obey their Masters at all times and in all places. Sam would decide everything for Maria: what to wear, what to eat, where she would sleep, and, of course, sex and sessions. She was afraid of that last part. Because even though she had personal taboos, she would have to go through everything with this man.

"All right, I'll give you the right to one safe word. If it comes to the second one, you can pack your bags right away," Sam continued lazily.

"I have taboos..."

"So, keep them to yourself," Sam cut her off abruptly. His threatening tone betrayed his irritation.

Maria decided not to argue. She needed this deal desperately.

"You must be ready for anything. Are you ready, Maria?"

Chapter 1

"Maria!" Mr. O'Dell growled with irritation.

"Coming, Dad!" a cheerful voice rang from the second floor. Not a minute later, a petite girl quickly descended the stairs. Her dark black hair was flying in different directions. A short white dress showed off her perfect legs. "I'm here!"

"Maria, I told you not to be late," her father tilted his head to the side in irritation.

Maria defiantly pouted her lips and pointed at the old man's watch, "I'm on time! Even a minute early!"

"All right, my dear Miss Punctuality," Mr. O'Dell softened. For the smile of his only daughter, he was ready to sacrifice all the money in the world.

It's a pity that there was almost nothing left to sacrifice...

"Mom! How do you like my dress? It's from the last collection!"

"Maria, you should say latest," the girl's father corrected.

"Come on, Dad. I don't believe in these things," Maria wrinkled her face in a funny grimace. The girl really did not believe in bad omens. At most, she read a horoscope if it appeared on her feed.

"You should listen to your father," the girl's mother smiled sweetly. She was in her mid-fifties, still looking beautiful as ever. Even health problems did not affect this strong-willed woman. Light gray hair gave her a special charm, and thinness, caused by the excess of medicine in her life, made Lena appear a bit younger.

"Okay," Maria rolled her eyes. She didn't want to argue with her parents today. The girl had a meeting with her friends, and they had planned her favorite activity, shopping.

"So, girls," O'Dell called his favorite women affectionately. "I have an important meeting today."

"Okay, Dad," Maria nodded indifferently, staring at her phone, and went to the kitchen.

"Will Paul be there too?" Lena asked cautiously.

"Yeah," the man changed his tone. He understood perfectly well what his wife was getting at.

Paul was a business partner of the O'Dell family. He and Andrew O'Dell started from scratch and grew into a successful holding company. The company was mainly involved in commercial real estate throughout England and America.

Younger than Andrew by a couple of years, Paul always seemed too cold and distant. He had a reserved look. Thin lips, always pinched, long skinny fingers, and a height of two meters made him handsome despite his fifty-two years old age. Fancy haircuts and tailored suits were his thing. Paul never spared money for himself. But he spared it for others.

Paul would often quarrel with Andrew. Paul demanded to cut wages for lousy work. To deprive people of bonuses and fire them for the slightest mistakes. Andrew always stood on the side of the workers. For this, he was loved and respected, while Paul was simply feared. There was no respect for him in the company.

Andrew, always kind and cheerful, looked like Santa Claus: short, gray-haired, with a big funny nose and an impressively big belly, resulting from his beloved wife's home-cooked meals. All that was missing was a red hat and a sleigh with reindeer.

"Try not to give him the floor," the wife muttered under her nose.

"Lena! Stop it! Paul is a good man! We've been working together for so many years," Andrew began to justify his business partner.

"All right, all right," Lena retreated. "So what's the meeting about?"

"Sam Williams is here," Andrew said, panting. At the mention of this surname, the man's cheeks flushed red. "We'll negotiate..."

Andrew wanted to add something else, but a phone call interrupted their conversation.

"The driver is in place. I'll be late. Don't wait for me."

"Good luck."

Kissing his cheek, Lena drew a cross in the air for her beloved Andrew.

It was a strange habit instilled in her by her grandmother. Lena had spent her entire childhood in Europe with her grandmother. At the age of eleven, Lena moved to New York with her parents. She met Andrew in college. Since then, they have had their ups and downs, but they have always been together.

Lena agreed to leave in London with Andrew to support his business. She never regretted her decision. And now she was trying to believe in his actions.

"Mom," the girl's voice rang. "Have you seen the car keys?"

"I have," the woman replied with a stern voice as soon as the cheerful Maria returned to the hallway.

"Where? Alicia is waiting for me!"

"Go tell Alicia that she'll have to wait another hour."

"Why!?" the girl objected.

"I won't let you drive!"

"Mom..."

"Don't even start! You scratched the door and almost had an accident! And what if someone got hurt!?" Lena reprimanded her daughter.

"It's just a scratch! No one was hurt!" Maria began to whine.

"Maria! You're twenty-four years old! I was pregnant when I was your age! My father worked hard! And you!? You're on your phone day and night! I don't like your friends at all! Isn't that Alicia a drug addict!?" With her arms folded across her chest, her angry mother didn't back down.

Her daughter's most recent foolish behaviour cost her a new batch of pills three times a day after meals. Maria lost control of her car and crashed into a guardrail. She was lucky she was driving at night, and there were hardly any people on the street. Her father had to persuade the police long and to let his daughter go. Thankfully, she was at least sober. No substances were found in her blood.

That accident could have already been long forgotten, but it was Lena who picked up the phone that time. The seizure happened faster than the policeman had time to speak. She was quickly taken care of by paramedics. But that was not what upset Lena. Maria was turning into a spoiled, rich girl.

A nasty, selfish, rich girl. Those who make you feel sick. Her mom noticed she was getting that sickness. Although Maria, claiming the opposite, did not stop buying shoes and clothes from the latest collections of popular brands. Andrew never limited his daughter to money, which she eventually began to abuse.

On Lena's attempts to exalt her husband, he would just say that the little girl was still young and that they should let her have fun. Just like that, their "little girl" was twenty-four years old. Already went through acting school, school of noble maidens, dubious friends, and one broken car.

"Mom!" Maria rebelled, but from the formidable look of her mother, she quickly tampered her mood.

"Either take the bus or stay home!" Mom retorted with an adamant look on her face and headed for the backyard. The roses wouldn't water themselves, after all.

Maria wrinkled her face defiantly. Even the formidable Frau Marta, the teacher of the school of noble girls, could not wean her from this pernicious habit.

"Stop frowning!" Lena squealed without turning her head. She knew her girl too well.

Exhaling loudly, Maria decided that her dress would not survive the bus ride. She canceled the meeting, changed into her favorite biker shorts, put on an oversized T-shirt (three sizes bigger), and went to watch a TV series.

Maria spent the whole day watching her favorite shows. Luisa, the maid, would just constantly run to the girl with a new plate of food or a drink.

"Well, she is getting paid, after all," Maria would reason and justify her behavior.

She heard the doorbell very clearly. She often laughed that even the neighbors heard it; it was just that loud. Maria knew that her mother or Luisa would open the door, so she would never hurry downstairs.

But she did, this time.

The girl heard voices. Male voices.

Everything else happened as if in slow motion. Maria heard a loud thud. She'd heard it before as if something had fallen. Or rather, someone. The girl herself almost broke her neck, flying down the stairs. Luisa was already running around with ammonia. Lena lay in the hallway and did not move. The uninvited guests turned out to be policemen. One was helping Luisa, while the other was calling an ambulance.

With a loud swear, the girl drew everyone's attention. Kneeling beside her mother, Maria stared at everyone with glistening eyes and hissed at the men like a wild cat.

"What's going on here? Who are you!? What do you want!?" the girl shouted furiously.

"Calm down, now," one of the policemen said in a gruff voice. It was clear from the menacing look on his face that he was in charge. "Your father is at the station. All your property has been seized."

The girl blinked rapidly. White noise seemed to turn on in Maria's head. One more word, and she would be the one needing ammonia.

"Dad? At the station? Property has been seized? What's going on!?" she stammered, trying to recollect herself.

"Mr. Williams? Everything's under control. I'll keep you posted," the cop reported to someone and hung up the phone.

"Williams? Williams who!? Who do you think you're talking to!? Who is this Williams?" Maria had no idea who it was, but she already hated the stranger.

Chapter 2

Maria sat in the kitchen, nervously twirling her mug in her hands. She was not allowed to go with her mother to the hospital by the police, but Luisa kindly agreed. The girl tearfully saw off the ambulance. Luisa promised to write constantly about Lena's condition.

"You will stay in the house," that one very rude man monotonously repeated.

"You have no right! I demand a lawyer!" Maria shouted. It seemed to help in the movies, but the scowling cop sent her to the kitchen and threatened her with a trip to the station if she did not calm down.

Tea didn't work. The mess in her head only thickened. Maria tried to keep a straight face and not show her fear, but there was plenty of it. For the first time in her life, she was incredibly scared. The most interesting thing was that the girl thought about herself only when she was alone. Before that, she could not stop thinking about her mom and dad.

Andrew was not young, either. Although his health was better than his wife's, such stress gave its imprint. As for her mother,

Maria was unable to even bear the thought of her condition. The mere idea that her mom could leave them forever made her eyes well up.

Yes, she may be spoiled, but Maria loved her family dearly and was ready to stand for them.

For the first time in a very long time, she washed the cup herself and put it in the kitchen cupboard.

"Something must be done!" Maria repeated restlessly to herself. "Who the hell are you, Williams?" she cursed quietly.

Then it hit her. There was something that could help her in this situation… the Internet!

"Where are you going?" one of the cops asked. He was sitting in the hallway, not far from the door, staring at his phone. Not the best security, the girl noted.

"To my room."

"No funny business, young lady!" the man growled menacingly.

"No funny business," Maria quietly mocked him in her own way. No matter how many times she tried to get rid of this bad habit, in a state of anger or confusion, it would undoubtedly appear as her defense mechanism.

The laptop was lying on her bed. Quickly opening the browser, the girl began her search.

The query "Williams" gave her more than a thousand options. Quietly cursing, Maria realized that this was a rather popular surname. But her wit didn't let her down.

"Williams, O'Dell," she changed it quickly in the search. Voila!

Maria opened the first link and saw a photo that was taken last year. It showed her dad, Paul, and an unknown man. A devilishly handsome and mysterious blond man.

If Maria hadn't known that her father's arrest was his handiwork, she would have fallen for him for sure.

The fashionable hairstyle suited Mr. Williams very well. Because of the high quality of the photo, Maria could see his stunning blue eyes. The kind you could stare into all day long. A masculine forehead, sharp cheekbones, and a straight nose. His tall stature and probably gorgeous, pumped-up body made Williams look like a dream come true for all women.

But his eyes were intimidating. Not repulsive, but ambivalent.

"I almost want to kneel in front of him," Maria thought and then laughingly pushed the thought away.

"Samuel Williams, founder and owner of Williams Incorporated, has held talks with top real estate companies. According to..."

Maria didn't read any further. She opened a new tab and quickly typed in his first and last name.

Samuel Williams, 31 years old.

Originally from Sweden.

Not married.

No children.

Height: 6'5 ft

Nothing but the standard information. Maria dug through almost every query for his name. Nothing.

Returning to the first tab, the girl read the article, but she found nothing worthwhile. Just a businessman. Rich. Smart. Looks like a Greek god.

Maria clutched her head and moaned loudly. Nothing helped. The bitterness of her own defenselessness crawled into every cell of her body.

Luisa wrote a short message saying her mom was okay. Requests to call or contact her father in any way were firmly rebuffed.

Sitting in her room and glaring at the wall, Maria was feeling like a delinquent child; she was under house arrest.

A quiet melody tore her away from her exciting pastime.

"Hey, Mary! What's up, baby?" Alicia giggled merrily.

"Hi, Alicia," Maria replied quietly and sniffed her nose.

"Hey, are you crying? What's wrong!?"

"Alicia... I... I... I don't know what to do," the girl decided to finally vent to someone. Sobbing quietly, she told her friend what had happened.

Alicia listened to her attentively. She didn't interrupt her and tried to calm her down when Maria was sobbing uncontrollably.

"Everything will be all right!" she reassured her friend. "Have you seen this Williams-guy?"

"No! I don't know who he is!"

"I see," Alicia answered thoughtfully. "What did you say his full name was?"

"Samuel Williams," Maria sniffed. "Why do you need it? I didn't find anything on him. Only general information."

"I'm not going to search on the Internet. Or rather, I won't be the one searching," Alicia said cryptically.

"What are you planning? Isn't it dangerous? Alicia, don't—"

"Maria!" she interrupted her friend, "First, calm down. Secondly, I'm not as stupid as you think I am."

"I never thought you were stupid," Maria grumbled resentfully.

"Trust me. We'll find something on this Williams."

"Thank you, dear," Maria thanked her quietly and burst into a new wave of tears.

Early in the morning, her father returned home. Maria almost strangled the old man in a tight embrace.

"Daddy! Daddy!" like a little girl, she repeated.

The old man could hardly contain himself from getting emotional. But still dropped a meager tear at the sight of his pale daughter.

"Have you eaten?" Andrew asked warmly.

He knew very well that in stressful situations, Maria, like her mother, stopped eating and slept badly. She turned into a walking ghost, just as pale and lifeless.

"Yes," she answered too quickly, which made him suspect something.

"Liar."

"I am," Maria saw no point in justifying herself.

"Maria..."

"I was waiting for you! Have you seen Mom? How is she?" the girl quickly changed the subject.

"No," the man lowered his head guiltily. Maria saw how difficult it was for him to speak. Tears clouded his eyes again. "But the doctor said that her condition has stabilized," Andrew added on a more positive note.

They ate in silence. Maria was reluctantly picking at her salad, but in order not to upset her father, she forced herself to eat.

Andrew, on the other hand, was deep in his thoughts. He frowned his eyebrows and rubbed the bridge of his nose. Maria thought for a long time whether to ask him about their situation, but her father, as if reading her thoughts, spoke first.

"Maria, I'm sorry for what happened," her father looked guiltily at his only daughter.

"Dad, what do you mean?" the girl asked with a surprised look.

"My dear, all of this," he drew a circle in the air, pointing at everything that surrounded them, "is no longer ours."

"How so?"

"I've lost everything. The company, all the money. We don't have anything anymore. I'm sorry, my daughter."

From the shock and bitter truth, Maria got a headache. Looking at her father, the girl could hardly perceive reality.

They lost everything. They were nobodies. Although not really—everyone knew about them. Their shame would be the most talked about news in London.

"What about..." Maria stammered. She didn't know what to ask. About the house? Cars? Clothes? Mom?

Mom! Who would pay for her treatment now?

The girl took a couple of deep breaths to calm down. She couldn't care less about shoes and clothes now. Yes, it was a shame, but Mom's health was more important than any brand. Her mother often joked about Maria and reproached her for being a pretentious rich girl. But now, Maria clearly understood that the most important thing in her life was family.

"Dad, everything will be fine! We'll think of something! I will think of something," the fragile girl said in a confident voice.

Andrew cried a bit once again. He saw his little Maria in a different light today. He was glad that she did not start begging for money but accepted it with pride and exuded support.

"Can you explain what happened?" Maria asked gently.

"Sam Williams."

"What do you mean? He did this?"

"Yes. As it turned out, he had been buying up shares in our company for a long time. Some of his men stole important documents. Documents with dirt on us. Don't get me wrong, I don't do shady business, but big corporations always have their sins. Sam recognized ours and used it against us."

"And Paul?" Maria asked. She didn't think much of that man. He was always throwing strange looks in her direction. Vulgar. Hungry. Maria tried not to think about it, but silly thoughts still popped into her head.

"He didn't show up for the meeting, and then I got arrested right in the restaurant. I couldn't call him. I'd spent my right to make a phone call on a lawyer."

"Mm-hmm," Maria said, deep in thought. "You don't think he's in on it with Sam, do you?"

"Maria! How can you say that? Paul is my partner; he would never do such a thing. It's his company too," her father said indignantly.

Maria only shook her head. Dad always defended him. Called him his best friend. Except that neither Lena nor Maria believed in that friendship.

The phone rang in her pocket. Looking at the screen, Maria quickly said goodbye to her Dad and ran to her room.

"Well, you found anything?" she went straight to the point.

"I'm glad to hear from you too," Alicia snorted teasingly.

"I'm sorry, I was just waiting for your call."

"And so I called..."

"Come on, Alicia!"

"Hush, tiger!" her friend chuckled. "Anyway, that Williams of yours is a real piece of work..."

Chapter 3

"Mr. Williams, please follow me."

A blonde girl with gorgeous curves wiggled her hips, almost hitting the walls of the narrow, dark hallway. Bowing his head, Sam gazed nostalgically at her white curls. No, they are way different...

"Is there anything else I can do for you?" Raising too many false eyelashes at the man, the girl bit her lower lip.

"No," Sam nodded dryly in her direction.

Just another promiscuous girl. She might be able to satisfy his hunger a little, but he didn't need temporary liaisons. For one thing, she looked shabby. Who knows how many cocks have been inside her. Sam didn't have time to heal from questionable ladies. Plus, he was in the mood for a good blow job and a little dominance tonight.

The strippers at the Rabbit Hole were great Submissives. However, they didn't realize it themselves. He would command them to obey. The perfect tandem he'd been missing these past couple of weeks.

Without a steady partner, Sam often left himself mentally exhausted. Only in his case, it was the other way around: the man worked himself to exhaustion, and everyone was affected by his bad mood. When he realized that he had no strength left, he came here—to the Rabbit Hole.

The girls here were quick to agree to "extra" services for an extra couple of hundred pounds. The owner of the institution knew about Sam's peculiarity, as he himself was a Dominant. Every time Sam would choose a new girl for himself. Quiet, skillful, and compliant.

Get on her knees? No problem.

Deep throat blowjob? Gladly.

Speak only when Sam told her to? That's fine.

The Rabbit Hole girls were a bit of a throwback. But Sam had long considered finding a permanent partner. That, as it turned out, was not so easy to manage. All the BDSM clubs in London knew Sam. Everyone also knew how smart and demanding he was as a Master.

A handsome blond on the outside but a demon on the inside. At first, all the Subs were almost pulling each other's hair out, so eager to go to his session. But as time went on, they started shunning him like he was a leper. Yeah, subspace and the best orgasm of their lives were assured for everyone. But when it came to punishment, Sam had no regrets.

He knew how to inflict a special kind of pain. Not physical, but moral pain. It turned girls inside out. Shredded in the meat grinder of their own thoughts and suffering. At the same time, Sam would be enjoying himself. Sam never crossed the line, but even that was enough to scare all the sane Subs away from him.

The second important problem was his work. Too much traveling, not only around the country but around the world. Not every Sub would agree to a constant life of living out of suitcases. It wasn't hard for Sam to provide for a girl, but he couldn't tolerate any insubordination outside the sessions. Quick to get annoyed and tear up the contract. He'd pay a penalty for the inconvenience and send the Sub on her way.

Today was one of those days when everything was annoying. Things were falling apart.

How long has it been since the last session? A week? Two? When he thought about his little experiment with Nina, Max, and Blackwood, his pants felt tight. His cock was filling up with blood at a disastrous rate, and he wanted to get off. Not every day you get to have a threesome with a gorgeous girl and two of your best friends.

Just as Sam was pouring his favorite whiskey into the glass, there was a knock at the door.

"Finally," Sam grumbled, fixing his belt. His patience was growing thin, and his desire to see a woman's lips on his shaft was growing.

"I asked for a blonde! What's that dark-haired misunderstanding doing here?" Sam noted at once, only to realize that something was wrong.

The petite girl looked like a teenager, which was a little disturbing. Sam immediately decided to make sure she was of legal age, just in case. She had a very inappropriate appearance to go along with her unclear age. Instead of slutty translucent lingerie and high heels for stripping, she wore a short black dress and the same color sandals. Finishing off this image was a small purse, which the girl clutched at with a dead grip.

She's afraid, Sam realized without much difficulty. So what was she doing here? Losing a bet to her friends? Determined to find herself a sugar daddy? Or just want to get laid with no strings attached?

"Wrong door?" Sam gave her an icy stare.

The little girl slumped even more. Her frail shoulders shook with tension. Her brown eyes didn't know where to look. Sam thought she was going to faint.

"Get out of here. I don't want any underage problems," the man growled harshly.

Sam looked away, letting her know he wasn't interested anymore. But the little bugger didn't budge a step.

"My name is Maria. Maria O'Dell. And I'm here on business," the stranger said confidently, lifting her chin.

Hearing the familiar and hated surname, Sam snickered.

The O'Dells.

Twenty years ago, it had been Andrew O'Dell who had ruined Sam's parents' company by deceit and blackmail. Humiliated and destroyed what was so dear to Williams senior, bringing him serious heart problems. Despite his fairly young age, Sam's father passed away a couple of years later due to a lack of funds for medical treatment.

For the young lad and his mother, this came as a major blow. Sam made a terrible promise to himself—to destroy the O'Dells. To make them go through what he and his family had to go through. He didn't wish death on anyone, but he wasn't going to have any regrets either.

Thanks to hard work and good wit, Sam was able to create his own empire. He put the Williams surname in a row with the top companies in Europe and England again.

All these years, he remembered. He remembered and hated the man who had caused him so much pain. And as soon as Sam had the opportunity to destroy him, he took it. He gained his trust and even offered a lucrative contract, motivated by good intentions to forget about the former enmity. And as soon as O'Dell let his guard down, Sam stabbed him in the back just as he had done at the time.

Not that Sam liked the gesture, but the anger and desire for revenge clouded his judgment. It ate away at him like a parasite, making him want only one thing: retribution.

O'Dell was arrested right in front of Sam's eyes. He looked calmly at the confused face of the elderly man. Not a single muscle on Sam's face trembled, but his soul wasn't satisfied.

Not enough! That's not enough! his subconscious kept repeating. Revenge didn't bring the satisfaction he needed. Yes, all of their family's assets had been seized. Everything had been taken from them, just as Sam's parents had been taken from him at one time. But the demon inside him remained hungry.

And then she shows up on the doorstep of the strip club. Maria. Maria O'Dell.

Sam had been given all the information about their family, so he knew she was twenty-four. She looked different up close than she did in the pictures. Innocent and weak. The Dominant in Sam licked greedily, wanting to bring the little girl to her knees and punish her. At once. Just for who she was.

"So?"

"What?" the girl was a little confused. But Sam noticed that her voice became more confident. She would regret that.

"What are you doing here, Maria O'Dell?"

Chapter 4

Maria had already opened her mouth for a prepared speech, but after realizing something, she closed it rapidly. Sam addressed her with the confidence of a person who could destroy only with one look. She wasn't prepared for that.

"I didn't know... oh... I mean... I didn't..." The girl's facial expressions gave her away. She was confused, babbling without a clear understanding of what to say. The man didn't stop watching her and only hummed softly. He was beginning to be amused by this girl.

"So what are you doing here?"

"I want to talk."

"Then talk."

"I know what you did to my family," her voice shook involuntarily, but to her credit, Maria didn't look away. She looked right at him. Was she trying to get through to him? To evoke compassion, which Sam didn't possess.

Do you know what your family did to mine? Sam growled to himself.

"Come to ask for mercy for you?" the man nodded mockingly, taking a sip of whiskey. His interest in the conversation was gone. He wasn't going to pardon anyone.

"Yes."

"Good luck," Sam said with a mocking snort.

"Please... "

"Get out!"

His patience was wearing thin. Sam got up from the couch and was next to Maria in two steps. Up close, she was even shorter, even tinier. You could take her under your arm, carry her wherever you wanted to go, and do whatever you wanted to do with her.

Sam's eyes read irritation and anger. A lot of anger. It was getting harder and harder to hold back.

"No," Maria replied in a whisper. Her voice trembled. The girl considered it pointless to hide her fear. Only a madman could pretend and be brave around this beast. Sam stepped on as if he was not affected by the difference in weight and the fact that she was a girl.

Maria could not understand why there was so much hatred and, at the same time, sadness in those blue eyes.

"Do you think I won't hurt you? Go away!" Sam threatened.

"I won't! I... I know what you like! I know about your needs." Maria said daringly. The man stopped for a moment.

Looking carefully into the face of the little brat, Sam stepped back. Without looking at Maria, he slowly returned to the couch. Taking a couple of sips of whiskey, he set the glass aside, crossed his legs, locked his hands together, and looked questioningly at her.

"So? Are you going to blackmail me?" He grinned. It became funny from his own words. No one would believe her, and if someone would, Sam would just buy their silence.

"No, the other way around."

"The other way around?" Sam was surprised for the first time in the whole conversation. "And what do you know, Maria O'Dell?" he asked with a sneer.

"You're a Dominant. And..." her voice trembled.

"And?"

"..everyone is afraid of you."

"And you're not afraid of me?" Sam answered sneakily, as if purring. In fact, Maria realized he was playing with her. She was a cornered rabbit, and he was a tiger who's gonna eat her up.

"I am afraid."

"So what do you want? To be my bottom? My personal slut?" he said and went into thought. Sam's eyes lit up. Suddenly, he wanted to play. Even the cock in his pants reminded himself as Sam imagined how he would punish Maria.

"I'll obey and do whatever you tell me to do," the girl gasped.

"Anything? Do you realize what you're saying? Have you ever had this kind of experience before?" Sam looked at her with a stiff grimace. His common sense was screaming at him that it was a terrible idea. She didn't look like a bottom. One smack on her beautiful ass, and the girl would run away screaming.

"Yes," Maria lied shamelessly. Her friend Google helped her learn the basics and terms. But in practice... she got nothing.

"And what is it?" Again, that fake, affectionate voice gave her goosebumps.

"I had a couple of sessions with Sheldon Mars. Light ones, nothing extreme." Maria answered proudly.

Alicia had prepared her well. As her friend explained to Maria, an acquaintance of her friend's acquaintance knew a local Master named Sheldon. He always agreed to all sorts of "requests" for a small fee. Maria had to give up her entire stash to pay for his alibi. From the same Sheldon, Alicia had learned about the fearsome Master Sam and that everyone feared him like fire. Now, Maria understood why.

"What exactly did you do?" Sam squinted at her. He refused to believe that such a beautiful girl would agree to a session with a tramp like Sheldon.

"Bondage, spanking, clamps, wax..."

"Sex? Anal stimulation? Knife play? Oral sex? Shibari?" the man deliberately interrupted her.

"No!" Maria grimaced, satisfying Sam's curiosity. "I told you! Light, no intimacy," she lowered her gaze.

Sam kept his eyes on her. He tried to see if she was lying, pretending anything! But Maria answered his questions confidently and knew the terms well. She even knew the difference between a whip and a stack. But something wasn't quite right. Sam couldn't figure out what it was.

The fact that she hadn't had intimacy with the other Master flattered Sam's ego. After Sheldon, he certainly wouldn't have her.

Pulling out his phone, he quickly typed something and sent it off.

Maria was still standing at the entrance, waiting for her fate.

"And what do you want in return? It can't go back to the way things were. Your father's assets have been seized."

"But you can withdraw your statement. My father is not a criminal."

"It won't bring everything back," Sam said. *And he is a criminal,* he kept this thought to himself.

"We don't need everything. Just withdraw your statement," Maria shook her head. She wasn't lying. If Sam took the statement, they could sell the house and the cars. It would be enough to pay for Mom's treatment. Maria would go to work, and Dad could start something new. Maybe. In any case, Maria's main concern was for her mother's health.

"It won't be the same as with Mars. It will be on my terms." Sam didn't know why he was talking her out of it. His palms itched to touch that soft skin. He wondered if it was that soft everywhere.

"I get it."

"Sex is a must."

"Okay," the girl shrugged.

Sam's cell phone beeped. A message came through. Without taking his eyes off his soon-to-be new toy, Sam quickly read the contents. The man's face changed immediately. The predatory grin horrified Maria. She didn't know what caused this reaction. She suddenly wanted to leave the room. To run and not look back.

But she was too late.

"Okay," he mockingly repeated her words. "I will fuck you day and night if I want."

"I understand," Maria mumbled, lowering her gaze. The pale skin of her cheeks flushed immediately.

"All right. I've wanted a slave for a long time," Sam sneered, with a very unkind smile that spread across his face.

Chapter 5

"A slave?" Maria asked in a hoarse voice.

"Yeah," Sam grinned. "And you thought I'd spank you once, and that would be it, all resolved for you and your family?"

Maria was silent. Her naiveté had played a cruel trick on her. She couldn't tell her family's worst enemy that it was exactly what she thought.

Trying to keep herself in control, she smiled with the corners of her lips. Such an innocent gesture made the man grin unkindly.

"You haven't changed your mind, Maria. Have you?"

"No. But I have a condition!" she lifted her chin again.

Sam could hardly contain himself. This girl had the nerve to set conditions. His rough palm itched again. The Master in him demanded to bend the little girl over and give her at least fifteen spanks, preferably twenty.

"Me too," the man said warningly.

"You'll write a letter in the presence of a lawyer, and it has to be notarized. You will confirm that you don't have anything against my family." Maria said, ignoring him.

Sam growled quietly at the anger that overwhelmed him. She was going to be a lousy slave. But that was good because he was going to make her life a living hell.

Maria had decided to play with fire. So it would burn her.

"I'll do it," Sam agreed calmly.

"I have taboos..."

"So keep them to yourself," Sam cut her off abruptly. His threatening tone betrayed his irritation. Maria decided not to argue; she was on edge anyway. "You must be ready for anything. Are you ready, Maria?"

"But Master and slave... it's trust and... and..." the girl tried to collect her thoughts in a heap, but she was desperately short of air.

"I know the rules," again that menacing tone, which made Maria's toes tighten. "I'm not a sick lunatic who wants to hurt you, but you should not do it through force. So this conversation with you is doomed to fail," Sam shook his head.

"No! I understand it too! If it's not you, then it would be someone else, but if I can help my family, why not mix business with pleasure?" The girl babbled. Tears welled up her eyes. Maria tried to hold on.

She lowered her head and took a couple of steps toward Sam. Frozen for a moment, she collapsed on her knees in front of the man. She put her hands behind her back and froze.

With such a sight, Sam almost choked on his whiskey. The sight of Maria on her knees in the position of the bottom caused a lot of emotions in him. Too many. Involuntarily licking his lips from such a sweet picture, the man could barely restrain himself from starting a session right in the club. All the more, he already had something to punish Maria for.

"Are you saying you trust me? The man who took everything from you?" Sam grinned. He didn't believe her.

"I want to help my family. And *you,*" she emphasized the last word, "I *can* trust you. You said yourself you wouldn't hurt me. I believe you."

The girl looked up. Their eyes met, and they each appeared almost glassy. Sam's with desire, Maria's with fear.

"Oh, I'm sorry! I'm not needed here anymore?"

A petite blonde in see-through lingerie appeared in the doorway. Maria's cheeks flushed with color from one glance in the stripper's direction. The stripper looked at Maria with displeasure. It was as if Maria didn't belong here.

"Come on in," Sam ordered the blonde. "You can start."

"And, uh…" she stared at Maria.

"You're paid to work, not talk," Sam hissed.

The stripper hastily climbed onto the small stage, turned on the music, and began to twirl around the pole. She smiled as she wriggled beautifully on the pylon, sending air kisses to Sam, clearly hinting at her interest in the man.

"Sit," Sam nodded to Maria as he noticed her start to rise to her feet. "I didn't permit getting up."

Maria returned to her original position. The dress was constricting her movements, and it was starting to get painful to be on her knees. Keeping her hands locked was not so easy. The girl mentally scolded herself for starting this whole thing. With her head down, she couldn't see Sam. Well, she could see his shoes, but nothing more.

Sam watched the blonde twirling on the pylon without interest. All his interest was down at his feet, in the form of the little annoying brunette. With the corner of his eye, he tried to catch any of her inaccuracies. And there were plenty of them. She wiggled her ass now and then and tried to raise her head a couple of times but quickly corrected herself. Not a good slave.

The music faded, as did the clacking of her heels. The blonde finished her performance and looked slyly in the direction of the strange couple.

"Should I go or...?" she said slowly.

"You can start," Sam grinned, setting the whiskey glass aside.

The girl, like a cat, gracefully approached Sam. Without any instructions, she knelt just as smoothly in front of his spread legs.

Maria breathed more frequently. Her hair hid her face, and neither the man nor the white-haired sucker could see her stunned eyes.

Is she going to give him a blowjob!? No! No! Maria panicked. Her brain refused to believe what was happening. Only the clinking of an expensive buckle and the distinctive sound of a zipper confirmed her guess. Her palms instantly became sweaty, and the pounding of her heart, like white noise, drowned out extraneous sounds.

"Raise your head," Sam commanded, "Look.... And learn," he hummed contentedly.

Maria forgot how to breathe. Even squinted, trying to get a better look at the man's face. What if he made a mistake? Confused something? Was he joking?

But Sam wasn't kidding.

The blonde had already reached the boxers and, with a triumphant glance at Maria, pulled down the elastic band.

Maria's gaze froze at the sight of Sam's huge cock. Giggling nastily, the blonde grabbed his cock at the base and began to lick it along its entire length. Turning her head, the stripper looked at Maria with a victorious look. Maria couldn't understand why the blonde was so happy licking a stranger's cock, but she also couldn't understand why she wasn't disgusted.

While the girls were exchanging glances, Sam was only watching Maria. He knew she couldn't last a week with him.

I will destroy you, O'Dell, he dreamed ominously, anticipating how he would see her tears and suffering.

That's what Sam was missing, dark-haired stupid girl, with a dream that he was meant to ruin.

Chapter 6

"Maria, are you sure this is a normal job?"

"Yes, Dad. I'm going to be a personal assistant for an aspiring artist."

"But I still don't understand why you'd want to live with your friend... what's her name..."

"Alicia!"

Maria couldn't stand it. Her father tailed the girl and questioned her about her new 'job.' Maria held on from the last strength, obediently answering her father's tricky questions. There was no time to come up with a coherent story, so Alicia, as always, came to the rescue.

"Say you'll live with me!" Alicia said.

"On what terms? My father will never let me go," Maria replied worriedly.

"He wouldn't let you go before, but now... you know," she shrugged her shoulders. "I know an artist; let's say you'll work for her! And live with me!"

"That's not much of a cover," Maria grumbled.

After the club, she went straight to her friend's house. When she entered the apartment, she went straight to the kitchen. That's where the alcohol was kept. Grabbing the first bottle, Maria took two big gulps. She was still pounding from her conversation with Sam and...as he said, her first lesson.

"Hey, girl, are you okay?"

An equally petite mulatto woman stood in the doorway. Dark curls sticking out in all directions. Her pouty lips looked fake, as did her firm breasts. Nature had given Alicia a great ass and a sharp tongue. She had a great wit and the ability to find a way out of any situation.

"Uh... I don't think so," Maria could barely reply. Taking another sip, she coughed loudly. "Can I take a shower?"

"You know the way," Alicia said and went to get a clean towel.

Maria stood under the hot water for a long time. Wrapping her arms around her shoulders, she tried to think about anything but what had happened at the club.

And this is just the beginning, Maria thought defeatedly.

The white-haired head and the huge head of the cock still flashed before her eyes. Maria had only seen such things in porn. The thought that Sam would be wielding his shaft between her legs was terrifying. What if he tore her up? Or worse, want to go up her ass!?

"*And he will,*" Maria said, completing her thought, almost sobbing. Trying to control the panic, the girl began to think about how to hold out for three months.

That was how long Sam demanded of her. If she didn't leave in three months and was a submissive slave, Sam would take back his statement.

"One safe word," Maria remembered. But it wasn't enough at all. She realized at once that Sam was deliberately testing her. She would have done the same thing.

"Fuck you, Sam Williams!" the girl raged at her own spinelessness.

"And if they ask me anything? I'll blab."

And fake it. But fake confidently, she remembered a famous quote from her mother's favorite movie.

"So Sam doesn't believe it either," the girl exhaled sadly.

"Feeling better?" Alicia asked, pouring red wine into cups. The girl had no glasses and no utensils in general. Working as a stripper in an elite club, she just didn't have time to cook.

"Not much."

"Is he that scary?" she started asking.

"No, not really. He's... He's unusual," Maria reasoned into her voice. "Rough? Yes. Straightforward? Yes. Arrogant? A hundred percent. He's an asshole!"

"Easy, easy, tiger. You still have to tame that asshole."

It's more like the other way around, Maria automatically started blushing from that thought.

"Well, the thing is..."

Maria briefly told Alicia about the conversation with Sam.

"Three months!? Are you kidding!?" The mulatto was stunned.

After that, they came up with a plan about the artist and moving in with Alicia.

"And if you lose?" her friend asked very seriously.

"I cannot afford to lose," Maria answered in the same serious tone.

"Yes… but what if!? Maybe he's completely sick! What if he'll tell you to go naked to the store!? Or better yet, he'll take you for a spin in some kinky-sick club! Do you know Tops can share their Bottoms if they wanna?"

"He's not like that!" Maria objected loudly, even though her friend's arguments frightened her. She had thought of it herself more than once during the evening.

"What?"

"I don't know!" Maria screamed. "I don't know, Alicia! But if I don't, Mom and Dad... they... they won't be able to..."

There was only a quiet mooing and a sea of tears. Alicia hugged her friend tightly. She was silent. Words were unnecessary.

After saying goodbye to her father, Maria went to her friend's house. Sam ordered not to take personal belongings. Only documents and a cell phone. About the latter, Maria rejoiced. Her father made her vow to call at least occasionally. Leaving her bag, Maria went to the elite neighborhood of London—Chelsea.

Sam's apartment was in a new condo complex in the downtown. Checking the route, Maria got to the right place by subway. The atmosphere of public transportation did not disgust the girl. The theater club, where Maria went, was located in the center, and the most reasonable way to get there was always the subway.

An hour and a half later, the girl stood at the entrance to the building. Everything around her screamed rich and expensive. Looking around, Maria realized how much she stood out. She deliberately chose a simple outfit: black pants, a cream blouse, and ordinary ballet flats. A small backpack held everything she needed.

"What can I do for you?" The receptionist, a nice middle-aged man in a perfectly pressed suit, greeted her warmly.

"I'm here to see Mr. Williams."

"How do I introduce you?"

"Maria O'Dell," the girl smiled nervously.

After checking the records, the man put on his fake smile and asked her to follow him.

"Penthouse number seven. Shall I show you out?" He asked at the elevator.

"No, thank you. Have a good day."

Saying goodbye to the receptionist, Maria stepped into the elevator. Her palms immediately became wet. The closed space made the girl shiver. The realization of what she had gotten herself into began to overtake her, causing an urge of nausea.

"Calm down," Maria barked at herself.

The elevator doors opened.

Taking a quick glance at herself in the mirror, Maria's face changed. The panic was gone. Her eyes stopped darting from side to side. Her back straightened, and her shoulders squared as if she had a ruler tied to her throat. Putting on the mask of an icy and obedient slave, Maria headed toward penthouse number seven.

"It's just a play. Just a play. Act well, and you'll win," Maria repeated over and over again.

Chapter 7

Sam couldn't gather his thoughts all morning. His slave should be coming today.

His whole body was aching for release. He'd always had at least a week's worth of sex, but now he was off the chain. Running around his own apartment like it was a cage. Waiting for his lunch in the form of one annoying, stupid girl.

The bell rang at two o'clock sharp.

"Good girl. Too bad," Sam grinned. He had hoped to punish her right in the hallway for being late. The man walked confidently toward the door, knowing that Maria would definitely stumble today, tomorrow, *and* the day after that…

Sam had an inexplicable thirst. A thirst to punish her. Everything, of course, would take place within the limits of what was allowed, but even with that, he knew how to drive his bottom to hysteria. He didn't like to do it, but sometimes the little manipulative girls deserved that. Clapped their eyes and thought they could bind Sam to them. They would always come to regret it. He didn't feel sorry for them.

That's why, he wouldn't spare Maria either.

When he opened the door, he was a little surprised, but he didn't let it show. Standing in front of him was a very ordinary girl. Ballet flats, which always made Sam cringe. He preferred girls in heels. Her dark hair was up in a bun. Very little makeup and a detached look.

There was no trace of that frightened girl in the strip club VIP room.

With a frown, Sam took another look at his new toy.

"Come in," the man ordered.

Maria slipped into the hallway. Stopping three steps away from Sam, Maria lowered her head.

I am a slave, she tried not to forget.

"Address me as a Master. But if we're in public, you can call me Sam. Is that clear?"

"Yes, Master," Maria repeated quietly. A chill ran down her body. Her brain was becoming more and more aware of the severity of the situation.

"I told you not to take anything but the documents," Sam glanced unhappily at her backpack.

"There are papers, a phone, a wallet, lip gloss, and pills," Maria said precisely like a soldier. She knew Sam would start nagging as soon as she walked in.

"What pills?"

"I don't tolerate my periods well, and I get migraines sometimes," she admitted honestly.

Sam was silent. She felt the weight of his gaze on her shoulders. She couldn't see his eyes, and she didn't want to. Her knees were already shaking from just being in enemy territory.

Sam was the enemy. Today. Now Maria fully realized it.

"Follow me," he commanded again.

The girl silently followed her Master. Only his bare feet and gray house pants were exposed to her gaze.

T-shirt. He's also wearing a T-shirt. What color is it? Shit! Maria scolded herself. First joint. She should notice every little thing. Study his habits thoroughly. This man didn't hesitate to say he wanted her to lose.

Lifting her head slightly, Maria took a quick peek at the edge of her T-shirt: white.

"I have to know everything about him," she repeated restlessly to herself.

"This is your room," Sam announced, coldly.

The man stopped at the closed door. Folding his arms across his chest, he glanced glumly at his companion once more.

"Annoying," Sam tsked. "Come in, take a look around."

With trembling fingers, Maria opened the door. She thought she was about to be confronted by a dark chamber or the red room from a famous movie. It was right to expect the worst, just in case. But it was not like that.

"Oh," the girl couldn't help but be delighted.

The first thing that surprised Maria was a lot of light. Windows on the floor opened a view of the center of London. The same light-colored walls did not bother her at all. She actually found them soothing. A large bed with many soft pillows, a couple of bedside tables, a desk by the window, a comfortable chair, and a small chest of drawers fit perfectly into the interior.

"There's the bathroom, and this is the dressing room," Sam went inside, touching Maria's arm. To his surprise, she didn't flinch. She stood there and studied her new home with interest.

"Thank you, Master," Maria lowered her head again, turning to Sam.

In her heart, the girl was exuberant. Not a basement and not a cellar with a mattress on the floor. There was also a huge balcony! So she would be able to be alone at least once in a while!

Maria mustered up some courage and spoke softly;

"Excuse me, Master."

"What?" the man looked at her with interest.

"Can I go out on the balcony?" Maria's voice cracked a little, and he could hear the joy in her voice. Too bad...

"If you're not embarrassed by your appearance, then yes," Sam grinned wickedly. Maria frowned, not quite sure what he meant. "You can look in the closet." Sam waved his hand dismissively and stepped aside. He wanted to get a better look at her reaction.

Keeping her appearance calm, Maria lifted her head and opened the dressing room door.

"What the..." The girl didn't understand the humor.

"Something embarrasses you?" Sam asked coldly, tilting his head to the side.

"No... I mean, yes. I don't understand... Master," she added hastily.

"This is your uniform. You will wear nothing but *THIS* in the house. Do you understand?" Sam spoke so calmly that Maria's toes tightened with fear and dread.

"Mary, but what if!? Maybe he's completely sick! What if he'll tell you to go naked to the store!?" Alicia's words came to mind.

"Take that off, too. That's it," Sam threw in her direction and left the room.

Maria stood staring at the completely empty dressing room. The shelves glistened with cleanliness. The hangers hung lonely, waiting for outfits that neither they nor Maria would see for a very long time...

"At least he doesn't want me to go to the store," she muttered and began to undress.

Chapter 8

"This is your uniform. You will wear nothing but **THIS** in the house. Understand?" Maria mocked Sam's words, taking off her pants.

In private, she decided to allow herself the full range of emotions. She would have to look cold and aloof in front of Sam.

"As if you can scare me!" she mumbled again, folding her things neatly. At the top of the pile, she placed a pair of lacy black panties and a bra of the same color.

Looking in the mirror, she saw a completely naked girl with sad eyes. Due to the publicity, Maria always tried to keep her body toned; jogging in the morning, yoga, and pilates. The girl even went to boxing a couple of times, but her mother protested, "It's not something a woman should do! You're a girl, after all."

The lack of appetite also had an impact. Maria ate very little, even though she wasn't picky.

Slender legs, flat stomach, firm standing breasts with pink nipples, small shoulders. Maria was one of those girls who were hated and desired.

She put Sam in the first category. However, she knew perfectly well that there would be sex.

She tried not to think about it yet.

"Do I have to wait all day for you?" she heard Sam's distantly displeased voice.

Picking up a stack of clothes, Maria quickly left the room. Walking down the hallway, the girl found herself in the living room. Sam was sitting on a huge leather couch and was doing something on his tablet.

"I'm sorry, Master," Maria joined the game. She lowered her eyes. She relaxed her lips and slumped her shoulders. Her whole appearance was one of resignation.

"Have you ever been punished, Maria?" Sam asked without looking at her.

"No, Master," she admitted honestly. Not even her parents had ever hit her, although as a child, she had done things that deserved punishment.

Sam set the tablet aside and finally looked up. It was a good thing Maria wasn't looking at him, or she would have been surprised at his reaction. An unkind glint appeared in Sam's eyes. Licking his lips, he brazenly began to look at his slave. He liked what he saw.

The man planned not to scare her from day one. To wait a little and then move on to intimacy, but at the sight of the young body, the cock in his pants began to rise.

Should I make her kneel? Sam pondered, not drifting his gaze away from her.

"Put your things on the chair."

Maria gawked in search of a chair and headed in its direction quickly. When she left the stack of clothes, she turned to face Sam, put her hands behind her back, and froze.

"Hands at the seams. Always," Sam corrected her. Little things like that undermined his faith that Maria had anything to do with BDSM.

"Sorry, Master."

"Can you cook?" Sam asked with a chuckle.

"Yes, Master," Maria replied quietly.

"Really?" he said, genuinely surprised. "What can you cook? Oatmeal?"

"Yes, I can make oatmeal. I can make soup, side dishes, and meat. Fish, too," Maria was naming all the things in order.

"The kitchen's that way," he waved toward the closed door.

"Excuse me, Master, you want me to cook for you?" Maria said quietly.

"Yes" Sam growled irritably, which sent big goosebumps across Maria's skin. He was angry. Maria had been in his house less than an hour and he was already growling at her.

"What do you like, Master? Do you have any allergies?" The girl inquired gently.

"Are you trying to poison me?" Sam asked calmly.

From such an answer, Maria forgot about her image for a second. Abruptly, she raised her head and stared at Sam with horror. *Is he serious?* She didn't even know what to say. She felt sick to her stomach, the thought was so disgusting.

"I...I just...don't know anything about you. Oh... I mean, Master. It's just a question. I am not a criminal," she blinked rapidly, trying to make some sort of response.

"Yeah, you already have one criminal in the family. I think that's enough."

Maria did understand his joke, which was more of an insult rather than funny. But she stayed quiet. She had to.

"What does Master want for lunch?" she tried to move the conversation in a different direction. Lowering her head, she tried not to cry from the resentment.

Sam watched her reaction carefully. Which, by the way, he liked. He certainly didn't think the girl was capable of such a thing. He wanted to see the real her. And he could think of nothing but threats.

"Eyes on me," he commanded.

Sam's palms itched again at the confused and worried look on Maria's face. She was like an obsession, just waiting to lead him into sin.

"You can cook whatever you want. I don't have any allergies," the man said dryly and then went back to his tablet, indicating that the conversation was over.

Once again, putting on the mask of a slave, Maria quickly slipped into the kitchen. Her skin was covered with goosebumps from not being used to all this. Not often, the girl flaunted naked around the house. She was consistently thinking to cover herself.

The kitchen was bright and spacious. Under different circumstances, the girl would have squealed with joy that she would be able to cook here all summer.

Quickly checking all the cabinets and the refrigerator, Maria started cooking. Her thoughts returned to Sam, who sat quietly in the living room. And also to her nakedness. Maria shivered at the thought of being naked.

"You'll get used to it," she said to herself encouragingly.

After an hour of effort, Maria set aside the pot of soup. The meat and potatoes were stewing in the oven, and a vegetable salad was already on the table.

Maria took the plate with the utensils and was about to put it on the table when she heard a cold voice behind her.

"Not bad," said Sam.

Everything Maria was holding in her hands flew to the floor with a crash. The sound of shattering porcelain echoed through the apartment.

Chapter 9

Maria stared at the broken plate, feeling her toes grow cold. Her heart slowed down, and her lungs ran out of air. The girl sincerely believed that she could hold out for at least a week. But to screw up on the first day!?

"Maria," Sam called sternly.

"S-sorry, M-master," the girl stammered with fear and despair. She really felt sorry for the expensive item, but she was even more upset for her ass.

Guiltily lowering her head, Maria expected screams and immediate punishment.

"Clean it up."

Having mustered up the courage to raise her head, the girl looked at Sam with a dazed look. He wouldn't punish her? But she'd screwed up!

"Okay," Maria said quickly. She picked up the larger pieces and swept up the smaller ones. She stepped carefully, trying not to cut herself. A kind of relief came over the girl in her heart. Even her nakedness was no longer embarrassing.

Sam watched her closely. While Maria cleaned up, she managed to show him all the most private places of her body. The man liked her well-groomed body. The lack of hair between her legs and on her legs. A flat belly on which he was sure to pour more than one candle of wax. Polished heels that he would tickle with a feather. And so much more.

Her joy didn't escape him either. No matter how hard she tried, Sam caught it all. He understood her thoughts at once, planting another seed of doubt.

Violation, disobedience, and any slip-up is punished. Always.

"Stupid," Sam tsked unhappily. Instead of joy, she should already be begging for forgiveness and asking for punishment herself.

Maria made quick work of cleaning up. Not knowing what to do next, she put on her slave mask and stood at the stove facing Sam. She didn't like the look in his eyes. It was as if Sam expected something from her, and was very displeased.

Feverishly recalling her actions, the girl tried to find the mistake.

"Am I going to eat today?" Sam asked again. "Serve the food."

In an instant, a bowl of soup, fresh bread, salad, and another empty plate prepared for meat and potatoes appeared in front of him. Sam sat down at the table, carefully examining the contents.

"What's this for?" He nodded toward the bread basket.

"For the soup," Maria shrugged. His question was strange to her. Her father always ate everything with bread. "This is for the meat; it's in the oven. With potatoes," the girl quickly added, pointing at the empty plate.

"Is that all?" Sam inquired enigmatically, looking at her.

Maria began to go over her every move in her head again. She was missing something. Sam had even condescended to give her a hint.

"I..." she stammered, not knowing what to say, feeling scared and anxious. She felt guilty.

Guilt! It flashed through her head. Exactly! All the blogs and articles about BDSM came to mind.

"I'm sorry, Master," her voice trembled. From the heavy sigh and relaxed posture, she realized she had hit the mark.

"You want me to forgive you?" Sam interjected.

"I've upset you, Master," she added faintly.

"What are we going to do, Maria? Huh?" Sam sounded amused.

"Punish me, Master?"

Sam was silent. He looked at the slumped girl and couldn't hold back a mocking smile.

A plan of punishment was already forming in his head.

"Eat," the man calmly changed the subject and began to eat.

"I'm not hungry... Master," Maria tried to refuse but quickly closed her mouth and lowered her eyes when Sam glared at her.

"It's not a question. And I didn't permit you to speak, Maria," Sam snapped at her. "You can eat after me. And clean up after me. After that, you're free to go. Keep the door to your room open. If I need you, I'll call you."

Maria listened attentively to the instructions and tried to hold back a gust of anger. She wanted to tell Sam to go far, far away. But instead of angry speeches, the girl only sighed heavily.

"Yes, Master."

"Go to the corner of the room," Sam nodded to the opposite end of the kitchen. "Face me. Eyes on the floor."

Maria almost choked at his order. What is she, a naughty kitten!? Anger made it hard to hold her image. Trying not to clench her hands into fists, she headed for her seat.

What a strange punishment, Maria thought, examining her toes.

With the soft clatter of the spoon, Maria realized that Sam liked the soup. The man grinned faintly and set his plate aside. It had been a long time since he'd had a home-cooked meal. A pleasant warmth from the hearty soup spread inside.

Leaning back in his chair, Sam began to look at his slave girl again. She had asked for punishment after all, but he was still concerned about her behavior. She was changing too quickly.

Let's see how you behave tonight, Maria, Sam thought.

"What about the second course?"

Maria fed her Master, cleared the table, and put the dirty dishes in the dishwasher. Sam left the kitchen as soon as he finished his meal, which the girl was extremely happy about. It was getting hard to breathe around him. Her slave mask wanted to fall off every time he looked at her with his piercing blue eyes.

Like I'm drowning, Maria twitched, remembering his gaze.

Taking a quick bite from unfinished baked potatoes, the girl cleaned up after herself and gingerly poked her nose into the living room.

It was empty.

Maria took a quick step toward her room, mentally praying to all the gods that she wouldn't run into Sam. Someone upstairs had heard her, though. Leaving the door of the room open, the girl began to explore her little place.

In the small bathroom, Maria found a robe, towels, and all the necessities. In the shower cubicle, there were jars with shampoo, conditioner, and shower gel. It was good to see that everything was new. Just thinking about another girl sent shivers down Maria's spine.

Finding no better entertainment, she decided to take a shower. The water helped wash away the smell of the kitchen and calmed her down a bit. Quickly wiping herself with a towel, she threw on a robe and headed for her room.

"Oh!" Maria shrieked for the second time that day and covered her mouth with her palms.

Sam stood at the window and looked at her. Disgruntled again. Angry again.

"I see you like to be punished, don't you, Maria?" Sam looked at her carefully and tilted his head to the side, his eyes on her robe.

Chapter 10

Maria wanted to scream and smash everything in her path. To swear and tell Sam everything she thought about him in a not-so-pleasant way. But she only lowered her gaze to the floor and began to untie the belt of her warm robe. Having thrown it aside, the girl immediately got goosebumps all over her body.

"I'm sorry, Master," she tried to show all her feigned remorse.

"And?"

"Punish me, please, Master," Maria involuntarily frowned at her own words.

"For what?" Sam began to fool around. He folded his arms across his chest and grinned contentedly.

"For breaking the rules," Maria said, surprised at his question.

"Be more specific, Maria," the man's voice became as cold as the air in January.

"F-for the clothes."

Sam kept his eyes on her. He slid his gaze over her steaming skin, her nipples swollen from the cold, and her thighs, which Maria squeezed so cutely. The spontaneous urge to visit her room led to another of Maria's missteps.

"That's it?" Sam rubbed his eyes tiredly.

Maria was silent. She stared at the floor and didn't move. His question caught her off guard. What else had she done wrong!?

Oh, the plate! But she'd already worked it off. Or maybe... The girl's cheeks flushed when she thought of her own silliness. There's no way a dominant like Sam would put her in a corner as punishment. It's too easy. Being so simple-minded, Maria took it as punishment.

"A broken plate," she added quietly.

Sam moved quickly beside her. Too fast. The girl squirmed in surprise and, by reflex, covered her breasts. Quickly realizing her mistake, she pulled her hands away, but Sam had already clicked his tongue in displease. Maria subconsciously felt his irritation. Her whole plan was going down the drain, where her family and reputation already were.

With the thought that there was nothing to lose, the girl collapsed to her knees and looked at her Master with puppy eyes.

"Please forgive me, Master! Please!" she began to beg. The girl was, in fact, saying that sincerely because if he kicked her out the door now, there would be nothing left for her but to go and throw herself off the bridge. That, or become a hooker. Maria did not see any other solution.

Tears rolled down her cheeks, and her chin treacherously quivered. She was about to be overcome by actual hysteria. Maria was looking for forgiveness in Sam's eyes. But it was empty—just an unwavering blue smoothness. The man looked at her as if she was nothing.

"Please," Maria grabbed Sam's pant leg without embarrassment or realizing what she was doing.

Sam calmly watched the girl's tantrum. This was what he wanted to see—remorse, guilt, pleading. And Maria didn't disappoint. Kneeling in front of him and begging. When tears appeared in her eyes, Sam struggled to hold back a satisfied smile.

No, he didn't like to drive his inferiors to such hysterics, but Maria was no ordinary slave. She was on a O'Dell, and seeing their pain and remorse was a delight for Sam.

"Follow me. Crawl," Sam ordered menacingly as Maria, still sobbing, began to rise from her knees.

With the look of a beaten dog, the girl followed her Master. She felt like an actual dog. She lowered her head to the floor and crawled in the direction indicated. The hysteria in her was calming down, but it was replaced by shame.

God, what am I doing? This is humiliating! Maria thought, shifting her knees and hands, following Sam. Biting her already bruised lips, the girl began to realize why this was called the punishment.

To humiliate. To show that you are inaccurate. To punish. That's what a Dom should do to a delinquent Sub. And Sam was no stranger to it. Absorbed in her thoughts, Maria didn't realize she was in a dark room not far from her bedroom.

"Stand up. Eyes to the floor. Hands at your side," Sam said calmly as he searched the dark wood dresser for something.

Maria did not have time to look around, but the girl saw a cross with locks, a small black sofa, and an ordinary chair. The soft carpet pleasantly caressed her feet, and the dim light prevented her from examining the room properly.

The girl quickly assumed the proper pose. Examined her toes and waited. Suddenly, every hair on her body stood at attention. The back of her neck felt his breath.

Sam came close. Warm breath tickled her skin.

"Close your eyes."

A tight band descended over Maria's eyes. Everything around her plunged into darkness. Being so anxious, the girl began to breathe through her mouth. Her pulse rumbled in her ears, preventing her from concentrating. Swallowing the collected saliva, she stepped from foot to foot, terrified of what awaited her.

Something tinkled very close by. The next second, Maria's wrists were in cold metal handcuffs. But she wasn't a criminal. The girl bit her lip to keep from screaming.

"*He's crazy! Sick!*" the girl was panicked.

"You'll have a choice," Maria twitched again, hearing Sam's rough yet calm voice to her right. "After your punishment, you can go to your room or—" He stopped talking. Maria felt an itch between her shoulder blades, wanting to know what "or" was waiting for her.

"Or?" she asked very quietly and carefully.

"Or you could ask for aftercare," Sam grinned, making Maria's insides shrink to the size of an apple.

Ask for!? Aftercare!? Fuck you! Maria immediately thought to herself.

"Do you understand?"

"I understand, Master."

Maria was grabbed by the shoulder and pulled in an unknown direction. Judging by Sam's movements, they were going somewhere again. A couple of steps later, strong hands grabbed Maria and easily sat her down on something soft.

A couch, she guessed.

Sam tugged the girl toward him. She awkwardly spread out on his lap, lying on her stomach. Maria's elbows rested on the soft upholstery of the sofa on one side, and her legs, slightly bent at the knees, on the other.

"What am I punishing you for again?" Sam asked hoarsely. His palm touched the soft and firm buttocks. He stroked them and then went deeper, touching her labia. Maria only yelped softly at the unexpected touch.

"F-for the broken plate and robe, Master," she repeated her sentence, her voice trembling. She was not ready for Sam's touch. Or rather, for his *soft* touch. The man gently crumpled her skin. He began to explore her lower back, and stroked her thighs. An incomprehensible warmth spread inside Maria. She bit her lower lip even harder. Her body betrayed her before she could even try to resist.

"Thirty slaps. Count out loud and repeat, 'Forgive me, Master, I am a stupid girl,'" Sam said in all seriousness.

Maria tried to breathe. But when a heavy palm came down on her ass, all the adjustments went out of her head.

"Maria," Sam growled menacingly, reminding her of her duties.

"One. Forgive me, Master, I am a stupid girl," Maria exhaled, squeezing her eyes shut. Her fingers gripped the edge of the pillow with all her might. Her knees trembled.

The pain is tolerable, she thought.

"T-two, forgive..." Maria repeated the whole phrase. The force of the blow increased slightly.

On the fifth, the girl was already hissing, tucking her toes. On the twelfth, she barely audibly moaned. On the seventeenth, tears flowed from her eyes, and the thought of stopping this madness was conceived in her head. But Maria kept silent, and swallowed her tears. She cussed to herself. She cursed Sam to herself, but kept silent.

"Twenty-" She froze. She lost it. Sobbing loudly, Maria, stammering, repeated, "Twenty... t-twenty..."

Her whole body was shivering. Sweat trickled down her back. Her ass was burning with pain. Tomorrow, Maria would definitely not be able to sit on the chair. And maybe even the day after tomorrow. Her thoughts were scattered and stubbornly did not gather in a pile.

"If you don't tell me the number, I'll add five more," Sam's calm voice made the girl roar even harder.

Twenty...three? Two? Think! Maria frantically recalled. The idea of getting five additional slaps had a sobering effect.

"Twenty-two-ah!" she shrieked as the heavy palm of her hand pressed painfully into her flushed skin again. "Forgive me, Master. I am a stupid girl."

"Is that twenty-two?"

"No, no! Twenty-three, forgive me, Master, I am a stupid girl," Maria retreated.

Sam's palm was a little sore. Looking at the reddish skin in front of him, he mentally berated himself for losing control. The last four blows had been particularly hard on Maria. He had to pin her legs between his own to keep her still. The girl squeaked, hissed, and sobbed but continued to take the punishment. On the thirtieth blow, she did not speak. She mumbled something and sank into the couch cushion. A loud female howl echoed throughout the apartment.

Sam reached for her small head out of habit but stopped in time. When he looked at the shuddering body in his lap, he felt no joy at the punishment. On the contrary, he wanted to caress and comfort the little girl.

Sam shook his head sharply, trying to get rid of that stupid thought. She was the enemy. Because of her father, he lost his own. He tried not to lose that thread of hatred, and his gaze turned cold again.

"Can you stand on your own?" Sam asked, doing his standard Master duties.

"Uh-huh," Maria sniffled. With her head between her hands, she was still crying quietly.

She realized from the man's movement that she had to get up.

Her whole body ached. It was as if a truck had driven over her. Her knees shook, her hands trembled. Her face was a mess of tears, snot, and saliva on her chin. Maria was afraid to move because of the slightest movement in the area of the buttocks.

Releasing the girl from the handcuffs, Sam touched her wrists as a matter of habit. He wanted to stretch the skin. Panicked that he was about to do something else to her, Maria yanked her hands away.

"I'm s-sorry, Master. I got scared," Maria wheezed the truth.

Sam didn't comment on her behavior. Taking a small tube from the table, he returned to the shaking Maria.

"Are you staying or going to your room?" Sam looked at her carefully. He waited patiently for her answer while the girl gathered her thoughts and tried to calm the trembling in her body.

"Can I go to my room, Master?" Maria asked gingerly.

"Go," Samuel replied irritably, shoving the tube of ointment into her hands. "You'll have to heal your ass, or you won't be able to walk tomorrow," he growled angrily.

Chapter 11

When she reached her room, Maria closed the door tightly. If she saw Sam again tonight, she would lose it.

"Mutherfucker!" the girl hissed, addressing all her resentment toward the owner of the apartment and her life for the next three months.

Three months! Maria almost exploded in loud sobs again out or irritation and annoyance. Only the anger to show this bastard that she did not need his affection and care stopped her.

I'd rather die! she screamed, unable to stop mentally cursing Sam.

The warm water was like a rough brush, scrubbing the remaining skin from her burning buttocks. Crying a little, Maria carefully blotted the injured part of her body with a towel. Both of her butt cheeks glowed a rich reddish-purple color. Trying not to make unnecessary and sudden movements, she gently rubbed in the healing ointment. She couldn't stop cursing and whining. Despite her flexibility, it was not so easy to treat the tortured skin.

Dragging her legs tiredly, the girl collapsed onto the bed. With only her legs covered, she hugged the pillow tightly. Closed her eyes in the hope of a sound sleep, but it did not happen.

Maria tossed and turned all night, hissed and yelping with every movement of her body. She replayed the past day over and over again. And when boredom and sadness completely overcame her, she took up the phone and began to study BDSM forums again. Even watched a couple of videos.

So, for studying the topic, the girl did not sleep a wink until the morning.

Exactly at eight, the door of her room opened. Being so tired, Maria didn't even get frightened. She turned her head and immediately met the dark eyes of her Master. With his hands folded across his chest, Sam stared intently at his slave. Still, the same disgruntled and cold gaze that Maria was beginning to get used to.

Dressed in an expensive dark blue suit and black shirt, the man radiated power, wealth, and success with his entire appearance.

"Good morning, Master," Maria couldn't think of anything else to say.

Hesitating, she began to carefully crawl off the bed. Her butt was still sore.

"Did you sleep well?" Sam asked indifferently.

"Yes, Master," she lied.

"Come on, I don't have much time," Sam ordered and, without waiting for Maria, left her bedroom.

The confused and sleepy girl decided to skip bathroom needs for later and quickly followed her Master.

Right behind the wall was his study. Just as stern and sullen as Sam. Dark brown walls, a floor-to-ceiling shelf full of books. An oak desk with piles of papers and a massive chair stood near a huge window and a door leading to the veranda.

"Read this and put your signature on it. I'll be back with the lawyer after lunch, and we'll finalize the agreement."

Sam shoved a couple of sheets of paper and a pen into Maria's hands. When she saw the word "contract," she grimaced in incomprehension.

"Is it a Dom-Slave contract? Why do we need one?" she thought but foolishly mumbled it out loud.

"I don't want any trouble. I don't think you do either. Right, Maria? I told you it will be on my terms."

His heavy gaze made her skin feel like ice. Maria clutched her thighs. For some reason, she felt the warmth between her thighs.

"No, Master. I don't want any trouble. I understand"

With a short nod, Sam let Maria know she could go.

Still sleepy and now, also confused, the girl quickly left the study to keep out of trouble. Tossing the contract on the bed, Maria went straight to the bathroom. A cold shower and a minute of meditation helped to refresh her head a bit.

The skin on her buttocks was still sore and already starting to change color. The ointment helped a lot, but Maria did not dare to sit on the bed. She laid down on her side and began to leaf through the contract she had been given.

The first page looked harmless and standard. Only one clause was confusing: Provision of Services (Note A). Maria made an invisible note to herself to read this and the whole contract from cover to cover.

While the girl was trying to cope with abstruse terms, a message landed on her phone:

"Can you call me?"

Dialing the number of her favorite friend, Maria waited with bated breath for her to pick up the phone. It happened instantly.

"Are you alive!?" Alicia chirped excitedly.

"Yes," Maria answered tiredly. The sleepless night and a nice shower had taken their toll.

"What did he do? Did you have sex?" Alicia didn't stop.

"No. N-nothing special," Maria shuddered, remembering last night and her tears.

She had just reached the confidentiality clause, where it was written in black and white about the importance of keeping "special" relationships secret; otherwise, the contract could be terminated, and the injured party, in this case, Sam, would be entitled to compensation.

The girl snorted even more unhappily. As if he hadn't already taken everything from them.

"You can't talk about that?" Alicia had figured her out at once.

"I'm sorry, Alicia," Maria excused herself guiltily.

"But you can say how you feel? You feel awful, I know, but just tell me: how much on a scale from one to ten?"

"Ninety-seven," the girl answered quietly. She had to do her best not to burst into tears.

"Baby," she tried to calm her friend.

"It's okay. It's okay," Maria smiled sadly into the void.

She felt really lousy. She tried her best to keep her head up, and after the first test, she just sat there and sulked.

Quickly saying goodbye to Alicia, Maria put the contract aside and, as usual, hugged the pillow, taking the most comfortable position on the bed.

"I'll sleep for half an hour," she thought to herself and fell into a deep sleep.

***

Sam looked at the sleeping girl and considered the next punishment.

Apparently, Maria had a special gift for messing things up.

He didn't know when exactly she'd fallen asleep, but judging by the red marks from the deposits, a long time ago. There was a contract lying carelessly on the bed. So she'd been so uninterested in studying it that she'd dozed off.

That brat also had the audacity to lie to him. When he'd entered her room in the morning, he'd realized she'd been up all night. Sam did not pity Maria. He only felt anger and irritation. Irritation at her presence. At her puppy dog eyes that mesmerized him. At her bitten lips, that made him want to bite them even harder.

Sam should've been thinking of ways to make her life hell, yet all he had in his head was a list of positions he wanted to fuck her and make her scream so she would tear her throat out in pleasure.

He wanted to play with her. To pleasure her, to see the gratitude in her eyes. But that's not why she was here.

Punishment was Sam's main job for the next three months. If Maria didn't fulfill the contract terms or say the two safe words herself, he'd kick her out the door. That was his goal! Not affection and pleasure, only cruelty, domination, and humiliation.

"Are you awake now?" he glanced unhappily at a sleepy and dazed Maria.

Without fully understanding what was happening, Maria began to rub her eyes with her fists. The corners of Sam's lips trembled at such innocent and childish behavior. He almost laughed at Maria.

"What time is it?" she mumbled in a sleepy voice.

"The lawyer will be here in fifteen minutes. Get dressed."

Throwing a huge bag from a rather expensive brand store on the bed, the man did not stop glaring at his poor slave girl.

"If you're late, I'll whip you more than yesterday!" he threatened, without turning around and left the room.

Chapter 12

Maria realized from Sam's menacing tone that she was getting into trouble again. Damn it!

Looking for her cell phone under her pillow, she was horrified to see the time. She had slept for almost six hours! Three o'clock in the afternoon! Now, Williams' anger was understandable.

The girl squinted at the parcel in front of her. Cautiously peering inside the package, Maria gasped in surprise. It was a brand new set of black lingerie and a knee-length house dress.

Quickly jumping up from the bed, Maria hastily brushed her tangled hair, took out the new clothes, and began to dress.

"Ouch!" she squeaked, trying to pull up her panties. Despite the thin lace, any contact with her tortured skin was uncomfortable.

There was almost no time left. Deciding to wear only a bra and a dress that hugged her figure like a second skin, Maria scrutinized herself in the mirror and picked up the contract as she headed for Sam's study.

"Excuse me," she knocked on the door. "May I?"

"Come in,".

Sam's voice sounded different. Maria could not hide her surprise as she took her place on the chair in front of Sam, who seemed less like an evil, Dominant Master and more of an ordinary, charming man.

A woman of about forty-five, wearing a strict black suit, sat adjacent to Maria. Dark hair, arranged in a stylish bun, made her look elegant.

"Good afternoon," Maria greeted the guest politely.

"Good afternoon, Maria," the woman replied in a sharp German accent.

"*Asshole*," the girl scoffed, trying as hard as he did to portray friendliness. A sharp pain immediately followed.

"Maria, dear, this is Frau Helen. She's my trusted lawyer," Sam couldn't hold back a slight smirk.

Dear!? What is wrong with him? Is he drunk? Maria's eyes rounded at this treatment.

"Did you sign the contract?" Frau Helen asked, her voice stern. She crossed her legs, revealing a view of her expensive red-soled shoes. The woman eyed Maria with a curious interest. She made no secret of her interest in her persona.

"I... ahem," the girl fretted. Not only had she not read it, but she also hadn't signed it. Sam was going to punish her for this.

"Can I have a pen?" Maria asked, running her eyes around the table looking for a pen.

Sam silently handed her a heavy personalized pen, to which Maria only smiled briefly.

"Thank you," she said, and without looking up, signed the contract.

"Are you satisfied with everything?" The woman raised her eyebrow questioningly.

"Yes," Maria answered hastily. She wanted to get to the agreement. Better yet, she wanted to be in her room under a blanket. The energy these two emitted almost weighed her down.

Maria thought she was getting paranoid because Frau Helen looked like a typical Mistress. Tall, with a straight back, and a penetrating gaze like Sam's.

"Mr. Williams, are you satisfied with terms?" Taking the signed contract from Maria, she handed the papers to Sam.

"Yes," Sam answered briefly, looking through all the pages and smiling enigmatically.

After signing his part, he handed everything to Frau Helen.

"Great, now about the agreement..."

Maria tried to catch every word, but Sam's incomprehensible gaze kept distracting her. He squinted at her enigmatically. Smiled dreamily. Briefly answered all the lawyer's questions. When all the points were discussed, Sam wrote down the main text on paper under dictation. Maria reread the content twice and signed the agreement with a trembling hand.

"I warn both parties: if the terms of the contract are violated, the agreement is invalid and void. Do both parties understand?"

"Yes," Maria answered quietly. It was getting more and more painful to sit. She wanted to get up as soon as possible. Her breath became heavier, and her forehead was covered with sweat. Maria wanted to scream, but she sat still and smiled with the corners of her lips at Frau Helen's next remark.

"In that case, my presence is no longer necessary." She adjusted her jacket and started to leave.

"Have a good day," Maria said with a sweet smile.

"I'll walk you out," Sam offered, rising from his chair after her. "If you'd be so kind as to wait for me here," he said with such tenderness that the girl's mouth dropped open in surprise.

"Is he drunk?" Maria whispered, barely audibly.

"O'Dell? Are you serious, Sam?" Mrs. Helen addressed him when they were already in the corridor.

"Have a good day, Helen," ignoring her question, Sam defiantly opened the front door in front of her.

"Good luck," the woman turned away and sighed heavily while heading for the elevator.

As soon as the couple left the study, Maria jumped out of her chair. She began gently stroking her ass through the thin fabric of her dress.

Standing with her back to the door, she did not immediately hear the approaching footsteps.

"Ahh!" she was frightened when a huge palm closed around her neck from behind and, with a jerk, nailed her breasts to the oak tabletop. Fear echoed throughout her body, twisting her insides into a tight knot.

Her first reaction was to lash out, screaming and kicking. Thankfully, Maria was able to gather herself quickly and collapsed obediently under Sam's onslaught.

Submissive. You have to be submissive, Maria kept repeating to herself in her head.

Sam was silent. He stared at his shuddering slave and wondered what to do. The brat hadn't read the contract, thus unleashing him. Now, he could do whatever he wanted to her. Anything she says *no* to will be considered a violation.

Spanking was not an option; she could barely walk after last night. She couldn't take that. She'd cry and run away at the mere sight of the whip. He couldn't physically abuse her, and he didn't want to. It'd be a sin to spoil such a beautiful body. There was only one thing left to do.

A sickly glint appeared in Sam's eyes. He grinned at his own deceit and reached for some papers.

"Read it out loud," he ordered, slipping a copy of the unsigned contract under Maria's nose.

"I-"

"Read it. And don't lie to me! Ever again!" Sam growled menacingly, squeezing his fingers a little tighter around her neck.

"I am sorry, Master," the girl whimpered fearfully. She didn't dare to argue with him in this position. Maria began to blush out of shame. How did he know?

Maria took the contract in her hands and, still in a bent position, began to read it out loud. After two pages of legal obscure terms, she reached the notes.

"Note A--oh!" The girl's body shuddered as Sam jerked the hem of her dress up to her waist, exposing her uncovered ass.

"Maria," Sam growled, "Who told you that you could go around without underwear!?"

Chapter 13

"It hurt a lot," Maria said, squeezing her eyes shut, afraid of his reaction.

Sam ran his fingers gently over the red marks of yesterday's punishment. Maria squirmed and hissed softly, trying not to draw his attention to herself.

"Keep reading," Sam ordered calmly but didn't remove his hand. Instead, he massaged her thighs, trying not to touch the bruises.

"Note A. Both parties agree to the following types of sex: vaginal, oral, which in turn includes blowjobs, oral sex and lingual stimulation, and an..." Maria stammered. Her cheeks flushed. She wanted to hide her head in the sand like an ostrich.

"Can't you read?" Sam's cold voice sobered her up a little.

Not just his voice, though. His hand slowly traveled down to the inside of her thigh. Maria threw all her strength into self-control because the first thing she wanted to do was to close her legs. To close off access to what was most important, but she didn't move. Her free hand clenched into a fist out of fear.

"Maria! So, what was that about sex?" Sam purred. He was amused by this game. It was a good idea to change tactics. The pain would be quickly forgotten, but the shame and embarrassment would haunt her for the rest of her life.

"Anal, which involves the partner's penis in front of or inside the anus to achieve orgasm," Maria read in one breath.

She had never been so ashamed. And scared. The same "penis" she had seen in a strip club. The size of it impressed her. *Yeah, cool, amazing, every girl's dream, but not mine*, she said. The thought of *THAT* going *IN* there made her sick.

"Do you understand?" Sam asked in the same sweet tone. His hand traveled higher, touching the edges of Maria's pussy. The girl only squeezed the contract harder, crumpling the paper slightly, and exhaled heavily.

"Lingual stimulation. What's that?" Maria asked quietly.

"Tongue caresses. You've never been tongue-fucked, Maria?" Sam brashly stroked along the folds, eliciting a quiet squeak from Maria. She jerked in surprise.

"N-no... Ah!" Maria jerked again at the hard pressure on her clit.

Her toes curled, her knees jerked up, and her whole body began to throb as the chills began to travel down her spine.

"How did you get fucked? Mm?" Sam calmly continued the smutty conversation.

His fingers never stopped lazily roaming her cunt. As if exploring every millimeter, Sam took his time driving her crazy. He simply moved his fingers up and down or "accidentally" touched her tender clit. Maria only sniffled loudly and whimpered softly, biting her lip.

"The usual way," the girl barely squeezed out of herself.

"Like this?" Sam asked innocently and inserted his middle finger into her without warning.

"Aggh!" came out of her tortured lips.

"Maria... Baby girl," the man tsked. The back of her neck felt his smug smile. He was grinning like a wolf who saw Little Red Riding Hood in the forest.

Maria only sobbed bitterly, crumpling the contract with her fingers until her knuckles were white. A stingy tear rolled onto the oak tabletop. Maria knew what he was talking about.

She was burning with shame. Barely contained the oncoming hysteria.

She was so wet.

The finger entered without any obstacle, like a hot knife through butter.

Maria was scared. Very scared because it felt so damn good! Yes, Sam was breaking down all the barriers of permissibility. He caused a wave of shame and embarrassment unknown to her before, but she did not turn away from his touch. Maria was afraid of the unknown, of his pressure. Instead of disgust, desire was building up in her.

And who's the sick one now!? the girl scolded herself. This shame swallowed her with even greater force. Enjoying the aftercare of an enemy! To be so wet because of a man who had destroyed everything her parents had! To want someone who didn't think you were human.

It would be better if he beat me instead! Beat me day and night! Maria wanted to roar and scream at her weakness.

"Unexpected, and-" Sam smiled contentedly and finished his thought out loud: "lovely." Moving his hand slowly, he roared, "Read on!"

"Non-traditional sex: petting, mammary, intercrural, gluteal, and several others, which involve breasts, buttocks, thighs, and other organs of the partner during sexual intercourse," Maria tried to read faster but stammered and stumbled over almost every word.

Sam watched her shuddering body mesmerized. Her reactions both amused and angered him. He couldn't figure out what he wanted more: to abuse her or to simply replace his finger with his already aching and eager cock.

Next on the list was a list of sex toys. Maria's shame and Sam's movements made her blush crimson red. She was biting and licking her lips, mooing when Sam picked up the pace and exhaled when he stopped.

Because of her voracious imagination and the forums she had read earlier, Maria began to imagine all these objects in Sam's hands. A small shiver began to cover her body again, for she knew for a fact that Sam would not spare her. Clamps, plugs, strapons, dildos, vibrators—all these things horrified Maria.

"Rules of submissive behavior."

"Read them carefully!" Sam growled unhappily. She'd broken two rules in less than twenty-four hours: she hadn't eaten enough, and she hadn't slept well. At this rate, he'd be driving her to hospitals instead of dominating her.

Maria understood his anger. She had a special relationship with obedience, sleep, and food. Or rather, she had no relationship with these things at all. She slept badly, ate only when someone forced her to, and always found herself in trouble. Having obediently read out loud all the duties of a slave, the girl calmed down a bit.

In turn, the Master, Sam, had no right to harm her. No violence or coercion. Strangely, Maria still didn't understand that distinction. Understandably, she had a safe word and the right to leave at any time. But then her family...

"I-I'm finished," Maria replied in a trembling voice as she finished reading to the end.

"Any questions?"

"N-no... oh!"

With a sharp jerk of her body, Maria slammed her hips against the edge of the table. Sam decided to spice things up and slid his thumb to the girl's anus. He took his time rubbing the tight ring, continuing the movements of his middle finger.

No! No! No! she clamped her eyes shut. Breathing loudly, Maria tried not to move.

"Maria," Sam began calmly but seriously, "Now, do you realize what you've signed?"

A short nod and silence confirmed her answer. Still crumpling the contract in her hand, Maria cursed herself and then the whole ordeal.

"You could have crossed out all your taboos. I gave you that chance, but now…" Sam deliberately didn't finish. He wanted the realization of her stupid act to fall on the girl with all its force.

Maria was silent. Only her heavy breathing gave away her tension.

"I understand... Master," she replied, gathering the remnants of her composure.

"You don't understand shit!" Sam only tsked irritably. Her answer pissed him off. How did she always manage to do it!?

Maria didn't even have time to squeak. Sam pulled out and pushed her toward him, turning her sharply around to face him. Fury burned brightly in his eyes. She had angered him again. The girl sobbed only faintly, for she didn't even realize what she had done wrong AGAIN.

Half-naked, red as a cherry, Maria clutched at her thighs to keep from instinctively covering herself. This was sure to piss him off even more. All her acting tricks didn't work when he was this close.

"If you understand," Sam tilted his head to the side and squinted his anger-blurred eyes, his fingers tightening around the girl's neck and lowering his hand, "Kneel, Maria... and open your mouth wide."

Chapter 14

Maria had been holding on somehow, but now, the harsh reality was upon her. The horror in her eyes made her condition clear. A stop word immediately popped up in her mind. Use this precious word on the first day? No. Maria couldn't do that.

"Take everything off," Sam ordered without regard to her inner hysterics.

The sight of Maria left him confused. He even wondered if she had ever given anyone a blowjob. Sam only grinned at his thoughts, not knowing he was completely right.

Maria, meanwhile, began to pull off her clothes. She got the dress off quickly but was struggling with the clasp of her bra. Her fingers wouldn't obey her. Her chin trembled, and her eyes flickered with anxiety. When she felt the familiar heavy gaze, she simply yanked one edge and seemed to tear the thin lace. The lingerie flew under her feet.

Completely naked, she stood there, afraid to look up. Feeling the gravity of the situation, Maria couldn't breathe properly. Her legs shook every now and then. Biting her lip, Maria looked away.

"Maria," Sam's voice grew quieter. Pulling the girl toward him, he forced her to raise her head and look him in the eye.

He had seen a lot of things in his life. But the amount of fear that gathered in those unhappy eyes was the first time Sam had ever seen it.

"It can't be," the man couldn't believe his hunch. "Have you ever pleasured a man with your mouth?" Sam asked in all seriousness. He wasn't trying to humiliate or embarrass her.

Maria was silent. A stingy tear rolled down her ruddy cheek. She didn't need to answer. Her emotions and condition gave away everything.

"You do realize that you will have to do it, right?" Sam asked again without a drop of sarcasm. He was talking to her like a top to a sub. The topic of enemies had been relegated to the background. No, he hadn't forgotten who she was. But forcing her to do something she didn't know about was nonsense.

"Y-yes, Master," Maria sniffed.

"I'll teach you, baby girl," Sam said calmly, moving her hand from her neck to her chin. It was necessary to calm Maria down. Taking her chin, he began to run his finger along her cheekbone.

"Thank you, Master," the girl sighed loudly. She didn't jerk her head. Didn't try to dodge Sam. She looked into his eyes and, like a snake under the guidance of an experienced snake charmer, calmed down. His slight touch made Maria float. She treacherously squeezed her thighs because it suddenly felt very hot and empty between her legs.

"You haven't eaten anything," Sam stated.

"No. Sorry, Master. I'll make it up to you."

Sam liked her answer. For whatever it was worth, Maria was a quick learner. For a second, he thought she'd make a good sub.

But not mine, Sam remembered the circumstances with annoyance.

After giving orders to eat immediately and apply more healing ointment to her buttocks, Sam stared at the closed door of his study and thought. Thinking about what to do with her for those three months. What should *he* do for three months?

Maria didn't quite realize it. Instead of tears and hysterics, the girl sprinted to the kitchen, not forgetting to take things to her room. She smiled like a fool and eagerly devoured an entire bowl of soup. She even ate a slice of bread and butter.

"*It's all right*," she kept telling herself. Maybe it wasn't that bad? Maybe Sam wasn't such an evil dominant? More like a nice one.

"A good Master," Maria laughed out loud. There's no such thing.

He could have put her on her knees and fucked her in the mouth without any sympathy. Remembering her condition, Maria stopped smiling. It was scary.

But he didn't. He calmed her down and told her to go eat.

"He said he was going to teach me," Maria gritted her teeth. On one hand, as stupid and naive as she was, she believed in good and that everyone had at least something light in their souls. On the other hand, when she looked at Sam, she had a doubt. A huge doubt.

Was she afraid of intimacy? *A little*. It was foolish to lie to herself. Far more frightening, though, was the unknown. In standard relationships, everything is simple, but in BDSM, wherever you turn, everything is an undiscovered territory. In twenty-four years, Maria had never knelt, yet this disgrace in the study had completely thrown her off-guard. The girl didn't have a lot of boyfriends—well, only one, actually.

Jack and Maria went to the same school. The guy followed her everywhere like a puppy since high school. Maria only smiled discreetly and flirted with the guy. She thought it was just a crush. When she got to university, Jack didn't give up. Gave her flowers and expensive gifts. Like a true gentleman, he took her to movies and restaurants. The interesting thing is Jack was in no hurry to get intimate. They rarely kissed. He didn't try to get in her panties. Even when they finally slept together, the guy remained cold.

He was not interested in any experiments in bed, and he did not ask Maria that very "take it in your mouth, baby girl." Lights out, blanket, a short prelude, and missionary position. Despite the boredom of their intimate life, they dated for two years. One day, Jack did not show up for their date, to which Maria simply shrugged. After that, they did not see each other and did not call each other. Their relationship ended as quietly as it began.

After that, Maria did not seek new acquaintances. Guys drooled over her, but she only smiled sweetly and pushed everyone away. Everything in her life regarding men happened quietly. Up until Sam. He turned everything upside down. Within a couple of days of meeting him, he'd made her feel everything from hatred to desire. And that was just the beginning.

The weirdest and most incomprehensible thing for Maria remained her reaction to his touch. There was no disgust. Her mind screamed that she should shudder and shake in agony at his touch, but everything happened exactly the opposite. She was burning with a cowardly desire. There, in the study, at one point, Maria had already opened her mouth to beg him not to stop. That was what was scaring her.

One day.

She'd been with him for one day, and she was already almost begging and pleading for him to fuck her.

What would happen in three months?

What would happen to her?

What would happen to him?

If Maria had been afraid of Sam before, now she was beginning to fear herself.

Chapter 15

"Come in," Sam said calmly as Maria peeked into the study.

She ate, washed the dishes, showered, applied the ointment, and even checked the messages on her phone. Afterward, the girl wasn't entirely sure what she should do. Sam didn't say when to come over or where she should wait. Doubting her actions, she still decided to return to the study.

"Excuse me, Master. I'm all done," Maria reported back, still at the threshold.

Sam was sitting at his desk, reading the documents intently while tapping his pen.

He's definitely reading everything, Maria rolled her eyes. She would remember her stupidity for a long time to come.

"Sit down. I'm still busy," he ordered without looking at her.

Maria looked around. There was a small sofa in the corner near the bookcase. She was about to approach it as she froze on half a step. With a shake of her head, the girl turned around and headed toward Sam.

"*He meant at his feet*," Maria thought wistfully. Bottoms and slaves always sit at their master's feet.

Going around the table, the girl was not at all surprised to see a small cushion near Sam's chair. Without looking at it, Maria carefully knelt down on it, tucked her head, and waited for her Master.

Sam could have left the paperwork for later and gone straight to "teaching," but his inner dominant wanted to give her another test. Maria had done well, which he was mentally pleased about. Constant punishments exhausted and made life difficult for both the top and bottom. The girl sat silently at his feet and waited quietly.

While Maria rummaged around in the kitchen, Sam thought about how to behave with this naughty slave girl. He could punish her all the time, but then again, that would be costly for him. And he didn't want that. After his little finger prank, Sam wanted more to hear her ragged breathing, pleas to keep going and allow her to cum.

Hmmm, this is going to be interesting, man grinned contentedly, having fully thought out the plan for the next three months.

"Eyes on me," he said to a sleepy Maria. The girl tried to hold back a yawn, but still, she yawned quietly once. Hearing her Master's cold voice, Maria immediately looked up.

Sam's enigmatic grin covered her skin with horribly huge goosebumps.

Straightening her back, Maria waited for instructions.

"How are the bruises?"

"They hurt," Maria admitted.

"They'll go away," Sam replied sternly. "Turn your whole body toward me. Put your hands here." He patted his legs just above the knee and leaned back in his chair, keeping his eyes on Maria. "Are you afraid?" Sam asked suddenly.

"A-a little," Maria stammered. The girl tried to look away, but strong fingers held her by the chin and returned her to her original position.

"Look at me. Eyes always on me, baby girl," Sam repeated with insistence.

"I'm sorry, Master," Maria tried to retreat. Licking her parched lips, she didn't twitch again.

Their "lesson" had gone by like a blur for Maria. Shaking like a frightened rabbit, she did everything Sam said. Smoothly stroked his legs. Carefully unbuttoned his pants and pulled back the elastic band of his boxers. She blushed when she saw his huge cock, and almost fainted when she touched it with her hand for the first time.

Maria was mesmerized by Sam's cock. It was already quite hard, wiry, with bulging veins. Swallowing loudly, she tried to ignore the tingling in her lower abdomen. Holding her breath, the girl shuddered as she imagined him inside her. A wave of arousal shot through her body at the thought.

You're sick, Maria chastised herself.

"Maria, breathe," Sam said mockingly, stroking her cheekbone.

Despite his tone and the absurdity of the situation, Maria calmed down a little and actually started breathing more often. Again, she didn't understand the reaction of her body and brain in general. No disgust. No anger. Fear of the unknown and fear of disappointment was what didn't leave her mind the entire process.

"Good girl," Sam exhaled heavily as her plump lips closed on the scarlet head. The wave of pleasure was so great that Sam could barely contain himself. Clenching his fists until his knuckles turned white, he threw all his strength into self-control, for the urge to wrap her dark hair around his fist and start thrusting all the way in was too great.

Not tonight. Let her get used to it, he said himself as he watched his obedient student.

Giving brief instructions, Sam couldn't take his eyes off her. He could tell by the small tremors that she was shivering and mentally exulted. She was getting aroused. She was wet, he knew for sure. His own lust was beginning to overwhelm him. Still, Sam raked her hair into his fist and thrust a little harder, causing Maria to cough loudly, trying to pull away. Pulling her away from his steaming cock, Sam looked at Maria languidly and a little absent-mindedly.

"Good, baby girl," he repeated hoarsely and brought her head back to his groin. Sam tousled her hair, feeling his orgasm approaching. Maria was already enjoying herself, sucking the huge length to the max, licking his smoothly shaved balls, and caressing the head with her tongue.

The orgasm hit Sam in full force. He arched his back and gripped the armrest until his joints crunched. Maria was more frightened by his animalistic growl. Relaxing her throat in time, Maria grimaced as she took every last drop.

Breathing in air loudly through her nose, the girl leaned her hands on Sam's legs and tried to come to her senses. Her body feverishly shuddered, thin trails of cold sweat running down her back and face.

"Not bad for the first time," Sam praised Maria, catching his breath and hiding his not fully fallen cock. "Stand up."

Pulling the embarrassed girl close to him, he stroked her hot buttock without touching the wounded skin. Because of her short stature, Maria didn't tower over him much. Her breasts were just at his eye level.

"Maria, what is this?" Glancing at the embarrassed girl, Sam inquired. His hands moved to her panting breasts. The standing nipples gave away her condition. Lightly pinching the small peas between his thumb and forefinger, Sam heard a quiet sob.

Maria kept her pleading gaze on him. Only she couldn't fully understand what she wanted: for him to let her go or for him to continue?

"Well?" Sam repeated his question.

"I... I don't know what to say," she blushed even more.

"Don't lie. I will punish you! You're horny, aren't you? You little slut."

"I am."

"Say it again," Sam ordered, twisting one nipple.

"Umhmh!" Maria took a step back, but Sam's strong arm around her waist brought her back to her seat. "I'm horny, Master," the girl squirmed in shame.

Sam slid his gaze lazily over her naked body. Dropping his palm between her thighs, he immediately felt the moisture on his fingers. *"You're wet,"* he said hoarsely. The fabric of his boxers stretched again, his desire piquing. Maria only rose on her toes, trying to make her plight at least a little easier. Clenching her hands into fists, she bit her lower lip, preventing the moans that were about to escape from her throat. But it suddenly stopped.

"Go. I'll see you tomorrow. And don't forget to eat. I won't remind you again," Sam folded his arms across his chest defiantly. "You'll go to the clinic tomorrow morning. I've made all the arrangements."

"The clinic?" Maria looked at him dumbfounded. Why would she go to the clinic!? A wave of indignation came over the girl.

"Yes. You'll get a full checkup. The gynecologist will prescribe birth control pills," Sam responded.

"I won't take hormone pills!" Maria blurted out in one breath. She was not going to harm her already poor health. "Why can't you use condoms?" she said and blushed instantly. Had she just accepted the fact that she had agreed to sleep with him!?

Sam looked intently at the bratty Maria. He even liked her little rebellion. It made him want to bring her to her knees again. But Sam resisted. Stifled the urge of anger. He knew his request was not simple, and her outrage was understandable.

"You will go to the clinic. The doctor will prescribe you the safest and most compatible birth control pill. I can't stand condoms.

Plus, they're gonna test you for STDs. I don't know who's been inside you, Maria. I care about my health," Sam said mockingly.

His speech made the girl's eyes widen. Was she the one who called him nice!? Maria took back all those nice words and thoughts she previously had about him. Asshole! He was a real asshole! How could she even think nicely of him!? He practically called her a whore. Life had taught her nothing.

Stifling the urge to claw his face with her fingernails and scratch him bloody, Maria ostentatiously lowered her head and, saying goodbye insensitively, left the study.

After spending more than an hour in the shower, she went to bed with her eyes red from tears. She remembered that she had forgotten to eat again, falling into a deep sleep.

Chapter 16

That night, Maria slept like a child. She even had dreams. The alarm clock, however, didn't wake her up. But Sam did.

She dreamt of home. She and her mother were sitting on the veranda and, like all girls, gossiping. Maria was actively saying something, sitting at Mrs. O'Dell's feet. She, in turn, listened attentively to her daughter and braided her hair.

"Can you imagine Mom!?" the girl squeaked. "Mom? Ouch!"

Maria was pulled sharply by her hair. The dream was beginning to fade. Everything was erased catastrophically fast until darkness came. The tension didn't go away. Opening her eyes, Maria stumbled into a new kind of darkness. A pair of angry blue eyes were drilling her. Maria didn't immediately realize what was happening or where she was.

"Good morning, sleepyhead," Sam said, watching her confusion. Maria frowned and tried to turn her head, but Sam held tightly to the dark hair.

Again. Maria broke the rules, again. At this rate, she'd wear him down; he'd let her go early and take her statement. But she didn't need to know about that.

Maria remained silent, watching him sleepily. It didn't take long for a chill to set in, and it quickly traveled down her naked back. She'd done something wrong again.

"Good morning," the girl replied drowsily.

"Maria, why am I here?"

A distracted look wandered across Sam's tense face. Maria tried to find the slightest hint of emotion in his facial expression. But she saw nothing but a horrified look, a tense chin, and compressed lips. The girl forgot his question at once. The sleepiness had not yet let go.

Seeing her condition, Sam only sighed heavily and pulled Maria toward him. With a loud yelp, she found herself in the familiar position for punishment—belly on his lap and ass up. Maria woke up instantly. She felt as if she had been splashed with cold water. She realized that she was about to get her ass kicked again. With her toes tucked in and her forehead pressed into the sheets, she held her breath.

"I'm sorry, Master," Maria tried to smooth the situation somehow.

"Why?" Sam asked calmly.

His palms had already started stroking the almost healed buttocks. With each touch, Maria twitched faintly. She was afraid.

"Why, Maria?" He insisted on her answering.

"I... I..." Maria began to get lost. She didn't understand why!

"Maria!"

"I don't know! Do you understand? I don't know!" It came out of her mouth as she threw her head back. She began to shiver with anger and fear. But more anger. "What have I done again?" she questioned pleadingly, her face pressed into the sheets.

"First of all, watch your mouth!" Sam growled and gave her a hard slap, which made Maria shriek loudly. "Second, what did I say about the food?" another slap followed.

"I don't eat three meals a day," Maria hissed, pressing her cheek into the mattress.

"Now you will! Otherwise, I'll punish you so much you'll run out of here naked and never look back! Do you understand me!?" Sam grabbed her reddened buttock, causing another wave of discomfort.

"Okay, Master. Sorry, Master. I'll make it up to you, Master," Maria sneered.

Sam only chuckled at her behavior. He would give her some time to adjust. But then there would be no mercy. In the meantime, an unkind glint appeared in his eyes. The sleepy and defiant Maria had caught his eye. He wanted not only to punish her but also to encourage her.

Maria concentrated on her breathing, expecting at least a couple more blows, but there were none. Instead, Sam touched the inside of her thigh, causing her to clench immediately.

"Maria, you are testing my patience."

She realized from his calm tone that she'd better not, and obediently spread her legs. His touch gave Maria a small shiver. Lying still became harder with each touch. When Sam touched her clit, she exhaled loudly, clutching at the sheets with her fingers. Sam was very compelled to fondle Maria's pent-up desire. He changed his pace, paying special attention to her clit and pressing lightly on the tight entrance without penetrating with his fingers.

Maria didn't last long. She started moaning loudly and tried to catch his fingers, wanting to feel him inside her like yesterday in the study. She bloody loved it, and she hated herself for liking it even more.

"Fuck," Maria cursed, feeling her orgasm coming on. She wanted to howl with pleasure and beg for more. But she just bit her lip and mooed into the sheets, trying to ease the tension.

When the glare began to appear in front of her eyes, the girl arched up like a cat waiting for Sam's final movements.

But he...stopped. Abruptly removed his hands. Maria almost burst into tears with frustration.

"It's a punishment, remember?" Sam was almost laughing. He liked what he saw. Pushing Maria up, he signaled it was time to get up.

She shook like a junkie who hadn't gotten her dose, but she stood up proudly from his lap and looked defiantly at her tormentor. Her legs burned with dissatisfaction. Her breasts ached, and her throat was dry.

"I don't need any pleasure or aftercare from you!" Maria snapped again.

Sam's face stretched at that loud statement. Had she forgotten her condition two minutes ago?

"Really?" Sam asked sweetly.

"Yes," Maria didn't back down.

"And you can endure all the punishments and games without aftercare?" the man was amused. Leaning back on his elbows, he studied his slave with interest.

Maria shuddered at his gaze. Her cheeks flushed again when she realized that he had come to her in only his house pants. It was impossible to look away from his muscular, perfect body. Muscles rippled at the slightest movement. The huge shoulders made her want to wrap her arms around him and not let go. For some reason, Maria wanted to leave a hickey on his massive neck. She'd never had such thoughts before. But with Sam, her desire only seemed to keep rising.

"I can," Maria answered a little more quietly.

"All right, Maria O'Dell. If you hold out, I'll let you go and withdraw my statement in two months."

Yes, she was always a bit stubborn, but what was he doing!? It wasn't BDSM anymore, just some nonsense! Sam had to stop. He should have stopped. But he was going as fast as Maria.

"Do we have a deal?"

"Yes!" Maria agreed without a doubt.

"Get dressed and go eat breakfast! You've got half an hour," Sam growled. He had just fallen for the little splinter himself. He, an experienced dominant! "And don't forget your panties!"

Chapter 17

Maria stared at the closing door and couldn't believe what was happening.

Two months without orgasms! Her own stupidity made her want to climb the wall. Even the shortening of her stay with Sam didn't make her happier. She couldn't do it! It was unreal! After what he did to her a few minutes ago, she'd lose before she could even squeak.

"Okay, focus!" Maria closed her eyes and rubbed her cheeks. The girl began to encourage and reassure herself.

"We'll get through this!" she couldn't stop saying the mantra, standing in the shower.

I can do it! she repeated, looking at herself in the mirror.

When Maria came out of the bathroom, there was another huge bag on the floor. In it, the girl found an exceptionally beautiful lemon-colored dress, white lace underwear, sandals on a small comfortable heel, and a purse. A couple minutes later, Maria was fidgeting at the mirror, examining herself from every angle. The panties caused a bit of discomfort, but she didn't dare leave the room without them. Putting her hair loose, she transferred her essentials into her new purse and went to the kitchen.

Despite their strained and strange relationship, Maria had a keen desire to thank Sam. She realized all these things belonged to her only for the duration of her time as a slave, but her parents had always taught her to say thanks, even if the person was a jerk.

Sam, too, had managed to change from his homemade pants to another expensive business suit. Maria could smell his cologne from the living room. The strong scent of orange and bergamot made her head spin. She wanted to snuggle into his massive neck and inhale this aroma until the smell disappeared.

Maria didn't like how she reacted with Sam. Those two days had gone like a non-stop roller coaster ride. From tears to mentally pleading not to stop, Maria had experienced almost the entire spectrum of emotions. After thinking hard about everything they had agreed on, she put on the mask of submission and obedience again, deciding not to take it off under any scenario.

Never had Maria imagined that her starring role would turn out to be like this. A role on which too many lives depend. She had no other choice but to cope with. Maria didn't see any other options. And she didn't want to.

Sam was consumed with the morning news and routine messages from lawyers and suppliers. The man was hastily eating and washing them down with good coffee. When Maria appeared on the doorstep, Sam paid no attention to the girl. She had already exhausted his kindness and condescension for the day.

Distantly hearing her cowering behind the kitchen surface, Sam forbade himself to look at her. He was still angry. That anger was directed at himself, but that girl was the instigator. Opening another contract, he completely immersed himself in studying the documents.

"More coffee, Master?" he heard from the second time. Maria had to come closer to repeat her question.

"What?" Sam frowned.

"I'm asking, do you want more coffee, Master?" Looking down at the floor, Maria repeated.

"Yes," he agreed.

Sam was watching her closely now. The dress and shoes looked perfect on her. She sparkled like a sun in the sky. He decided not to ask about the underwear. He hoped she'd learned her lesson.

Maria frowned amusedly, scratching her little nose and mumbling something faintly. After making him a fresh pot of coffee, she returned to the refrigerator. Looking into it, she wrinkled her nose again and closed it. Maria crumpled like a schoolgirl in front of the principal's office, obviously hoping to ask something.

"I'm sorry, Master. Can I ask you a question?"

"What?" Sam said irritably.

"Can I just have coffee with milk? I'll make myself a cappuccino. I can't eat in the morning. If I do, I'll be nauseous all day, and my stomach will hurt. Peanut butter toast at the most, but... but you don't have any. I don't eat much. I don't eat much at all. I'm not trying to disobey by any means, but I'm just not much of an eater. My mom makes fun of me all the time. But sometimes I get a craving, and I can eat a box of doughnuts by myself," Maria rambled on.

Sam could sense her excitement from the way she nervously tugged at the hem of her dress. He also cringed at her formality. Usually, the lower ones always addressed the Masters that way, but this one pissed him off.

"All right. But if I see that you're not eating at all, you will be punished."

"I understand, Master. You explained it very well."

They ate breakfast in silence. Afterward, Sam gave Maria a credit card and ordered her to buy all the groceries she needed.

"Get some fresh air."

Maria dismissed the idea of walking around London, especially in the center of the city. There was a high probability of meeting acquaintances or some of her mother's friends. Then the problems would become even greater.

The girl started refreshing her memory of the stores that made home deliveries.

In the lobby, the two of them were again met by a friendly bellman. He looked at the transformed Maria with interest. On the street, two cars were waiting for them. Having assigned a silent driver, Steve, Sam left for the office without even saying goodbye.

A little relaxed, Maria went to the clinic. There, everyone spoke to her extremely politely and explained each nuance. When it was time to visit a gynecologist, Maria became visibly nervous, but the elderly woman doctor quickly calmed her down. She did not ask unnecessary questions when she saw the marks on her buttocks. She did not ask why she needed contraception for three months.

"I can recommend a contraceptive shot. It works for three months. With your test results, it's the best solution. If you take the shot today, you can have physical contact with your partner in two weeks," the woman said slowly. Then, she went through the list of contraindications. Maria tried to listen attentively, mentally rejoicing that she would not have sex for another two weeks.

"Everything is clear," Maria smiled.

"There can be menstrual irregularities," the doctor warned her.

"Okay. Let's do it!"

Chapter 18

Maria spent the next two weeks like she was at a resort. The girl tried to stay positive no matter what.

Forced to walk around naked twenty-four hours a day? At least it's good for the skin!

Can't go outside? It's too hot out there anyway!

Have to give a blowjob to the enemy of the family? Experience! And pleasure, too, but no one will ever know.

Want sex or basic aftercare so much that sparks are flying from your eyes? Stamina!

Haven't had your ass kicked in thirteen days? Personal victory!

On rare occasions, Maria still wore a house dress. Sam allowed her to cook in the kitchen, but all the cleaning was left to the lovely Mexican Rosita. The woman spoke a little English and generally did everything quickly and silently. To Maria's surprise, Rosita even cleaned *the room*. The same room where all of Sam's sex toys were kept. Only Rosita had the right to enter his bedroom and study without Master's presence.

In these rare hours, Maria sat on the veranda and watched the bustle of London. The girl never dared to leave the apartment during all this time. The thought that she might be met by acquaintances chilled the blood in her veins to a negative degree. Sam did not insist on long walks, especially since Maria managed to burn her nose by sitting on the balcony too long in the middle of a sunny day.

Alicia stormed the phone with constant messages. Worried. It was probably thanks to her constant encouragement that everything went so smoothly. Maria called her father once. Told him how "work" was going. She had to lie a lot. A LOT. That day, she didn't even eat but defiantly smeared her plate with meat sauce and purposely left it in the sink. It worked.

Lying to her family turned out to be very difficult and painful. Maria was torn apart with each new lie. Her father marveled at her successes and constantly repeated that he missed her and that he would fix everything. Maria only smiled sadly and looked behind her back. She cried a lot, too.

There was also hatred and disgust. The girl attributed all these emotions to herself. When Sam called her into the office a second time and ordered her to kneel, she thought she would vomit in disgust, but she didn't. Maria was overwhelmed with lust and arousal. Like a cat, she licked her lips at the sight of the huge cock as if it were a bowl of milk. And, of course, Sam hadn't forgotten about their arrangement. He did incredible things to her body. Patting, pinching, tickling, squeezing, and stroking in places Maria didn't even know about. Who would have thought that the erogenous zone could be under her shoulder blades!? Maria's constant sexual tension had turned her into one solid erogenous zone.

Sam also loved his toys. Maria hated them. Again, because she couldn't have any rewards. The feather stack had become her personal hell. The nipple clamps made Maria bite her lips until they turned bloody, and the Wartenberg wheel still gave her nightmares.

90

But the worst of them all were Sam's barbed phrases. His thoughts out loud made Maria shake. He phrased her a lot.

Ramming her with two fingers, tied to St. Andrew's cross, he did not stop whispering in her ear all kinds of vulgarities. He told her in detail how he wanted to fuck her. Where and what to stick in her. When to use flogger on her gentle skin. At such moments, Maria only convulsively gulped air and shuddered under a new portion of hateful pleasure.

Each time, he mockingly pissed her off with the question, "Yes, or no?" It was getting harder and harder to refuse.

But there were some things Sam never allowed himself. No kissing or tongue fucking at all. That job was entirely Maria's responsibility. No sex.

The doctor hadn't forbidden intercourse, and there was still an option of interrupted intercourse, but Sam didn't even try to stick anything but his fingers inside Maria. She was, of course, happy about this course of events, but as he had promised, sometimes she wanted to howl and beg to be fucked.

Almost every day, she would go back to her room, fall on her bed with her face in the pillow, and just howl. The fact that Sam could hear her didn't bother Maria. She could help herself quietly in the shower, but this Cerberus could see right through her. The slave mask helped with household chores and simple orders, but with sexual matters, everything fell apart as soon as he was near.

Unlike Maria, Sam remained more or less satisfied. The girl didn't disappoint. She braved, huffed and puffed at the urge, and howled into the pillow, but did not give up. O'Dell became his personal challenge. And the more she tried to cope with the arousal, the more he wanted to make her give up. However, something kept stopping Sam. In two weeks, he'd gotten used to the glimpse of her bare ass and her constantly sleepy face in the kitchen in the morning.

Sam remembered their evenings in the study with particular fondness. Her mouth would work wonders. Who would have thought Maria would be so capable? He didn't think about the stinky strip club or the lippy strippers. And when an old acquaintance called to ask about the date of his next visit, Sam politely declined because now he had Maria.

He liked to touch her. Corrupting her young body. The sight of the goosebumps on her skin made his cock flinch. Every time he saw her in agony, Sam suffered with her. He would blindfold her to hide his condition. After a couple of days, Sam made it clear to himself that he would not let Maria go after two months. All her suffering would be for nothing; she would only hate him more, but Sam was not going to change his mind.

That's why he wouldn't have sex with her. He knew she couldn't take it. She'd lose.

The issue of her father was still open. Sam hired the most expensive detectives to re-investigate the incident that happened twenty-five years ago and the dark deeds of the O'Dell company. The man was confused by the forged signatures of O'Dell Sr. on some contracts. If you are an accomplice, why forge your own signature? This thought parasitically lodged in Sam's head.

The feedback he got from everyone at the company was also bothersome. They received Sam terribly, constantly gossiping behind his back about how good it was with Mr. O'Dell. Comparing all the facts, Sam realized that something was amiss.

He did not share his hunches with Maria because it could all be a well-planned performance. The thought that Mr. O'Dell might have deliberately put his only daughter under Sam's thumb made his eyes darken. Only the realest scumbag could have done such a thing. The only thing left to check was whether O'Dell was indeed a scumbag or not. Life had taught Sam not to trust anyone. Not even the people closest to him.

For the last couple of days, Sam had been in the office late at night. The idea of sending a driver to pick up Maria even crossed his mind. He needed a release more than ever and had already thought of a scenario for that day's session.

The car was waiting downstairs when there was a knock on his office door.

"Jacob," he shook hands with his security chief, "Have a seat."

"Excuse me, Mr. Williams. But I thought you might want to see this."

A tall, stocky man with a formidable face, wearing a businesslike black suit, handed Sam a yellow folder.

"Thank you, Jacob. Have a good weekend," he said, looking into the folder.

"Have a good one, sir."

As soon as the door closed, Sam sat back in his chair and began to study the contents of the folder. With each new page, Sam's face crusted with anger. His eyes darkened with rage.

"You are a bitch, Maria O'Dell. Little lying bitch!"

Chapter 19

As she heard the sound of the door opening, Maria quickly jumped out of bed and ran to meet her Master. Once in the hall, she stopped in the center of the room, put her head down, and waited.

"Into the Room," Sam growled as he walked past.

Damn it, he's angry again, Maria thought, annoyed as she took her time heading into the playroom.

Still pausing in the center of the playroom, Maria waited with bated breath for her Master. Sam reeked coldly and angryly, probably because of his work. At least that's what she thought. Her father would often come home in such a state, but a couple of hours passed, and he would be all sunshine again.

The door opened with a crack. A disheveled Sam stood across from Maria. By the clenched fists and bulging veins in his arms, Maria realized he was truly furious.

Should I slip him some peppermint and chamomile tea? Maria chuckled to herself. However, the fun evaporated as soon as he approached. She didn't even have time to blink.

Grabbing her chin firmly, he yanked Maria toward him. A barely audible squeak escaped her throat. The sight of his crazed eyes made her ears blare.

Something is wrong. Maria unmistakably read his emotions. An unpleasant sticky sweat protruded under her shoulder blades. Intuition never failed Maria, and right then, it was screaming that she needed to be extra careful.

Sam remained silent. Continued to burn his slave with his gaze. Looking for even the slightest hint of his mistake. But he saw nothing. A blank space.

"Hands in front of you," Sam commanded, moving toward the toy dresser.

Maria watched his actions with hidden panic. Putting leather bails and greaves on her, he began to quickly lower the chains attached to the ceiling. Panic came to Maria in waves. He had never played with her like this before. He had almost always blindfolded her, which was not strange but a bit frightening. But not today.

Securing her arms, Sam fumbled for a hidden carabiner on the floor and, forcing Maria to spread her legs wide, secured the greaves. Stretched like a frog, Maria struggled to breathe and stared into the wall.

Behind her, there was a noise again. Sam was looking for something on the shelves. Facing the couch, Maria didn't know what he had taken. When he finished his search, Sam strode defiantly to the couch and laid out the contents so that Maria could get a good look. With each new device and toy she saw, Maria flinched. When she saw the last item, she sobbed.

On the black leather couch was a whole set called "Maria, you're fucked": metal nipple clamps, ordinary wooden clothespins, a Wartenberg wheel, a paddle, a stack, a vibrator, lubricant, and, as it seemed to Maria, a huge anal plug with a pink stone.

"Do you remember your safe word?" Sam asked spontaneously.

"Red," Maria nodded with a strong feeling that she may use it today.

"Maria, why don't you tell me about your sessions with Sheldon Mars?"

Chapter 20

"Did you not hear me?" Sam asked calmly after Maria said nothing.

"That's nothing interesting," Maria's voice trembled. Like a true slave, she lowered her head guiltily.

Sam didn't comment on her answer. He approached the sofa and thoughtfully ran his gaze over the toys lying there. Maria watched his movements. As his fingers reached for the anal plug, everything inside her twisted with fear. But Sam quickly changed his mind in favor of the stack.

"Describe it," Sam demanded, scrutinizing the device. He still wasn't looking at Maria. He swung the stack a couple of times, cutting through the tense air. Maria only squeaked quietly, realizing that it was bad.

She hoped that the Master had just had a bad day and now he needed to blow off steam. *But why these questions about Mars!?* Maria refused to accept the fact that Sam knew her little secret.

"Maria!" Sam reasserted himself and circled around like a shark.

Maria pulled herself together. On the fly, she began to make up delusional scenarios of the sessions she supposedly had with

Mars. Meanwhile, Sam did not stop walking around her. He stroked her buttocks, her thighs, her breasts with the soft tongue of his stack.

"Say that again, I didn't hear you," he asked quietly.

Exhaling heavily, Maria began to repeat her story, trying not to stumble.

The first blow came on her back.

"And also... O-o-u-ch!" she shrieked.

"Go on."

Tearing up her breath, Maria continued. Sam continued, too. With each new phrase, anger spilled poison throughout his body, paralyzing his mind and common sense. For the first time in his life, Sam wanted to hurt someone. Intentional physical harm. The remnants of his mind wouldn't let him. But he was close. Again, unable to physically harm her, he played with her mind. He chose the scariest toys and didn't blindfold her, but avoided eye contact.

Stack, like a brush, applied short but sharp strokes to her trembling body, which was now a canvas. Maria flinched, hissed, and shrieked unashamedly when Sam paid attention to particularly tender places. Her nipples were dark red, her ass was reddened in some places, and her crotch whimpered from the greatest number of spanks. Maria tried to bring her legs together, but the greaves wouldn't allow it. Arching her legs and balancing on her toes, she struggled to do the job.

Sam demanded she repeat it all over again. And again. And again.

After an incalculable number of strokes, Maria hung from the chains as her legs were no longer holding her up. Seeing her condition, Sam returned to the couch. Putting the stack aside, he picked up another "toy." Maria didn't immediately realize what he had in his hands, she was so distracted by the pain and Sam's glare.

"Did he fuck you?" Again, that calm voice, which Maria feared most of all.

"N-no," she wheezed. "I already told you... a-a-ah!" she jerked sharply.

A rough palm came down on her moist crotch. Painfully pinching her clit between thumb and forefinger, Sam watched her agony.

"He didn't touch you here?" Sam grinned. He let go of the tender pea and began to fondle it roughly.

"N-no," Maria clenched her teeth and frowned at the emotions overwhelming her. Pain and pleasure merged together, slowly driving her insane.

"And he didn't do that?" Sam whispered softly in her ear.

The next minute, sparks flew in Maria's eyes. She tried to pull away, but a rough hand grabbed her neck from behind and pulled her back. With his other hand, Williams stroked the clothespin he had attached to one of her labia. The pain slowly passed, but when he "casually" flicked the clothespin, the agony returned.

"Please!" Maria whimpered, mentally cursing Sam and everything associated with him.

"He didn't fuck you?" Sam asked innocently, stroking his cold, sweat-soaked neck and shoulders.

"No!" Maria almost sobbed. The realization had come long ago, but she'd been trying to believe she was right until the last moment.

He knows.

He knows and wants to hear it from me.

Maria had clearly given herself her word not to give up, but with each passing minute, it became more and more difficult to keep that word. Her limbs were stiff, and her tendons began to shiver because of this foreign affair. Her whole body was trembling. Her skin was covered with sticky, unpleasant sweat.

"Please," she moaned, staring at the floor. Her conscience wouldn't let her look him in the eye.

"All right," Sam replied calmly, and, without sparing Maria, put the second clothespin next to the first.

"Ouch! Ouch! Take it off! Please!" She was losing control. Tears spurted from her eyes. Her teeth chattered like she'd been shoved into a freezer.

"Maria, baby girl, you are fucking…" Sam was dangerously close again. Wrapping his palms around her face, he forced her to lift her head and look at him.

What Maria saw only horrified her more. In contrast to her, the expression on Sam's face was startling. A paragon of calm and composure.

"Breathe, Maria."

Putting his arm around her shoulders, he began stroking her dark head affectionately. Instead of feeling calm, Maria almost howled with fear.

This was how killers said goodbye to their victims.

Sam wasn't going to kill her, but he could kick her out. And that would be twice as bad.

"Take it off, please," Maria tried to get through to him. She only wheezed, her body was too worn out to say something on the decibel scale.

With a loud sniff of air through his nose, Sam slid one hand down. Not wanting to ease her plight, he jerked both clothespins, holding her head down. Throbbing and shuddering with sobs, Maria lost control of herself completely.

It was time for the final performance.

"How did you two meet?" releasing from the girl's rigid embrace, Sam again returned to the sore subject.

"Who?" asked Maria, barely moving her tongue.

"Mars. And you."

Frozen in anticipation of the answer, Sam mentally decided her fate. Everything depended on her.

"On the Internet," Maria answered.

"You know, I've always admired a woman's stupidity," Sam reasoned. He defiantly took a tube of lubricant, an anal plug, and turned to Maria. "You think you are the smart one here? You think you can fool me?"

Maria looked at him without raising her head. She knew what was coming in next. The blood in her veins ran cold with fear. For some reason, for her, anal sex was the scariest. Had it happened with someone she loved, it would have been different. But Sam wasn't trying to make her first experience easy.

Stepping around her in a circle, Sam ran the cold metal over her hot skin. She twitched again, though there was almost no strength left. Once behind her back, he pressed in close, letting her feel his arousal. Despite the fabric of his pants, his rock-hard cock rested against Maria's lower back.

"Look what you've done, dirty bitch" he whispered disparagingly in her ear, pressing even harder against her.

Shoving the items into his pants pockets, Sam began to stroke her firm breasts. The long-hardened nipples whimpered with desire, the areola covered in tiny goosebumps. Embracing both hemispheres at once, Sam began a new torture. He twisted, pinched, and pulled her nipples, confusing her desire and disgust even more.

"You like it, don't you? Hmm? The real whore you are," Sam's voice grew rougher. Maria didn't immediately realize what he was asking.

"I-I..."

"Admit it to yourself!" Sam shouted, making the girl's ears pop. "You're a damn masochist, Maria! You like to feel pain!"

"No!"

"No?" Williams tsked angrily, running one hand between Maria's legs. "Then explain to me what this is!"

Sam injected two fingers abruptly inside, ramming into her at an incredible speed. Like a shockwave through her body, Maria could barely keep control of her breathing. Her whole body spiraled into invisible spasms and chaos. The only sounds heard were moans and a slutty squelching sound.

But like every other time, as she almost cummed, Sam stopped everything. As abruptly as it started, it finished before Maria could regain control of her body.

"Fuck!" Maria couldn't stand it anymore.

"Yes, Maria, fuck." Sam radiated cold calmness again, so cold that Maria began to freeze. She even felt like steam was coming out of her mouth as she exhaled air.

"I'm not a masochist," she cried.

"You are. You're lying to me again."

Hearing the word 'again' made Maria cringe at her own helplessness. Before she could digest his words, something cold touched the hollow between her buttocks.

Lubricant, the girl squirmed all over with fear.

"You see, Maria, masochists, especially women, like it rough. You know that in BDSM, even rape can be played up. Some people like it. Screaming, fighting back, and then cumming so hard you feel high. Almost everyone likes anal. You'll love it too. You're a masochist."

"I am not..."

"Shut the fuck up!" Sam snapped. He just didn't have the energy left to pull the truth out of her. Giving her one chance after another. His own words and actions made him sick, but he wanted to teach her a lesson. A cruel lesson. She didn't fully realize what she'd gotten herself into.

Sam was shaking with anger. He tried almost everything, but she just wouldn't confess!

For the first time in his life, he didn't like what he was doing. He was disgusted with himself, but he wasn't gonna let it go.

"I'm gonna fuck you, Maria." Pressing his cheek against her temple, Sam began to unzip his pants. Hearing a heavy sob, he continued, "Long and hard, just the way you like it. I'm going to pound into you until your nose bleeds and your crotch burns with the friction."

Maria howled softly, washing away her tears, exhaling loudly with each new word she heard. Sam tried not to react to her suffering, continuing his story, "And when you can't even get a word in edgewise, I'm going to fuck your ass. It's very sweet and definitely very tight. That's how you fuck masochists and bloody lying bitches. So if you have something to say, say it now!"

She couldn't take it anymore. In that moment, nothing mattered.

"Red," she said.

Chapter 21

The sun shone unpleasantly in her eyes. The silence was crushing. Maria's body ached with all the pain from yesterday. Every side she turned, her bones would crack. When exactly did she stop crying? And how did she fall asleep? The girl did not remember. Nor could she remember how she got to the bed.

After the safe word, Sam unbuckled the handcuffs, removed the restraints, and silently left the room, leaving Maria on the floor, shuddering and sobbing. She struggled to get up and made her way to her bedroom.

Unable to shower or even just wash herself, she went straight to bed. When Maria woke up, the first thing she felt was aching muscles and the urge to stand or lie in the shower for a couple of hours. With a loud groan, Maria climbed out of bed and made her way to the bathroom, trying to stay close to the wall in case she collapsed. She couldn't stand straight.

She sat down on the cold tile and pulled her knees up to her chest. The hot water brought her back to senses a little and relaxed her muscles.

Rewinding the events of last night, Maria tearfully recalled every word Sam had said. Like needing to be angry. To wish him to die the most horrible death. But she only got mad at herself.

"Why should I blame him? I'm the one who tricked him! I am the fool! Fool!"

Tears mixed with water, running down her cheeks. Sighing loudly, Maria looked at the closed door. She was afraid it was about to open. Maria wasn't ready to face him. She was not ready to look him in the eyes. She was afraid to see him now.

Her plan had failed miserably. All she could do now was ask for her clothes back, go back to Alicia, and start looking for a job. Maria forced herself to get up, stretching her stiff muscles a little. She washed herself with trembling hands, wrapped herself in a soft towel, and carefully went back to bed. Now that she was being kicked out, she didn't have to flaunt her nakedness around the house.

There was a knock on the door as soon as she was on the soft mattress. Maria held her breath in fear. Her heart sank deeper. She wasn't ready.

Her inner voice just roared with fear. *What to say? How to behave?*

"Maria, are you asleep? It's Rosita, can I come in?"

Rosita? The girl frowned. *It's Saturday. What is the Mexican doing here?*

"Please come in, Rosita," Maria wheezed.

The governess opened the door and appeared with a tray. The room immediately smelled of food. The seemingly frail woman had managed to bring a bowl of oatmeal, fresh toast, butter, jam, berries in a small bowl, and herbal tea.

"Mr. Williams ordered me to make sure you ate it all."

Maria shivered and wrapped herself tighter in the warm blanket.

"Thank you, Rosita. Can I have coffee? I don't eat in the morning," she said politely. She couldn't get a bite down her throat because of her worries.

"So don't eat in the morning," the woman smiled sweetly. "It's five o'clock in the evening!"

Tilting her head to the side, Maria first thought that Rosita was laughing at her. But she confirmed her words by showing the time on her phone. She even checked her own phone, just to be sure. She had slept for almost twenty-four hours. Already doubting everything, Maria carefully asked,

"Is today Saturday?"

"Yes, nina."

"Nina?" Maria asked.

"It's a *girl* in Spanish," Rosita explained. "Eat. Don't make Sam angry," she tsked unhappily.

Rosita looked sympathetic to Maria, but her eyes read something different, *"You've made a mess of things!"*

Maria had no choice but to silently eat everything on the tray. Hot tea was better than her favorite coffee. Rosita admitted she'd added mint and chamomile to it. The woman sat silently on the edge of the bed and watched the pale girl.

"Master... Sam," Maria corrected herself quickly, "is Sam at home?" She waited with bated breath for an answer.

"No. He left yesterday," the Mexican replied calmly. "I got here last night. I watched you all night. You were shivering and crying in your sleep. Calling for your mum."

"I'm sorry," she lowered her head guiltily. She felt terribly ashamed in front of the woman. She had made numerous people uncomfortable with her lies.

"Calm down, nina. I don't know what happened here, and it's none of my business. I was asked to look after you. You look like a *puta*, but you have a good heart. And sad eyes. Like Sam's. You both have the same look in your eyes... lost. Who broke you children like that?" Rosita pondered in her voice, rubbing the edge of her apron.

Maria listened to the governess, mesmerized. She was not even offended by the famous *puta*. She had learned at school that it meant *bitch*.

Maria was surprised at the look in her eyes. She'd never noticed any sadness in Sam's eyes. Only rage, constant anger and hatred. In rare moments, lust. But sadness? Maybe she was feeling too sorry for herself, so she didn't notice his feelings.

"Did he say when he'd be back?"

"No, he doesn't report to me," Rosita smiled cheerfully. Maria understood the humor and smiled faintly too.

"You can go now. I feel better already. I'll manage on my own," Maria tried to convince her that she was adequate. She didn't want to bother the Mexican anymore. She had already been guarding her bedside all night and all day.

"I can't," Rosita said flatly. "I won't disturb you. I'm going to make soup now. For dinner. And then Mr. Williams will call, I will tell him you're better."

"All right," agreed Maria reluctantly. If Rosita was going to make soup, then she would make her eat.

Taking the tray with empty dishes, the woman quickly left the room, leaving Maria alone. The food and the flavored tea really brought her to her senses. Even the pain in her body was better. But there was a burning in her chest. Rosita's words stuck weeds in her head.

Sam hadn't left her alone. He took care of her in his own way.

"He has to!" Maria sighed heavily, remembering the contract. Sam was a responsible dominant, unlike Maria.

Pondering her parting words, Maria didn't immediately hear her phone. Someone was calling.

It was Luisa.

A chill ran down her spine. Luisa was staying with her mum and monitoring her treatment. Horrible images immediately popped into the girl's head.

Quickly answering the phone, Maria spoke in a trembling voice:

"Hello, Luisa?"

"Maria, good evening," Maria's fingers were numb from the tired tone of her mum's slop. She gripped the phone with all her might.

"Luisa, what's wrong? What's wrong with Mum?" forgetting all measures of decency, O'Dell Junior demanded answers in a trembling voice.

"She is still in the hospital." Maria mentally exhaled, but not for long. She realized that there was a second part to the story. Luisa sighed heavily and continued, "She needs to go to rehab. Insurance won't cover it. She doesn't want to ask your father for money. Or rather... um... please forgive me, Maria, but both you and I know that your father has no money. If your mother doesn't take this course soon, her condition will deteriorate considerably...."

Luisa began to tell in detail the kind of treatment Lena required. But Maria was no longer listening to her. Her mind had already started tracing ways to retrieve the amount needed.

The pain, resentment, anxiety and worry about the situation with Sam lingered. The girl couldn't believe her luck. One problem after the other. But now, her priority was different. She'd still have time to talk to Sam. For now, she had a new problem, a problem on which her mum's life depended.

Quickly regaining whatever scraps of her strength were left, Maria said only one more thing before she could put the phone down and get to work.

"I'll get the money."

Chapter 22

The taste of whiskey was gone. Sam felt like he was drinking water.

Mistress Helen shook her head tiredly but did not kick him out of the private room of her club. Sam rarely visited her. But when he did, he was very popular. At first, Helen would send her delinquent sabots to him, and Sam would play with them. They would tremble, roar at the harshness of the punishments, and then moan loudly at the Lord's mind-blowing encouragement.

This time, the man refused the sessions. He asked not to be disturbed and requested a bottle of whiskey. Then, a second.

Listening to Maria's howls proved unbearable. No, she wasn't annoying. It was just that, for some reason, Sam wanted to take her into a tight embrace, to stroke her and kiss her until she calmed down. But he couldn't afford it. If Sam showed any weakness, Maria would climb around his neck even more.

Sam had left the apartment with the firm intention of kicking Maria out. He decided he'd wait for her to recover and then kick her out the door. The girl had broken the terms of not only the contract but everything that could be broken.

Anger overshadowed Sam's mind so much that he almost called an acquaintance from the police to speed up the O'Dell case. But he stopped in time. Immediately, his anger routed back to himself. Next to her, he was losing the thing he was most proud of: self-control. Maria was like a toggle switch going off in him.

The ever-faithful Rosita had agreed to look after the trouble while Sam recovered. The Mexican didn't speak up, but she took a liking to Maria. In the morning, she had reported on her condition, which was quite deplorable.

That's when the third bottle came into play.

Sam never worried about the condition of the lower ones. He'd always had his measure and had never crossed the line. But then again, with Maria, everything was going to hell. Things could be complicated for non-BDSM people. Some people would get a simple slap, while others would tolerate a suspended shibari or medical needles.

Maria turned out to be a masochist. Sam couldn't believe it for a long time, but you can't fool the body's reaction. The girl was flowing with the feeling of pain. Without realizing it, she was torturing Sam. Her stubbornness had backfired on both of them.

Saturday night, Rosita called again. Maria woke up towards the end of the day. Surprisingly she ate whatever the Mexican had prepared and had even asked about him. Sam was not amazed. He understood her condition: confusion, fear, ignorance. To the question, "What should she do?" Sam briefly ordered her to wait and then disconnected.

"Wait?" Helen asked mockingly, standing in the doorway.

"Do you often eavesdrop on other people's conversations?" Sam asked tiredly.

"Only when it's about the strangest couple in the whole world," the Mistress answered in the same way.

Without waiting for an invitation, she silently sat down in the chair opposite Sam. As always, she was dressed strictly with perfect styling and shoes on the finest stiletto heels. Helen filled her glass and took a single sip.

"How do you drink that?" Helen set the whiskey down squeamishly.

"I don't know," the man admitted.

"Am I allowed to start my speech with *I told you so*?"

"Helen..." Sam's cold stare gave Helen's skin goosebumps.

"I'm not talking. I won't," she raised her hands in a conciliatory gesture. "What are you going to do?"

"I'll kick her out!" Sam growled like a wounded animal. There was more pain in his words than anger.

"Yeah? Does she disgust you?" Mistress arched an eyebrow.

"That's not the point..."

"What is it, Sam?" she dared to interrupt.

Sam went silent. Helen always asked the right questions. Questions that most people didn't have the answers to.

"She seems afraid of you, but she's not afraid to stand up to your orders. It makes the blood run cold in your veins, doesn't it, Sam?"

Squinting, Mistress Helen wasn't looking into his eyes. She was looking into Sam's soul. She saw all the darkness, the wounds that no one could mend and cleanse.

"If you let her go, you'll regret it."

Chapter 23

Maria listened attentively to Rosita as she finished her second mug of tea. The Mexican woman had a difficult fate. All of her stories made her laugh or cry. A frail-looking woman and a mother of five managed to make her way from a terrible neighborhood in Mexico to a successful governess in London. She even admitted that Sam paid her enough money to support the whole family, but Rosita continued to work six days a week.

Over the constant talking and cooking, the weekend passed. Sam didn't show up on Saturday or Sunday. Every time the phone rang, Rosita quickly left the room. Maria looked at her with anticipation each time. But she only smiled briefly and always started to change the subject.

Maria could not forget about the conversation with Luisa. As luck would have it, all the pawnshops were open on Monday, so she had to wait. Although Maria did not fully understand what exactly she was waiting for. Staying alone, the girl flinched at every rustle. She was afraid of Sam's appearance, the demand to get out of the apartment, and the refusal to take a statement from the police.

Rosita stayed until Monday. She made fragrant tea and began to treat the still-pale Maria with pancakes, who devoured them with pleasure, spreading jam or honey on each one.

"I can't cook that well. These are delicious," Maria smiled.

"You'll learn!" Rosita responded.

"Mm-hmm," Maria agreed, putting another pancake into her mouth.

At that moment, the kitchen door opened. Rosita dropped her spatula, and Maria jumped up in her chair, dropping the bite back onto her plate. The temperature in the room immediately dropped to three degrees Celsius. In addition to the heavy air, Maria felt the icy stare of her possibly former Master.

"Good morning, Mr Williams," Rosita chirped, trying to ease the tension.

"Good morning, Rosita. You can go now. Thank you," Sam's face suddenly changed. He looked at the Mexican with a kind of warmth and respect. Maria had never seen anything like that towards herself. It made her chest ache.

Maria immediately noticed Sam's two-day unshavenness. In addition to the usual look in his eyes, she saw tiredness. His appearance was no better than Maria's. She couldn't her mind wander to the thought: *Was Rosita right? Are we both unhappy in our own way? I certainly am, but Sam... what or who made him so?*

"Always a pleasure. I'm just frying up some pancakes," Rosita said.

"You can go," Sam insisted, and the woman didn't dare disobey. She glanced sadly at Maria.

"Thank you," Maria rose abruptly from her chair as Rosita began to leave the kitchen. "Thank you very much, Rosita."

Without moving, Maria just lowered her head, looking at her uneaten breakfast. The fabric of her homemade dress clung to her back, wet with cold sweat. She was scared. Terrified.

"I'll be in the study at three. See you there," Sam uttered, without a warning.

His commanding voice sent a warm wave through Maria's body. Maria tried to even out her breathing and not give away her state. Clutching the hem of her dress under the desk, she squared her shoulders more firmly and leveled her back. She couldn't let Sam know, even if there was a hurricane in her soul.

Half past nine. She had six and a half hours.

"Can I go outside?" Maria asked, immediately shrinking back in fear. Addressing Sam was much harder than she had imagined.

"Do whatever you want," Sam nodded indifferently, without looking at her, and walked out.

Maria stared at his back and tried not to cry like a little child. If someone had told her a fortnight ago that Williams's indifferent gaze would make her chest burn, she would have spat in that person's face. Had she been hurt by his words? Denial came in waves over Maria, already exhausted from the emotional race.

She glanced at her watch and decided not to waste any time. London was not small, and it was not easy to find a pawnshop that would accept gold and diamonds of the highest grade.

Hastily cleaning up after herself, Maria headed for her room. She had already put all the jewelry she had with her into a small bag. The rest had to be picked up from Alicia's apartment. Maria was afraid to tell her friend Sam's exact address. She remembered confidentiality.

From clothes, Maria had only sandals and a lemon dress in her wardrobe. Under different circumstances, the girl wouldn't refuse trainers and a tracksuit, but she had no choice.

Gathering everything she needed in her purse, she took a quick step towards the exit, hoping not to meet Sam on the way. She was lucky this time.

***

Dumping his dirty clothes on the warm bathroom floor, Sam rubbed his face tiredly. He needed a hot shower, rest, and an obedient slave girl. Of the above, the only thing he got was a shower.

After his conversation with Helen, he decided not to rush into it but to weigh the pros and cons. He'd been thinking for a long time. He'd left the club with a confident decision to chase her away, but when he'd seen her, it had all turned to mush.

There, in the kitchen, Maria was afraid and confused. Her trembling voice made Sam almost groan. Everything that had been sleeping peacefully at the sight of the most loyal and obedient girls in Mistress Helen's club woke up in his groin. Why was he having such a strange reaction to that brat? Sam was starting to get angry again.

Unable to decide everything, he gave himself over to fate.

If Maria came into the office dressed, he'd kick her out. If she came in naked, he'd keep her. For three months. No more arguments. Everything would be just the way he wanted. On his terms!

At two fifty-eight, there was a quiet knock on the office door. "Come in."

Sam put the clipboard aside and slowly raised his eyes to Maria.

Chapter 24

"Have a seat," he pointed to the chair with his eyes.

Sam kept his eyes on her. He was trying to see whether he had made the right decision or not.

His piercing gaze made Maria squirm in her chair. It's uncomfortable to sit on any surface when you have a bare bottom.

Naked.

Maria was afraid she wouldn't make it in time. She flew into the apartment, taking off her dress as she went. Quickly rinsing herself off, the girl headed straight for her execution. Warm steam still emanated from her damp skin. A few drops of her wet hair fell onto the soft carpet.

"Maria, we got off on the wrong foot," Sam exhaled heavily, leaning back in his chair. A hurricane was raging inside him. He had hoped for a different outcome. He'd hoped for another, and he was glad for this one. Pushing the silly thoughts aside, he continued,

"Firstly, you shouldn't have lied to me. Secondly, I understand what drives you."

Maria did not raise her eyes. Clenching her thighs tighter, she glared at the edge of the table. His words weren't getting through to her very well. Intentionally or accidentally, Sam was speaking in riddles, for which she had no time or energy left. Gathering more air into her lungs, she mumbled quickly without looking, "Are you kicking me out?"

"Do you want to leave?" The man asked ironically.

"No."

"Good."

"Good?" she interjected, raising her huge eyes sharply at Sam. A palette of emotions played across her face. Sam could see it: confusion, fear, hope, and even joy. The last one confused Sam.

"Yeah. But now it's gonna be on my terms."

"Good."

"Good?" Sam raised one eyebrow. He was clearly hinting to her that the game was on. Again.

"Okay, Master," Maria mumbled and lowered her head. "I'm sorry, Master."

"Three months. The new countdown begins today. Your next stop word is a ticket home. No bickering. Total obedience and submission. You don't talk to anyone without my permission. You don't look at anyone without my permission. You don't eat without my permission. You don't sleep without my permission. You don't fucking brush your hair without my permission. Understand?"

The more Maria listened, the more her fists clenched. Sam was basically turning her into a puppet. Now, she had no choice in the matter. Sam had created a real hell for a feminist. Maria's favors didn't apply to them, but all his rules were frankly annoying. But he gave her a chance. The girl mentally thanked him for allowing her to stay in this hell for another three months.

"Yes," Maria wheezed. Her voice failed at the most inopportune moment, giving away her condition.

"Questions?" Sam asked with cold calmness.

"When you're not here, what do I do?"

"You can write messages."

"Can I talk to Rosita?"

"No," Sam said.

"Can I call my family today?" Maria slumped, afraid of hearing the same answer.

"Yes."

"Thank you, Master," Maria breathed out in relief.

Sam immediately noticed her shaking shoulders. Her eyes were glassy.

Sam had no desire to play with her today. Friday was enough for him. Though what he'd dumped on her was already a punishment of sorts. For a rookie, that many restrictions were catastrophic. His plan was to make Maria suffer for a couple of days and then slowly remove the restrictions if she behaved well.

But still, his discomfort persisted. And again, it was because of this girl. However, Maria's battered appearance had him concerned. Rosita had said that Maria had been eating well and socializing a lot with her. Why, then, was a hunted and battered kitten sitting in front of him? One more second, and she'd just cry. Why?

"Is everything okay?" Sam asked for some reason. He didn't realize how he'd said those words in his own voice.

"Yes..."

"Maria," Sam exhaled heavily. She was going to lie again. "Despite all these rules, I'm responsible for you. Morally and physically. Let's at least try not to lie to each other," he shook his head, not believing his words completely.

"I'm sorry, Master," the girl sniffed her nose. "I'm just still not feeling well, honestly," she opened her eyes wide, trying to show her condition. "Tomorrow, I'll be good as a new penny," Maria joked stupidly.

"A new penny?" Sam smiled.

"That's what Dad always says..." Maria stammered. Memories of her old life, which turned out to be a happy life, caused a wave of sadness. A lone tear rolled down her cheek. "I'm sorry, Master."

"Go rest," Sam nodded at the door.

As soon as Maria left the office, he cursed softly. Fate had played him again. Too many contradictions. Sam didn't know what exactly he should grab onto.

Hate or try to live in peace?

Before Sam could fully ponder on that point, he was interrupted by the phone.

Blackwood? he wondered.

Sam rarely interacted with old dominant friends. The exceptions were Blackwood and Max. Similar in personality, they quickly found common ground.

"You're out of ideas, and you're calling me?" Sam started mocking his friend right off the bat.

"Not today, Williams. Not today," the man on the other side grinned.

"What is it then?"

"Nina."

Samuel's blue eyes darkened. His face grew serious, and his whole body tensed. Blackwood had said the forbidden word. No one had ever discussed *her* with him.

His personal secret. The blond obsession. The girl who made him shiver. The girl who made Sam's heart break into a thousand pieces every time he left her. And no one but she herself could put it back together. His unrequited, eternal love.

"What about her!?" he didn't ask; he growled.

"I'm sorry, mate. Nina's fell in love with someone."

Chapter 25

"Sam," Blackwood reminded himself after a long silence on the other side.

"I got it."

He couldn't get anything else out of himself. An unknown weight pressed against his chest, making it almost impossible to breathe. Sam could barely contain himself from throwing the phone at the wall and smashing everything around him.

He couldn't believe it.

Nina couldn't love! She couldn't! Anyone but her. With her "special" attitude towards men, love was something unacceptable. She'd made her peace with it. Sam accepted it. He never judged her lifestyle because he had his own secrets.

But they were so good together! Sam had dreamed of spending the rest of his life with her. Instead, he was content with infrequent meetings and long sex. He himself tried to keep their dates to a minimum. He knew he couldn't let go if he saw her too often.

Sam didn't believe in love. Maybe in another life, he would have been happy for Nina, but not in this one. Anger made his teeth grit. Anger. Envy. Rage. Even hatred for someone who dared to take away the one thing that kept him on the bright side of this world.

Nina had always laughed and called him a good man. He wasn't. It had always been wrong. But Sam didn't argue with her. Played the part of the good guy. Really enjoyed being happy when she was happy.

Now, that'd been taken away from him. The last flame that warmed his already cold heart had gone out.

"Was that all you had to say?" Sam asked calmly.

"You need to talk to her."

"And you need to stop prying into other people's lives!" Sam couldn't help himself.

"Don't forget yourself, boy," Blackwood replied with the same calmness.

In fact, it was a squabble between two dominants. All the fury of the universe was hidden in the quiet and calm phrases. Each of them had enough of it.

"I'll be there," Sam said, which was what Blackwood wanted to hear.

"You're coming to visit?" his friend grinned ironically into the phone.

"Yeah. I won't be alone."

"Mm? Who is she?" Sam felt Blackwood smile.

Last time, he'd come with Nina, and now she wasn't his anymore. What was going to happen to Maria? Remembering the girl, Sam shook his head. He didn't want to think about her again today.

"You'll see."

Having exchanged a few more phrases, the men agreed to meet, touching on a couple of work issues. After saying goodbye to his American friend, Sam was left with a mixed feeling.

Fury was quickly replaced by sadness. After a glass of his favorite amber liquid, Sam opened the balcony door. Evening

London was awake. The lights illuminated the endless roads going into the distance. Remembering the most vivid moments of his acquaintance with Nina, the man did not immediately hear a familiar, quiet voice.

Opening the door a little more, Sam saw Maria naked in the reflection. The girl was sitting on the threshold of the door leading to the balcony, her knees tucked up to her naked breasts. She was talking on the phone. Sam did not intend to eavesdrop but, hearing the first phrases, froze to a halt and began to catch in every word.

"I don't know what to do, Ali!" Maria exhaled loudly. She could not stop shivering with anger and annoyance. "He only gave me seven thousand! Seven! Luisa said Mum need twenty-five thousand pounds for treatment. I haven't got half that," she sobbed.

"Yes. I was at your house today. I'm sorry I didn't tell you. I was in a hurry." Maria was silent, listening to her friend's lamentations. She tried to answer all her questions briefly. "No, it's fine. No, he doesn't hurt me. Beats…the notion is stretchable, Ali," the girl grinned bitterly. "It's all right, Ali. No one oppresses me or humiliates me. No, he's not evil. And no, he's not a psychopath! God be with you, Alicia! No, he's not raping me! Where did you get that!?" Maria was outraged.

Maria patiently listened to her friend's crazy speculations, denying each one. Sam was surprised by her answers. She talked about some nice man, but not about him. Even defended and justified his actions.

"Ali, listen," Maria said almost in a whisper. "Can you help me? Yes, I know you don't have that kind of money. Can you sell my things?" she stopped abruptly. After listening to Alicia's loud indignation, Maria continued, "I understand, Ali. Yes, I know that all my stuff was worth at least a thousand pounds each. Yes, I realize that they will buy them for two hundred pounds at the most. But understand!" shouted Maria, in order to ennoble the moody friend.

"I need money! Lots of money! My dad hasn't got any. No one has it, but if I don't get it right away, Mum...."

Maria gasped at the pain that clenched her insides. She had to cover her mouth with the palm of her hand to keep from screaming, so much so that she was twisting with hopelessness. She only quickly switched off the microphone and howled softly, resting her forehead against her trembling knees. Quickly brushing away her tears, she returned to the conversation.

"Sorry. Something's wrong with the connection," Maria brazenly lied. "Yes, Ali. That's it. Sell everything. Don't worry. I've got some trousers and a T-shirt left. I've got enough. Take what you can get. Thank you very much. You too. Bye."

There was a stifling silence. Sam kept his eyes on Maria. He stared at the reflection in the balcony door, head bowed. He was confused about a lot of things. Firstly, she didn't say anything about money problems. Second, he realized it was in her DNA to deceive everyone.

However, Sam understood her actions. Sam had made it abundantly clear that he hated all O'Dells. Why would she ask him for money for her mother's treatment if he himself took it away from them? An unpleasant bitterness arose in his mouth and bitterly burned his throat. He felt disgusted with himself. After all, he also had a sick mother, and for her sake, he would do anything.

After taking a couple of sips of whiskey, Sam was about to close the door when he heard her phone ringing again.

"Fuck," Maria cursed, to which Sam grinned.

I should totally whip her for swearing, he thought.

"Hi, Daddy," Maria replied cheerfully.

Sam almost choked when he heard her tone. There was no trace of her former hysteria. She was smiling and talking colorfully about her 'job.' The more she talked, the angrier Sam got.

"It's great! I love it! Yeah, Matilda's great! Oh, Dad. It's modern art. You wouldn't understand. No, I'm not saying you're old. I just don't get it myself sometimes. I don't know. We're still in Liverpool. Yeah, it's a long way. I don't know, Dad. Matilda has a lot of meetings. I won't be in London for at least another month. I know. I miss you too," Maria's voice didn't betray her condition, though she was shaking. She didn't feel cold. Only a terrible emptiness and guilt. Deceiving her father wasn't easy for her. Every now and then, she bit her fist until it was red.

"Daddy, it's gonna be okay. Of course, it is. I know it's not your fault. It's gonna be okay," she kept repeating this phrase over and over again. Maria was trying to reassure herself more than her parent. Taking the phone aside, she bit her lower lip and squeezed her eyes tightly shut. A panic attack was starting to creep up on her. She slapped the cold tile a couple of times, brought the phone back to her ear, and spoke in a ringing voice, "Daddy, I have to run."

"Daddy, I have to run. I have more papers to print out for tomorrow. I love you! Yeah, I'll be sure to write. Yeah, and I'll send a picture!"

"Fuck!" she slammed her fist on the tiles again.

Throwing the phone away, she couldn't hold back. She wrapped her shaking hands around her head and started howling like a wounded animal.

Sam closed his eyes. Turned away. He was torn apart. On one hand, he wanted to comfort her. On the other, he wanted to leave it at that because this was none of his business. Taking a final gulp, Sam set the glass aside and headed for the kitchen with a heavy gait.

"Not my family, not my problem," he repeated the phrase like a mantra, trying to believe his own words.

Sam made himself some tea and spent a long time relishing the mug of hot drink.

Blackwood's news had blown a hole in his armor. Maria's conversation with her dad and friend had blown it all to hell.

"Fuck!" Sam cursed loudly, regretting his action in advance. Putting the untouched mug in the sink, he quickly left the kitchen.

The balcony door wobbled in the breeze. Taking a couple of steps, Sam froze in place.

Right at the entrance of her room, curled up in a fetal position, Maria slept. The girl had her arms tucked under her head. Her hair was disheveled and hid part of her tear-swollen face. She was still sobbing, pushing her knees harder against her stomach. Her whole body was covered in goosebumps from the cold.

Cussing softly, he squatted down beside O'Dell.

Chapter 26

Sam was frustrated. Maria had asked to be punished again. Sam nudged her, trying to wake her. For a minute, he just watched her facial expressions; watching her forehead frown and her full lips quiver.

"Stupid," he uttered.

Rubbing his neck tiredly, Sam began gently lifting the sleeping body from the floor. As soon as his hands touched bare skin, Sam cursed with anger.

Ice cold.

From head to toe, Maria was ice cold. If Sam hadn't come to check on her, she could easily have frozen to death.

Light as a feather, she fit perfectly into his strong and warm embrace. Feeling the heat coming from him, the girl snuggled even tighter against Sam. Her frail arms wrapped around the man's massive neck. She nuzzled her nose into Sam's shoulder and sobbed softly.

Once at the bedside, Sam tried to tuck her under the covers, but Maria wrapped her arms around his neck and pressed herself against his hot chest.

Without thinking, Sam sat on the edge of the bed, pulled down the blanket, and covered himself and Maria with it. Feeling warmth throughout her body, Maria exhaled faintly. Sam knew from her swollen face that she had been crying for a long time. He hugged his slave tighter as he closed his eyes.

Unlike Maria, he didn't have such a difficult situation with his relatives, but Blackwood's news had hit him hard. His chest ached at the mention of his unrequited love.

Immersed in pleasant memories, Sam did not immediately realize that he had begun to calm Maria to sleep. She sobbed softly, but at some point, tears sprang from her eyes. She began to toss and turn in Sam's lap, trying to get the blanket off her.

"Mummy! Mummy!" Maria began to repeat, becoming more and more hysterical.

Sam quickly orientated himself and threw the out-of-control girl onto the bed. Pressing down with his whole body, he was afraid of hurting her. Wrapping his arms around her thin wrists, Sam pressed down even harder on Maria. She wriggled like a cat. Calling for her mum and roaring like a baby.

Sam tensed up himself. The sight of her pain turned everything inside him upside down. Clenching his teeth together to a nasty grind, Sam tried with all his might to choke down all the pity he was feeling.

He was starting to feel like a junkie, wanting so badly to calm her down and help her. The thought of paying for treatment even crossed his mind, but he quickly pushed it out of his mind. But Sam wasn't going to let the situation go.

He remembered well all the pain and agony he had gone through in his youth. His father's death hadn't been easy for him. He'd dealt with it, but he'd paid too high a price.

He forgot what goodness was.

He rejected the very existence of love until he met Nina. Alas, fate had dealt him a piggyback.

"Mum!" Maria cried out once again through the terrible dream she was having. She pulled out one hand and swung it at Sam's face.

With a loud curse, Sam jammed his forehead into her neck, causing Maria to wake up abruptly. Not fully aware of what was happening or where she was, she wrapped her free arm around the body looming over her. She was afraid to breathe. By the distinctive color of her hair, which she saw with her side vision, she knew she was being pinned to the bed by Sam.

Still, with a loud exhalation from the weight of his body, Maria gave herself away. Sam slowly rose up on one elbow. His other hand still held hers in the same way.

Maria didn't understand what he was doing there. Why was she in bed?

Sam turned his head towards her. There was a thin mark on his cheek from her sharp nails.

As soon as Maria saw what she had done, her heart sank into her heels. She knew her sad fate. The gravity of her accidental act came over Maria in full force. Everything had taken its toll: the conversation with Luisa, the failed pawnshop deal, her father's lies, her mother's lack of money, the deception Sam had uncovered.

It was the look in his eyes that killed her. Cold. Detached. Warning. With his whole look, the Master radiated his usual emotions toward Maria: anger and resentment. Closing her eyes to the white glare before her eyes, Maria sobbed shamefully, choking on her own saliva. Her free hand clutched at the sheets as if it were her last hope for salvation.

"He'll be gone now. He's going to leave," Maria repeated to herself.

"Maria," Sam's voice, like a bullet, hit her right on target. She could not hold back any longer.

"Don't! Please! Please! I am sorry. Please!" Maria cried again, covering her eyes with her hand. She pulled desperately with her other hand, but Sam wouldn't let go. Turning to the side, Maria tried to escape her Master's clinging grasp. "Don't!" she repeated, panting. She slid her heels across the bed, turned her head away until her neck crunched.

Sam did not immediately realize his actions. Whether it was fatigue or his inner dominant in a deep sleep, he woke up as his usual lonely self. He grabbed the still-howling Maria by the chin and turned her head forcibly to face him. She only opened her mouth like a fish, looking for air.

Sam helped her.

He plunged a passionate kiss on her lips. The kind of kiss that made your heart sink and your toes curl.

Chapter 27

Maria froze. She didn't want to scream or break free from the tight embrace. Sam reminded her to breathe by exhaling loudly into her mouth. And when his tongue began to skillfully explore the cavity of her mouth, Maria had no explanation for his action. She only moaned softly in response.

Maria's body, which had been cold until then, was instantly inflamed. She wriggled against his hands, afraid she wouldn't be able to catch another touch. Rough fingers slid gently along her narrow waist, crumpling the skin as if exploring it anew.

It was entirely different from before. Sam didn't subdue. Didn't leave red marks on her body. Didn't order her to bend over or what to do.

Maria simply surrendered herself to her fate. After such an emotional race, Sam's actions seemed like a breath of fresh air. Air she hadn't breathed in a fortnight.

Daring, she wrapped her trembling arms around his neck. Every second, she worried he'd become an emotionless monster again. She was terrified to see his cold and detached gaze. She couldn't bear it.

Sam flinched only slightly when she wrapped her arms around his neck. He pulled her even tighter against him. He ran his fingers along her spine, pulling her off the bed and breaking the long kiss. She didn't realize at all how she'd settled on Sam. Still wrapped her arms around his neck, she squeezed her eyes shut, not wanting to open them.

"Look at me."

Maria felt as if she'd been splashed with cold water. Biting her lower lip, she hoped she'd heard him. She couldn't look into his eyes. Didn't want to see all that darkness and gloom there. The girl needed warmth and affection now more than ever.

"Master, please."

"Sam," he interrupted her. "I'm Sam now, baby girl," he added quietly.

Maria opened her eyelids sharply, not believing what she heard. She couldn't believe it, and she didn't understand what was happening. But once she got a better look, she immediately realized the reason. Sam's appearance was no better than Maria's. The same tired and sad look. A relaxed face and no smile or smirk.

A man as miserable and broken as herself sat in front of her. Maria felt it in her subconscious. She felt like crying again, not because of her problems, but because she was not the only poor and miserable person in the world.

"Rosita was right," the girl thought sadly, not taking her eyes off Sam.

"About what?" Sam whispered.

"Nothing, Master," the girl nodded.

"Maria, it's not a session now. It's just me and you," Sam repeated calmly, and Maria almost had a micro-orgasm from what she heard.

Breathing heavily, she was afraid to move. Their foreheads were almost touching, their lips trembling from the resulting vibration. Fully aware of herself, Maria realized that she wanted him. Wanted to give herself to this man to forget for one night the feuds, grudges, and hatreds. She ached to feel desired.

Sam couldn't take his eyes off her. Maria hypnotized, attracted, and, most importantly, didn't make him feel disgusted. She didn't shake like an aspen leaf but looked at him with dignity and even defiance. Despite the thin layer of clothing that separated their bodies, Sam could feel her desire. The entire universe had shrunk to the size of a small room where two people looked at each other with a different gaze. It was as if nothing had ever happened before.

Inside Sam and Maria, a time bomb was ticking in sync. And when the arrow reached the right mark, there was an explosion.

Maria only had time to moan in between his frantic kisses. Sam's hands roamed her body, afraid to miss the slightest spot. Kneading her ass, stroking her thighs, pulling her against him at the waist. Maria only responded to his tender touch and arched her back to meet his skillful fingers.

As soon as the big palm touched her breast, Maria instinctively clenched. She squared her shoulders. Could barely keep her hands from covering herself. Her body remembered the roughness, bordering on pleasure. But she didn't want to relive it again tonight.

"Shh, relax, baby girl," Sam whispered in her ear, biting her earlobe with his lips.

Remembering the trust, Maria straightened her back. All her movements radiated apprehension and fear, but she dared to believe him.

Sam had exceeded her expectations. It turned out that this stale, wicked man could not only bring her to her knees but also elevate her above the ground. With the first touch, Maria realized that everything would be different. Sam skillfully massaged one and the other breast. He pinched, pulled and twisted her nipples to the point of slight pain.

Stifling her real emotions, Maria moaned softly, but when Sam's hot lips took in a hard pea, she didn't hold back. She wrapped her arms around his head and pressed her breasts into his face.

"Ah!" she let out a loud moan. Maria was afraid of her own reaction. Afraid of the excessive liberty she had allowed herself. A hundred times, she regretted it.

Sam immediately recognized the change in her movements. He realized that the girl was frightened because everything they were doing now was completely contrary to his nature. Sam was not surprised to feel a small tremor in her body. That proved to be the final straw.

Maria obeyed him completely. Perhaps she didn't fully understand it yet, but her behavior and her body's reaction confirmed Sam's guess. The girl was writhing with desire in his arms, wanting more but not forgetting who he was and who she was.

Pulling away from her soft breasts, Sam looked at her with a slightly distracted gaze. Both of them were pounding with arousal. Maria averted her gaze again. Nervously biting her lips.

Touching her red cheek with his fingers, Sam turned the girl around to face him. There was still a flicker of fear in her gaze. Sam ran his knuckles along her cheekbone to her swollen lips and down the graceful curve of her neck. The soft touch soothed Maria. Her lips opened in search of comfort, and there was an uncomfortable whimper that Sam had touched. Maria wished for more.

"Remember, Maria," Sam's serious voice brought her to her senses, "I want you to not hold back. I want to see you cum. Over and over again. Don't stop yourself. If you want to scream, scream. If you want to beg, beg. You want to curse, curse."

Without averting his gaze, Sam began to take off his T-shirt.

Chapter 28

Maria couldn't take her eyes off him. She watched his every move. She licked her lips like a cat in anticipation of tasty milk. She had seen him without clothes before, but now everything was different. They were different now. Not master and slave; two people, two bodies in anticipation of intertwining.

No holding back. She could and wanted to. As soon as the T-shirt flew in an unknown direction, Maria began to study the man's body brazenly. She ran her fingers along the tense abs, lightly scratching the perfect forearms. She was afraid, but she did it.

Sam watched her with interest. Maria, like a curious little animal, was prying everywhere she could reach. He only smiled demurely and exhaled loudly at his slave's timid touches. He himself began to stroke her thighs. He didn't direct it on purpose. Waited for her to ask for it. He couldn't quite suppress his dominance.

"What?" Sam asked quietly when Maria's hand stopped at the edge of his trousers. Like an innocent sheep, she ran her finger along the elastic of his boxers.

With a loud gulp, Maria lowered her head, trying to hide her face behind her hair, but Sam did it his way again. He took her by the chin, forcing her to look at him. The lust-clouded eyes were filled with desire. Looking into those amber lakes, Sam saw the reflection of his own equally lustful eyes.

"Do you want it?" he asked huskily.

"Do you?" Maria answered in his tone.

His whole plan burned to the ground as soon as he heard her voice, just as gray and shaky. Acting purely on instinct, Sam rolled Maria onto her back and began covering her with hot kisses. She purred softly in pleasure. Getting high as he heard Maria's loud moans. Doing his best to keep her going.

Sam had already started to pull his trousers down. He let his tongue travel down Maria's smooth body. From her collarbones to her navel, Sam let his tongue conquer every inch of her body, but when Maria spread her legs wide apart with a long moan, he was completely blown away.

"Sam!" Maria's dry throat let out a hoarse renunciation as she felt a hot, slightly rough tongue on her crotch. He wrapped his arms under her trembling knees, drawing him in a tighter close. Sam had already begun to taste Maria, enjoying her trembles and responsiveness. He gently stroked her pussy and sucked on her clit with such tenderness that Maria could barely restrain herself. Sam was growling with pleasure. He purposely kept his hands away, wanting to fill her with his cock.

"I... Oh my God!... Sam! I... I... I... A-a-a-a!" the girl couldn't formulate her thoughts.

Leaning back on the sheets, Maria began to thrust herself onto his tongue. She gasped with pleasure and felt the pleasure twisting stronger and stronger inside.

"Yes!" Maria shrieked and arched her back until her vertebrae crunched. The long-awaited orgasm covered the girl to the point of semi-fainting. Her whole body was covered with cold sweat, and her eyes rolled back under her eyelids. Sam didn't stop, prolonging her pleasure to the maximum. To his own surprise, he liked this state of her.

Like a well-fed bear, Sam sat back on his heels, wiping his lips with the back of his palm. Soaked with it, he watched the still-shuddering Maria with pleasure. Covering her eyes with one hand, she clutched at the sheets with the other. Her thighs twisted involuntarily from the ecstasy she had experienced, and her breasts rose and fell sharply as she tried to steady her breathing.

"You okay?" Sam asked without a trace of mockery. He did care about her condition, at least because he wanted to continue. Maria made a half moan, half squeak.

The strength to look at the perfect Maria was becoming less and less, and so was her patience. Having thrown off the rest of his clothes, Sam gently grasped the thin icepicks. Slowly spread them apart and bent her legs at the knees again.

A loud gasp escaped Maria's mouth as the head of his cock touched her still-wet labia.

Sam, again, took his time. He rubbed his perfectly-hard cock's head against her folds, pressing it against the throbbing entrance. Maria howled with desire again, as if it hadn't happened a few minutes ago and she wasn't the one squirming from the orgasm that was tearing her to shreds.

Taking the lubricated shaft in his fist, Samuel began to slowly enter her tight womb. He growled, swearing, shuddering with the desire to fuck Maria to the point of hoarseness in her throat.

Maria was choking on her own moans. She moaned and whimpered but did not pull away. She mumbled something and clenched her fists tighter and tighter. She thanked Sam in her mind for the tenderness with which he was plunging into her, though she could feel his beastly desire. Wrapping her legs around Williams, Maria arched herself toward him. Accepting him fully until she felt him resting against something.

Giving her time to get used to him, Sam gripped her waist tighter and began to move. He plunged into her hot and wet womb with unprecedented pleasure. Maddened by her tightness. Feeling every cell, just as she felt his blood-soaked shaft. Every vein. The throbbing head.

Sam tried to keep his cool, but things didn't go according to plan again. Maria was so tight inside that he was swept away again. With an inhuman growl, Williams pounded into her body, taking his breath away and covering himself in sticky sweat. Maria adjusted to his movements and whimpered quietly. There was only enough strength for that.

Pressing Maria onto himself, Sam was lost in the euphoria. Lost control of himself. Tightened her to the limit. Squeezed her narrow waist until it bruised. And when he felt her muscles contracting and wrapping around his cock, he almost went insane from the orgasm that overtook him.

With each jagged movement, his semen flowed out of Maria, and Sam continued thrusting like a mesmerized man until he was completely exhausted. Piling on top of her frail body, he struggled to balance on his elbows. He tried not to run over Maria with his weight. He rested his head against her thin neck, which was wet with sweat, and breathed heavily.

Maria was afraid to open her eyes. It still seemed to her that it was all a dream. That if she opened her eyelids, everything would be a fantasy. A pleasant negativity spread all over her body, along with fatigue. The girl felt Sam's sweaty body on her. She tried not to move. She almost wanted to beg him to stay. Despite the hot evening, Maria needed his warmth.

She exhaled quietly and almost yelped when Sam scooped her up and pressed his body against hers. He was like a missing puzzle, joined to her as one. He pressed his chest against her breasts and nuzzled into the dark top of her head. Pulling Maria as close to him as possible, Sam fumbled for the edge of the blanket he'd thrown aside earlier and covered their tired bodies.

Everything suited him at that moment. The quietly sniffling Maria. The ache in his muscles after an unplanned sex marathon. The lightness and freshness in his head. Thanks to Maria, Sam was able to forget about all the problems that had piled up in such a short time. Even the girl lying next to him was not disgusted or angry. Today, he saw a different side of her, and he liked it a lot. He wanted to see and hear her like that always.

Smiling through his sleep, Sam couldn't even think that this fragile girl would save him today. It would help numb the pain in his heart. Nor did Maria suspect that this seemingly horrible person would give her so much tenderness and warmth today. He would save her from the cold and pain that weeds had crept into her chest.

Maria woke up early in the morning with a wild urge to shower. Her skin was unpleasantly tight with Sam's dried seed. Her whole body was sticking to the blanket and sheets.

The only thing in the way was Sam's still tight embrace. The man hadn't moved all night, thus restricting Maria's movement.

Quietly, with the utmost care, Maria twisted in his arms. With her back to Sam, she tried to free herself from his arms.

"Nina, stop it. Go back to sleep," Sam growled menacingly, pulling the dazed Maria against his hot body.

Chapter 29

Sighing heavily, Maria decided not to play with fire. She snuggled more comfortably in his arms and tried to sleep. It amused her a little that he, like Rosita, had called her 'girl' in Spanish. There was no indication anywhere on the vastness of the internet that Sam knew Spanish.

"Not many people know about his dominance either," Maria smiled, thinking.

She still managed to fall asleep for another couple of hours. She woke up already alone. Feeling around the bed for another body, Maria realized that Sam was gone.

The sun was blinding, making it hard to concentrate. After sitting in the middle of the bed for a while longer, Maria remembered to shower. She threw back the blanket and was on her way to the bathroom. Stopping abruptly in the middle of the room, she remembered Sam's menacing speech.

"You don't fucking brush your hair without my permission. Understand?" she remembered his words very well.

Asking permission to water seemed absurd, but she didn't want to test his patience again. Shrugging her shoulders, Maria went in search of Sam.

After going around all the allowed rooms and knocking on the study door for a long time, she decided to check his private bedroom.

"Yes?" she heard as soon as Maria knocked softly.

"Master… can I come in?" Her voice trembled uncertainly. She had never been in his room before. She didn't even know what it was like there.

"Come in," he said softly.

Slowly opening the heavy door, Maria peered into the spacious room. A huge bed with a leather headboard up to the stream took up most of it. A couple of armchairs near the window, a small table with a mirror, and two more doors leading to the bathroom and dressing room. All in calm brown and beige and blended in perfectly with the overall décor of the flat.

Wearing only a towel, Samuel stood beside the bed, actively typing a text message. Maria stood quietly by the door and waited for the Master to look at her.

"What?" he sounded cold and distant. Like nothing had happened last night. It was like Sam's amnesia had worsened. He wasn't even looking at the girl.

"Good morning, Master," she tried to ignore his detachment. Her voice sounded surprisingly calm.

Sam still took his eyes off the phone and looked at Maria. Carefully, with a squint, he looked over her body, hovering over the places where small bruises were already showing.

The weight of what he had done had fallen on Sam early in the morning. He didn't want to call Maria by another woman's name. It came out of his mouth. And as soon as Maria obediently settled back into his arms, Sam began to count the minutes and even the seconds to leave her room. Shame overwhelmed the man. Despite her position, Maria was in no way a replacement for Nina.

And now, instead of anger or resentment on her face, he saw only a barely perceptible smile. Apparently, she did not hear him or masterfully hid the offense.

"Morning." Putting the phone away, Sam approached Maria with the grace of a lion.

The closer he got, the faster her poor heart began to pound. The strangest thing was that Maria was frightened by the lack of fear. There was a hurricane going on in her chest for a different reason. Licking her parched lips, she obediently lowered her eyes to the floor.

"Can I take a shower, Master?" Her voice trembled.

There was a faint chuckle. Sam almost groaned with the joy that overwhelmed him. Finally, Maria stopped tugging at the tiger's whiskers and gave in. Still looking at the scattering of small bruises on her wrists and thighs, Sam decided to reward her efforts.

"You can do that."

"And brush my teeth?"

"And brush your teeth."

"And even comb my hair?" The last one came out with a little chuckle.

"Yes," Sam exhaled, holding back a smile. Sam realized the absurdity of the situation as well as she did. Quickly hiding his amusement, he added seriously, "Don't ask me that again. Your job is to look after yourself. Remember?"

"I do, Master."

"You can go now. I need go to work."

Having received all the necessary information, Maria quickly left his territory. In the shower, the girl thought for a long time. For the first time in all the time she was near him, it seemed to her that she could succeed. She could help her family.

Chapter 30

Before Maria could rejoice, Sam once again painfully sealed her to the hard reality.

Every move she made, she coordinated with her Master.

"Can I have coffee?"

"Yes."

"Can I watch TV?"

"No."

"May I go out on the balcony?"

"Yes."

All day long. By Tuesday evening, Maria hated Sam again and her phone to boot. If it hadn't been for Luisa with the good news, the girl would have had another breakdown.

As it turned out, the clinic where her Mum was admitted had a new sponsor and all the patients were given the most necessary courses of treatment at no extra cost. Having learned the news, Maria squeaked and jumped with happiness for almost an hour. She decided to hide the money she had received for the jewelry. There was no telling when she might need it again.

"Good evening, Master!" Maria was glowing with happiness when she met Sam in the hallway.

"Hi," Sam smiled sweetly.

He knew the reason for Maria's cheerfulness. This reason cost him a tidy sum, but seeing Maria's carefree smile and joy in her eyes, he realized it was worth it. Besides, he had made the clinic happy by paying for the treatment of most of the patients.

That night, Maria obeyed his orders without question and didn't even object when Sam took her right in his office. With her breasts spread out on the table, she moaned softly as she moved in time with his thrusts. Remembering her little secret, Sam remembered to slap his palm on her red buttocks. Maria only hissed softly but didn't ask him to stop.

That's how most of the week went. Samuel slowly began to allow Maria more autonomy. She decided what she wanted to eat, she could choose and read a book and once a day she could switch on the television for half an hour.

On Friday, Maria woke up early. She planned to have a great day in Rosita's company. After a quick rinse in the shower, the girl raced to Sam's room. She hoped he would let her talk to the cute Mexican woman.

"Come in."

"Good morning, Master! How did you sleep?" Maria was no longer shaking in front of him and even allowed herself little more than a meager "yes, no."

"Good," Sam grinned, arching an eyebrow questioningly. In his years, he'd learned the behavior of women. If she was petting him, she wanted something. "I'm listening to you, Maria."

So arrogant, Maria could barely contain herself from rolling her eyes.

"Rosita is coming today!"

"Yes, I know."

"Can I talk to her?"

"No," Sam told her calmly.

"But..."

"Maria," he said with warning in his voice.

"Why? Why not?" she almost cried.

"Because I say so. Go to your room! This is out of the question!" Sam growled coldly.

Maria flew out, slamming the door at the same time. Bitter tears rolled down her cheeks. She was already in a golden cage. She couldn't talk to Ali. There were too many questions her friend asked and too few answers Maria had. Dad was not an option either. And the girl had no other friends or even just someone to talk to. Rosita had become an outlet for her in this realm of submission. And now Sam has taken away Maria's only ray of light.

When she burst into her room, collapsed on her bed, hugged her pillow, and began to cry. Maria stopped hiding her real emotions. She wanted to show this dry man all her grief and sadness.

Having lost any hope, the girl did not immediately notice the figure in the doorway. Putting his hands in his pockets, Sam calmly watched her sobs. Wiping her tears with her hand, Maria sat down on the bed, covering herself with a pillow. She realized she had to calm down, or she'd be punished.

"Excuse me, Master," Maria asked, stammering.

"So, you want to talk to Rosita?" Sam asked with undisguised curiosity. He was surprised by her reaction. He knew how quickly Rosita could get people to like her.

"Yes," she mumbled quietly.

"Then I have a proposition for you," Sam's voice became softer. That softness made Maria shiver. She knew it meant nothing good.

"What?" Her voice went hoarse at once.

Sam silently approached the bed. His hands were not the only ones in the pockets. The man carefully pulled out the contents and threw them beside Maria. The girl's eyes rounded in an instant. A cold wave ran down her back, and droplets of sweat appeared on her forehead.

No! No! No! No! Her mind immediately howled.

She couldn't take her eyes off the tube of lube and the small anal plug with the pink pebble.

"As long as it's in you, you can talk to Rosita."

Chapter 31

Maria was puffing like a steam engine. She looked furtively at the things he had brought and then at Sam himself. Her amber eyes showed obvious fear and, to Sam's surprise, curiosity. She bit her lip, pressed her pillow harder against her, and fidgeted with her feet on the carpet.

"Does that hurt?" she blinked toward the anal plug.

"No."

Sam had chosen the smallest plug. It didn't even need lube, but he decided not to traumatize the already wobbly Maria. For her, anything that touched her ass was horrible, scary and painful. Being an avid lover of anal sex, Sam simply could not leave her untouched from the backside. For a long time, he'd been walking around looking and dreaming about that sweet, tight hole.

Their strained relationship kept preventing him from getting to that part. Sam thought that as soon as he touched her anus, Maria would run out of his apartment through the window. The girl had shown how afraid she was of anal play when Sam had tried to beat the truth out of her.

But now, they'd developed a kind of trust. Very shaky, but still something. Like the way Maria had started to respond to his actions and obediently follow his instructions. Sometimes, she frowned and pouted her lips, but she did it. She herself did not realize that she was behaving like a real slave.

"You can refuse. It won't count as a stop word. You just don't talk to Rosita. And by the way, she can't talk to you either."

The already round eyes got even bigger. Maria opened her mouth to say something but quickly closed it. Apparently, she prevented the flow of harsh words that were bursting out.

"Do I have to do it myself?" she looked at the cork with doomed eyes.

"No. Lie on your stomach. Butt up."

Taking her question as agreement, Sam smiled involuntarily. The cock in his trousers began to wake. The man got to shake with overwhelming delight. The sight of Maria in the kneeling position brought out the darkest and most vicious in Sam. His palm began to tingle, wanting a sweet spanking.

"Relax, baby girl" Sam said quietly.

Maria shuddered as Sam ran his knuckles along her spine. She tried to breathe evenly and think of anything but the foreign object in her ass.

With his other hand, Sam began to knead the firm hemisphere. Fumbling for a tube of lube, he squeezed a small amount onto his finger. The room was filled with the pungent smell of orange.

Spreading her buttocks with two fingers, he gave himself access to the tight ring. As soon as the cold gel touched her skin, Maria pitched forward. Just in time to catch her by the hip, Sam gave her a loud slap on the left hemisphere.

"Ow!"

"Don't move. That didn't hurt. You'll remember what I said when you begged me not to stop," Sam kept massaging the tight entrance as he bared his teeth. Slightly pushing in and out with his finger. He alternated the movements until Maria stopped shuddering with each pressure on her anus.

"Oh," Maria blurted out as Sam pushed a little harder and inserted his finger one phalanx in.

"Shh, Relax, baby girl."

Stroking her trembling back, Sam began to slowly plunge his index finger into Maria.

Exhaling loudly, Maria decided to obey his advice. She relaxed and tried not to think about the pain. With the last one, she managed to cope with the hurrah. The girl decided to hide the fact that it didn't hurt her at all. Unusual. Unpleasant at first. But the longer Sam massaged Maria from the inside, the faster the girl got used to it.

As soon as Maria relaxed completely and stopped squeezing Sam's finger even harder, he quickly removed his hand and inserted the plug in one motion. Before she could even utter a word, Maria only shuddered quietly.

"That's it. While you're walking around with this beauty," he deliberately pressed the pebble, eliciting a muffled groan from Maria, "You can talk to Rosita as much as you want. Get up."

As soon as Maria moved, a fine shiver ran through her entire body. There was a whole chasm between her legs and a lingering desire. Her loins were shooting because of the plug and the sensations this thing brought. Squaring her shoulders, Maria took a deep breath. Her hands were eager to touch the brightly colored pebble. But she was embarrassed by Sam.

"What was to be said?" Reaching behind her, he barely touched her temple with his lips. Maria stretched out like prey before a predator, trying not to make any sudden movements.

"Thank you, Master!"

"Good girl. Get dressed." With a gentle slap on her buttock, Sam smiled contentedly and quickly left the room.

He couldn't stand to be around her like that. He was afraid of himself. He knew what he was capable of. He didn't want to destroy what they had both worked so hard to build. Watching Maria, Sam became more and more convinced of the wrongness of his decision. He chastised her for her frivolity and thoughtlessness.

Letting the lower one go was never a problem for him. The exception was always Nina. But she was not his slave. They just had sex together. Sam had always introduced elements of BDSM into their 'relationship,' but they never even had a full session. What happened at the club, he didn't count. They hadn't been alone then.

Now, when he looked at Maria, he started to get a cat scratch on his soul every time he looked at her. He was getting used to her. Starting to give her too much attention. Making plans.

More and more often, he forgot that their time was running out.

Chapter 32

Maria didn't regret the opportunity to socialize with Rosita in the slightest. Although the little thing in her ass was uncomfortable, the girl calmly endured the whole day. The Mexican looked at the shuddering Maria with surprise without commenting on her behavior.

"Is everything all right, Nina?"

"Uh-huh," Maria smiled pretentiously in response.

The realization of her own stupidity and naivety came to Maria a couple of days later.

Still sleepy, the girl obediently stood at the entrance to the master bedroom and waited to be called. Tonight would be the third time she would set her heel for Sam's amusement.

Over the past few days, Sam had very rarely spoken to her. He sparingly answered her questions, got what he wanted and retreated to his office in silence. Behaving with a sickening restraint and detachment.

Maria should've been happy, but instead, the girl began to fall into a kind of depression. She was offended and sulked around because of the lack of attention. She even cried in the shower a couple of times when Sam didn't say goodnight to her. She couldn't sleep, going over in her head what she'd done or said wrong. The morning came with anger and disgust at herself and her own thoughts. Maria, as if waking up from amnesia, remembered who Sam was and what he had done to her and her family.

At some point, she just had to force herself to think bad thoughts about him.

"May I?" Maria asked quietly, peering into the room.

"Come in." Sam was holding his phone, as usual. Coming out of a shower, a faint vapor was emanating from his body. The white towel sat low on his hips, revealing a view of his perfect oblique muscles and the trail of blond hair that ran downward. Maria had completely forgotten the purpose of her visit to his bedroom, brazenly studying all the naked parts of the man's body.

"Ahem," Sam reminded her.

Tearing his gaze away from the phone, he grinned involuntarily. Over the past month, he had come to learn Maria's habits well. He had cracked her pretense like a nut and could not distinguish the truth from another game. Found all the erogenous zones. Knew by heart the location of every mole on her body. Calculated the time in which she reached orgasm, as well as how long she could tolerate and keep herself in control. Even recognized the intonation of her moans and screams. The unknown and mysterious Maria was now an open book that Sam read and discovered.

Her body was defiantly revealing the state of her mistress as she stood there in the room. Small goosebumps on her breasts and protruding nipples gave away the excitement Maria was in. The glint in her amber eyes and deep breathing confirmed his guesses.

Seeing all this beauty in front of him, Sam could not resist the temptation to eat such a sweet prey. To top it off, another plug was already on the table for tonight's permission to communicate with Rosita.

"Come here."

Rolling her eyes mentally, Maria obediently walked to the bed. The sparseness of his answers and orders always spoiled her mood. Without a word, the girl immediately rested her elbows on the hard mattress. Resting her knees on the edge of the bed, Maria lowered her head and concentrated on breathing.

Hoping for the standard Master's actions, petting-plug-free, Maria tried to relax.

"Ah!" she burst out as soon as Sam's finger entered the narrow opening. She couldn't get used to the feeling. Sam moved his finger smoothly, touching places she had never known before, making her eyes blurry. Her breathing quickened, and her thoughts became a mess.

Fully concentrating on the movements in her ass, Maria didn't immediately feel the touch on her already wet womb.

"Maria," Sam exhaled softly.

With his free hand, he fisted her dark hair and pulled her towards him. Her fragile body arched up, obeying the movements of his firm hands. Tilting her head back, Maria exhaled loudly. She didn't realize what was happening. Sam wasn't acting according to plan, and panic was rising in her throat.

"What..." Maria didn't have time to finish. In the next second, a lightning bolt of pleasure struck her entire body.

With one sharp thrust, Sam entered her completely. He continued to fuck her with his finger in her ass and slowly moved his hips, plunging into Maria up to his balls, which smacked against her crotch.

Clenching the white sheets in her fists and shuddering her whole body from what was happening, Maria whimpered louder with each of Sam's movements. The sensations were much more vivid and unusual. Continuing to stimulate the girl with his finger, Sam saw and felt how good she felt. He himself was getting high and trembling with overflowing excitement. The thought of making this part of the morning ritual flashed through his mind.

"Please!"

"Please what?" Samuel gritted his teeth. He was beginning to lose touch with reality himself.

"Please, Master! Can I cum!?" Maria squeezed her eyes shut in shame. She still had a hard time with these phrases.

"No!" he growled, picking up the pace and thrusting even harder. With his head tilted back, he could hardly hear outside sounds, only the white noise in his ears from the overwhelming pleasure.

"Please!" Maria was almost crying, biting her lip. A fire was igniting in her that made her whole body whimper, and between her legs ached and burned terribly with dissatisfaction.

"I beg you!" Maria kept whimpering and begging.

Sam didn't answer. Maria felt every vein on his blood-soaked cock, and a cold chill began to run up her spine. She kept begging and mumbling, caught between brutal reality and euphoria. Everything turned into a thick fog before her eyes.

Feeling her from the inside out, Sam didn't hold back, swearing loudly and cumming into the slave girl trembling with frustration. Abruptly changing his cock to two fingers, Sam began to massage the front wall of her vagina.

"Beg more, baby girl," he ordered, still reeling from his orgasm.

Chapter 33

Maria howled like a wounded animal. She collapsed chest down on the bed, moving towards him herself. Seizing the moment, Sam thrust his middle finger sharply into her tight ass.

"Aggh... Yes!" Maria whimpered, exhausted. Desire mingled with pain, rose the girl to the heavens.

She continued to scream and move her ass in time with Sam's movements, receiving the most vivid and long-awaited orgasm of her life. With each new thrust, she put out the fire burning from within. Enjoyed the pleasant wave of heat that covered her entire body. Shuddered at the final thrusts. She forgot how to breathe but opened her mouth like a fish looking for water.

There was an unpleasant ringing in her ears. Her knees were shaking, and she was unable to hold her body up. Her fists were still clutching the sheets painfully. Maria breathed loudly without opening her eyes. There was a boundless emptiness and wetness in her lower abdomen. Taking a couple of deep breaths, the girl struggled to get out of bed. Leaning her arms on the mattress, Maria didn't immediately realize why the sheet was stuck to her stomach.

Slowly lowering her gaze, Maria was astonished at what she saw. A huge wet stain mixed with Sam's semen was on the spot where the girl had been. To the last second, Maria denied what she had seen until a thin, transparent trickle ran down the inside of her thigh to confirm her guess.

WHAT IS THAT!? No! It can't be! Everything swam before her eyes. Embarrassment swept over the girl headlong. Her face and neck were red from shock.

"God! No! No! No!" she sobbed loudly and covered her face with her palms. She couldn't believe she had wet herself during sex.

Taking a step back, Maria slammed into Samuel's stone chest. Scared even more, the girl deliberately averted her gaze. The shame of what had happened had completely knocked the ground out from under her feet. She only cried quietly and backed away from Sam, hoping not to come into contact with him.

"What are you doing?" Sam wondered.

Quickly dashing to the bathroom for a dry towel, he had in no way expected to see such a picture. A crying Maria kept her back to him, her back turned to him.

The girl bent her knees and clenched her thighs with all her might as if something was hurting her. With a frown, Sam quickly shortened the distance between them.

"Stay back!" Maria shouted, resting her side against the wall. She almost folded in half from the fear of being touched.

"Maria! What's wrong? Are you in pain?" Sam asked seriously, ignoring her hysterics. He came close to her and forcefully pulled her hands away from her face. Her tear-red eyes looked anywhere but at Sam. Maria continued to cower, unable to hear her Master.

"Maria!" Sam shouted, and it helped.

As if hearing a forbidden command, Maria glared at him. She looked like a frightened child with her lower lip puckered and her arms crossed over her chest.

"Why are you crying?" Sam repeated calmly.

"I...I didn't mean to. I don't know how it happened. I'm sorry! I'm sorry! I'm sorry!" The girl lowered her head, her voice shaking as she repeated the same thing. Unable to contain her emotions, she started crying again.

"Maria, explain! What did you do?" Sam frowned. Looking at her intently for an answer.

Maria tried to cover her face with her hands again, but Sam stopped her. Stared menacingly straight into her eyes, to which Maria stopped throwing a tantrum in an instant. Without words, she realized she needed to explain her hysteria and shame. She shuddered at the thought of saying those words out loud.

"I don't know how it happened," she repeated quietly, glancing toward the bed, where the sheets were wet.

"What?" Sam glanced at Maria in confusion.

Personally, he was completely satisfied with everything that had happened. He hadn't had such a release in a long time. He was also impressed by Maria's giving. Her moans and screams would be in his sweet dreams for a long time to come. Memories of how she cum on his fingers a couple of minutes ago awakened the man's carnal hunger again.

"Don't make me say it out loud!" she pleaded softly. "The last time this happened to me was when I was a child," she added even more quietly, calming down a little.

Sam digested her words slowly. He looked down at the bed again. With all the puzzles in his head, he didn't know what to do first: laugh or explain to Maria what a squirt was.

Abruptly pulling her against him, he exhaled heavily into the dark top of her head. Maria was surprised again. Scared of her own pleasure. Cumming with such force that she flooded Sam all over the bed and even his legs. For a dominant to bring his slave to such a state was on par with a gold medal for an Olympic champion.

And she burst into tears and thought she had wet herself.

Still unable to contain his laughter, Sam laughed out loud, pulling Maria even tighter.

Confused and hurt, Maria did not understand his amusement. Her lower lip quivered with annoyance, and her hand itched to slap Sam sweetly.

"Maria, do you know what a squirt is?" Sam asked with a laugh.

"I've heard of it," she answered warily. Her cheeks turned crimson again. His words came quickly to Maria.

"Well, congratulations, you got a taste of it today." With another giggle, he added, "Well, I got it on me too."

The shame was gone. It was replaced by anger and resentment. Maria began to puff like a locomotive from a desire to send Sam, or even better, to hit him painfully. Neither the first nor the second she could not afford so obediently stood like a statue in his arms.

"Can we finish this so I can go? Rosita will be here soon," Maria asked distantly.

"No."

Lifting Maria, light as a flake, in his arms, Sam, ignoring the woman's squeals, headed for the bathroom. Afraid to fall, Maria wrapped her arms around his strong neck and snuggled against him with her whole body. Again, the uncertainty and randomness of his actions shocked her.

Once in the spacious room, Sam and Maria walked into the huge shower cubicle. It was large enough for five people at once. Putting the still-wobbling girl on the floor, Sam began to wash his grief-stricken slave.

Maria twitched every now and then from his touch. She waited for a trick or another instruction. But Sam simply helped her wash away all traces of their recent love crime and then demanded that she wash him.

Lathering the flannel with fragrant shower gel, Maria took her time following his instructions. Following the flannel, she walked over the clean skin with the palm of her hand as if looking for flaws. Although, in fact, the girl was quietly rejoicing and enjoying the process. And when Sam handed her a towel, Maria automatically began to wipe his wet body.

Sam decided not to stop her. Covering his eyes, he enjoyed Maria's smooth movements. But when it came to his groin, he sharply took the towel away. His cock was already starting to rise again from a too-long stay of defenseless and docile Maria next to him.

"I'll do it myself," he said hoarsely and nodded towards the second towel.

Once in the bedroom, the man began to get ready for the office. He quickly went into the wardrobe. He put on his underwear and chose a suit and a shirt.

"What are you still doing here?" Sam was startled when he saw Maria standing in the center of the room.

"The ..." Maria crossed her arms under her breasts, causing them to rise, and looked down at the table where the anal plug lay lonely.

"Button my shirt."

With a lazy command, Sam moved close to Maria. When her small, trembling fingers reached the top button, the man stopped her. Taking her palm in his hand, he touched the back of it with his lips. Maria's eyes widened to half her face. An uncontrollable hurricane of emotions arose in her stomach. She was overwhelmed with joy, delight, desire and curiosity. Sam clearly read it all in her gaze. He smiled faintly at the corner of his lips. He had snapped again without realizing it. He just did what he really wanted to do.

"You've done your time. Go get dressed. Rosita will be here soon," Sam said intimately without averting his eyes. Maria stood up on her toes at the sound of his tone. Her mouth was dry from the bottomless blue eyes in which she kept drowning. And the longer she stared into them, the more she sank to the bottom.

Chapter 34

After that morning, Maria walked around like she was in a fog. Distracted. Always in herself. Silent. Even Rosita's entertaining stories didn't help cheer her up. Maria only came out of her inner self when Sam was around. The man was like a breath of fresh air. She'd become timid and would smile stupidly. Followed his orders and didn't hold back her emotions when it came to encouragement. Moaned and begged him not to stop. Shuddered in the most unforgettable orgasms she'd ever experienced. Running off to her room, happy and sleeping like a child. And when her periods came, she cried that she wouldn't be able to please Master.

Sam didn't bother her. Even ordered her to wear clothes at all times. Worried about menstrual pain, he was meticulous about what painkillers Maria was taking. Watched her diet, though he didn't force her to eat when she didn't want to. He understood her condition.

Maria rejoiced like a child at such attention. She quietly thanked her Master.

At times, when her brain reminded her of the purpose of her stay at Sam's house, Maria would get sad. She would sit on her bed for hours, staring at one point. Rewinding her life over and over again. She blamed fate for being such a pig. Regretted that they'd met under these circumstances. Hardly, but she was beginning to admit it. She was drawn to Sam. She was starting to like him. And not just like him. Maria was horrified to realize that her feelings for Sam were much stronger than mere sympathy.

The girl longed for him to leave. She thought of ways to please him. Worried if he didn't smile, she would rejoice with him.

Alicia's comment was clear and cruel, *"You, my friend, have turned into a trained puppy!"*

Maria didn't deny this similarity. One time Sam decided to have a pet-play, and Maria's ass was decorated with a cute plug with a tail. Not a dog, but definitely a graceful kitty.

Sam's condition, on the other hand, swung like a pendulum. Rashness and irrationality had become his best friends. The previously reserved and stern Dominant had turned into an impulsive boy.

He would get angry, then actually pounce on Maria from the doorstep. His anger was mostly directed at himself. Sam was annoyed by the feelings that arose around Maria. He even began to contemplate suggesting that she stay after two months. He didn't know how to ask, but he was thinking about it more and more.

The question of O'Dell Senior's scam remained open. But his people did not stop looking for any facts of his innocence or participation. A lot of things did not add up. Again, the employees of his company never stopped praising their former boss.

A couple of times, Sam heard rumors about his partner. Paul Stance was repeatedly involved in various scandals, including the forgery of documents. Being completely infatuated with Maria, Sam overlooked the main O'Dell partner. Paul disappeared in an unknown direction. Even Sam's men could not find him, which further fuelled the man's doubts.

Blackwood reminded again of himself and the conversation with Nina. Sam couldn't put off the trip to New York any longer. Firstly, his friend was right. By severing his relationship with Nina, Sam would be able to focus his full attention on Maria. She would definitely be able to distract him. Secondly, the partners were starting to remind him of long-standing contracts; among them was David Blackwood with his long-time friend and business partner, Henry Nicolson.

Sam was about to go home when suddenly his phone rang. For this man, Sam decided to allocate a special ringtone.

"Did Blackwood tell you to call me?" Without saying hello, Sam got straight to the point.

"Sam, can't I just call you?" The owner of the velvet baritone was offended by the man's statement.

"Woolf, cut it off," Sam exhaled heavily. He had no energy left after a hard day of work to listen to his old friend's moralizing. He wanted to stroke Maria's soft skin, not talk to Max. "Let's just cut to the chase."

"All right, mate. When can I expect you? Oh, and Blackwood asked me to call. I don't know why he's so hung up on you, but you know him. That old fox won't let go," Woolf said sarcastically.

"I've already figured that out," Sam rubbed his eyes. If Blackwood got Max Woolf involved, it was a serious matter.

"So when?" The annoying friend kept up.

"A couple of days."

"Be specific."

"Max, don't get cocky," Sam snapped at him warningly.

"All right," the friend smiled into the phone. "Blackwood said you wouldn't be alone. Will you bring her to the Kink?" he asked craftily.

"Maybe," Sam pondered in his voice.

"If she's as sweet as Nina, I'd love to have her....."

"No!" Sam shouted. He didn't realize how he'd snapped. He squeezed the phone until it crunched. The thought of someone else touching Maria made his eyes darken with anger. Taking a couple of deep breaths, he pulled himself together quickly, "She's my slave. Only mine."

"Understood," Max replied calmly.

The men did not speak of BDSM again. They quickly discussed their work and said goodbye. Lastly, Max once again reminded him of his visit to New York.

All the way home, Sam pondered the trip. He could not decide whether to take Maria with him or leave her in London.

"Good evening, Master!" The girl's sonorous voice brought Sam out of his trance.

As soon as he looked at the naked girl standing in the middle of the room, he realized he couldn't go a day without her.

"Shit," Sam cursed to himself, realizing how much trouble he was in.

Chapter 35

"Has Rosita left?"

"Yes, Master," she blushed. As of late, he'd ordered the girl to remove the anal plug herself.

"Good. Get ready, we need to buy you some clothes. We're leaving London for a couple of weeks. I hope you've got a passport," Sam asked her smartly. Without looking at Maria, he paced the room, listing in his thoughts all the things he needed to buy before the trip.

The girl's eyes widened as he announced the whole list. When he said they were going to Oxford Street, she almost fainted. She couldn't go with him to the busiest part of town, where all her friends hung out, and even worse, her parents' friends. If a single living soul found out about her connection to Sam, her father wouldn't stand for it. Maria tried not to think about her mother's reaction.

"Get dressed," Sam repeated calmly, noting with surprise the pallor on her face.

"I can order everything online. I know all my measurements," Maria began to dissuade him. From the fear of appearing on the street with Sam, the girl's fingers and toes turned cold.

"Maria, I said go get dressed. I've had a long day. I want to finish with this and have dinner," a note of irritation and threat crept into the man's voice. He looked closely at the trembling Maria.

"I can't," Maria shuddered at her own answer. Lowering her eyes to the floor, she shrank to the size of an atom. Or rather, she wanted to very badly. She wished Sam wouldn't glare at her, not look at her with such anger and hatred.

"Why?

"I can't," she repeated with tears in her eyes. She was ashamed because she knew what he was getting at.

"Maria," it sounded so menacing that Maria's teeth chattered in fear, "why can't you go shopping with me?"

The weight of this conversation came upon her in full force. Sam, whom she had seen off to work that morning, was gone. The formidable dominant stood before her again. And she was... back to being the lying Maria O'Dell. Or rather, she could have. Everything depended on her answer. Having learned the past lessons of life well, Maria decided to tell the truth. The bitter truth.

"If we are seen together, there will be rumors. People will be surprised," she replaced the last word. The word that was on her tongue was *"freak out."*

"You care about what people you don't know would think?" Sam chuckled contemptuously. The mood had completely soured. Maria was surprised again. But not in a good way.

"I don't want anyone to know ..."

"Shut up," Sam snapped.

His eyes darkened. Sam took a couple of deep breaths through his nose to regain his composure. Not to do anything stupid, but the man was approaching a state where he was doing the worst things to the lower ones. Bringing them to the thinnest line without breaking the rules. And looking at the shuddering Maria, he knew she couldn't take it.

She'd say the stop word.

He'd made that rule himself, which he'd repeatedly chastised himself for. There was an inexplicable panic in his soul every time he thought she'd leave early.

"Go to your room," Sam ordered with a cold voice and walked past Maria as if she were nothing.

As she stared at her Master, Maria couldn't understand the feelings that overwhelmed her. She wanted to run after him and, despite the absurdity of the situation, fall to her knees, begging for forgiveness.

She had been rude. She had disobeyed.

She deserved to be punished.

Sobbing loudly, she covered her eyes with her hands. She wanted to hide from everything, to find herself in a warm embrace. But worst of all, she couldn't imagine anything but Sam's embrace.

She couldn't imagine. Every time she went back to the night they'd had sex for the first time, she'd remember how he held her in his arms and soothed her like a small child, giving her warmth. But now Sam felt cold and painful to be around.

After gathering her thoughts a little, Maria slowly wandered back to her room. The tears were still flowing, dripping down her chest. The trembling in her body didn't stop, as if a very important thing had been taken from her.

Rushing to the bathroom, Maria washed her face with cold water. She tried to calm down and think about how to fix the situation. But no sooner had she made a plan in her head than the door to her room slammed loudly.

"Maria!" hearing her name, Maria flew into the bedroom.

Still angry, Sam looked tiredly and coldly at the flushed slave girl.

"Order everything online." Tossing the tablet and credit card on the bed, he quickly withdrew.

Pouring three glasses of whiskey into himself at once, Sam was able to cool down a little. He grinned at his own stupidity as he realized the meaning of her words. The girl was just afraid for her parents. He'd really overreacted. He'd demanded to take his pet out for a walk in the busiest part of town.

But he was not going to forgive Maria. He would, later. For her attitude towards him and being ashamed of their acquaintance.

Sam had never been interested in the feelings of his slaves. It was purely business between him and the girls. He took. They gave. Everyone left happy. But with this brat Maria, it had all turned upside down.

Sam was thinking about the future with Maria too much. He was feeling too much.

That's why Maria's words hurt him. Stupid thoughts popped into his head.

She thinks she's better. You're just a sick man to her! She's only with you for the money! She's just like her father!

Sam turned ferocious and stone-cold with every new idea he had for himself.

The whiskey saved him. Cooled the heat, for the time being, at least.

He would punish her. Maria had no idea what terrible fate Sam had in store for her. He'd remind her who she was and where she belonged. She wouldn't say no. The price was too high.

Sam looked out over the evening London. Holding a glass of his favorite drink, he smiled slyly at his own madness.

There was a darkness brewing in the man's eyes. A darkness from which he could never escape, the darkness he was going to throw Maria into.

Chapter 36

For the first time in her life, Maria was sick of shopping. Every dress and blouse added to the basket made her hate herself. A couple of times, the girl simply threw the tablet far away on the bed and began to measure the room on trembling legs. Who would have thought that a shopping trip would turn out to be a disaster?

Maria's gaze kept returning to the ajar door. In her time in this house, she'd learned the rules: You mess up, you get punished.

But Sam didn't come. Maria kept expecting to hear heavy footsteps in the corridor. But there were none. Not an hour later. Not in the morning. After sitting on her bed all night, Maria didn't sleep a wink. Instead, only listened to the silence and the beating of her own heart.

Guilt burned in her chest, spreading poison throughout her body. Her fingers ached with the desire to open the door of his bedroom and appear for punishment. But the remnants of common sense stopped her.

Washing herself with cold water, Maria reluctantly went to the kitchen. Sleep didn't come, and neither did her appetite. But again, the habit she had developed was taking its toll. With leaden hands, Maria brewed coffee and took out yesterday's pancakes. Rosita had made more on purpose so that Maria could eat the leftovers the next day.

She got rid of the cover and put the plate in the microwave. The coffee machine beeped, reminding her of the aromatic coffee. Maria almost reached the mug, and suddenly, a cold wave of horror ran down her spine. Her back straightened on its own, and her butt clenched involuntarily. She didn't need to turn round to see the look in his eyes. She knew there was anger, hatred, and contempt there. The latter was particularly jarring. It was like an invisible slap in the face, for Maria did not have contempt for Sam. At first, yes. But now, there was a different feeling in her heart.

"Good morning, Master," she said quickly and turned around.

Eyes to the floor. Arms at the seams. Shoulders slumped. Sam stared at her very carefully, trying to figure out: was this a game, or did she really feel guilty? After yesterday, her credibility had dropped to zero again. Sam didn't believe her. Questioned her every move, looking for a catch.

Crawling back into his cocoon of hatred and detachment, he refused to accept Maria. *She's not a person; she's an enemy,* he said to himself. Another temporary toy. And the longer he tried to convince himself of that, the lousier he got. Anger at his own thoughts and actions clouded his judgment. The experienced dominant acted irrationally, thus returning to the mode of constant punishment.

"Did you order everything?" Sam said dryly, ignoring her greeting.

He pushed himself off the doorjamb and walked lazily toward her. Just as tired and disheveled, Sam kept his predatory gaze on Maria. He didn't look like an ordinary man in his house trousers. He looked like a Greek god.

Resting her buttocks on the edge of the tabletop, the girl dared to look at her Master. She couldn't even utter a word. She only sighed loudly, opening her mouth. The words stuck in her throat as Sam's hand sank hard into her hair, gripping a huge section of strands in a vise.

"Are you suddenly deaf, Maria?" His murderous stare left Maria completely confused. Sam pulled on her hair, forcing the girl to stand on her toes. Pressing his hips into the tabletop, Sam waited for an answer.

"Y…yes, Master," Maria managed to squeeze a short answer out of her trembling body.

"Too long," Sam growled, forcibly turning her back to him.

"Oh!" was all Maria could manage to breathe out. She was lost. She didn't understand the purpose of his movements. His voice was frightening. It was as if they were back in that terrible first day of their acquaintance. "What are you..."

"Shut up," Sam growled.

Maria didn't dare object; Her body shuddered unpleasantly, but between her legs, she was suddenly hot and empty. Biting the inside of her cheek, Maria breathed loudly, trying to push her thoughts away. It was failing miserably. Sam's vibrating voice was hypnotizing and putting the girl into a trance. Fear mixed with excitement and anticipation of something unknown and pleasurable. She knew he wouldn't hurt. Knew that despite all his anger, he would take care of her. And that warmed her inside out, an inexplicable flame of desire and lust.

"I'm sorry, Master," Maria blurted out quickly.

"I told you to shut up," he pulled on her hair a little harder, causing Maria to arch her back.

Her buttocks rested against his groin, clearly feeling his arousal. The slightest friction against his trousers gave her an invisible electric shock. She clawed her fingers into the tabletop until her knuckles were white, and threw all her strength at the remnants of her self-control. She was on the verge of a breakdown. She wanted so badly to feel him inside her. To feel the hot throbbing of his cock. She was even ready for his favorite anal games. She suddenly felt the need to merge with him. But there was one annoying feeling that wouldn't leave her.

"Punish!"

"What?" Sam grinned, wincing at what he'd heard.

"Punish me, Master," Maria begged, gritting her teeth.

"For what?" Sam whispered quietly in her ear. Maria began to shake even more. His voice crept under her skin. Teased every nerve.

"I've upset you! Please punish me and forgive me!"

His free hand clenched into a fist. Sam could barely contain himself, so eager to get on with what she was asking. But no. He'd been up all night plotting his revenge. Hatching and sucking up every little detail. So he was not going to give Maria an easy pardon just yet. He suffered himself, but he made a firm decision to see it through.

To break her completely.

Hoping for his love of punishment, Maria was anticipating the sweetness of his heavy and rough hand that would now fall on her ass.

"Punish," she echoed in his ears.

Maria arched herself even more. Preparing for the much-needed release. She shuddered faintly as Sam's palm stroked her buttock. She was prepared for his next move, only she didn't expect for him to withdrew his hand. She gasped when Sam let go of her completely, and took a few steps back.

"Go get dressed. I don't want to look at your naked body anymore," his words, like a shot to the heart, penetrated very deeply. The pain became so unbearable that Maria felt as if something had cracked inside her.

Chapter 37

Maria had never put on panties with such hatred. She wanted to tear the thin lace and throw it in the bin. But the girl obediently pulled the underwear over her naked buttocks. The house dress unpleasantly prickled her skin, which made Maria constantly scratch her ribs and lower back. Everything irritated and pissed her off. She wanted to kick the annoying pouf with her foot. She wanted to throw a cup into the sink and make it shatter.

Sam was to blame for her mood. In one phrase, he'd ripped her heart out, ground it up in a meat grinder, and thrown the rest out the window. If someone had said that to Maria a month ago, she would have run to get dressed, but it was different now. Sam had managed to get her used to this way of life. He showed her that shameful things weren't shameful, unleashing her inner beast that'd been sleeping all those years.

Now he was putting her back in a cage; a short leash and taking away the bone he gave her.

Maria wasn't the least bit embarrassed by the comparison to a dog. She came to him to be submissive and do everything he said.

To kneel, sit in the corner, and wait for her master. Wiggle her arse when she got a treat.

"Just a dog. Wet bitch," the girl scolded herself, swallowing her tears.

Fully dressed, she collapsed on the bed, continuing to whimper quietly with resentment and guilt. It hadn't gone anywhere. Maria herself didn't notice how she began to need his forgiveness. She laughed and scolded herself. But she couldn't stop feeling that pain inside.

Close to lunchtime, her orders arrived. It took the courier fifteen minutes to bring in the different-sized bags. Maria didn't even check to see if everything had been delivered. She carried it all from the living room to her room with her head down. The girl did not feel delighted or happy about the new items. She unpacked the outfits and, without trying them on, hung them in the wardrobe.

When she put the shoes on the shelves, she realized at once that she was not alone. She didn't even turn round. She felt the heavy gaze on her back. She exhaled loudly, hoping to get away with a slight fright.

"Did you buy a suitcase?" Sam asked tiredly. With his whole appearance, he radiated indifference and detachment. Maria felt it; as if the temperature in the room dropped as soon as Sam entered.

"No," Maria answered quietly and a little fearfully. The gears in her head started working at once. The girl frantically recalled whether he had ordered her to buy a suitcase. "You didn't command to buy it, Master."

Sam tsked unhappily as if a mosquito had flown near her ear. She poked him again. Stared at him with frightened eyes. Flinched at every sharp look. Shaking his head, Sam once again forbade himself to feel, locking all emotion away. Cut the already thin thread that bound him and Maria together.

"Don't be so shaky," Sam growled harshly. He didn't mean for it to be like this, but it was just the way it was.

Maria stretched as if a ruler had been tied to her shoulder blades. Her eyes became glassy, and she could barely hold back the tears.

"I'll buy it myself. Pack your things. We're leaving tomorrow for a few weeks. Give me your passport."

Hearing the last, Maria frowned. Her imagination immediately drew a lot of terrible pictures, from selling her for organ farming to renting her out as a slave. The girl did not hurry to leave the small dressing room, continuing to look at Sam with a sidelong glance.

"I need to book tickets," Sam explained as if reading her mind. He was amused by her reaction. Somehow, he was mentally glad that Maria wasn't a complete fool.

She is not mine to keep, the man reminded himself.

Hearing the purpose of his demand, Maria pulled the documents from the shelf in the dressing room with shaking hands. Glancing at the dark blue cover with gold lettering, she handed the passport to Sam.

"Will you give it back later?" Maria asked apprehensively.

"Yes. I'm not going to sell you into another slavery," Sam grinned wickedly, making Maria's legs give out. Every word he said hurt her. Every phrase hurt. Every look killed. If a cat could spend nine lives, Maria managed to spend more than forty in a month. And this, the girl knew for sure, was not the end.

Maria spent the rest of the day alone. No one touched her, no one punished her, no one called her. Gathering her things into neat stacks, Maria tried to concentrate on working out her looks and outfits. She wasn't going to wear just anything. For some reason, she wanted to show Sam a different side of herself. To capture his gaze while fully clothed. She spent hours rearranging dresses, blouses, skirts, shoes, and bags. Standing out complex schemes of fashionable and stunning images.

Completely absorbed in packing, Maria did not immediately notice two huge suitcases by her door. On one of them lay a short note: *"Wear something comfy tomorrow,"* Maria read aloud. A silly smile lit up her tear-stained face. There was a pleasant prickling in her chest. Too bad the girl didn't realize that it was her soul that was falling to pieces.

The next morning, everything happened as if in a fog. Maria quickly got ready, even faster, had breakfast alone and, like an excellent slave, waited for her master, fully packed and ready suitcases.

She was still upset that Sam hadn't come out for breakfast. She'd heard his voice in the study, but she'd been afraid to look in. In a hurry she finished her coffee and went back to her room. She left the doors open, waiting for further instructions.

"Are you ready?"

"Y..yes," the girl almost choked on her own saliva as she looked at Sam standing in the doorway.

The black T-shirt was tight around a sculpted torso that made her want to run her fingers over it. Tight dark blue jeans emphasized his slim and equally well-trained legs and narrow pelvis. He didn't even need to turn around. Maria already knew that his arse looked stunning in those trousers. Comfortable dark trainers completed Sam's enticing look.

Maria couldn't take her eyes off her Master. In her heart, the girl exulted that it all belonged to her. Yes, a slave she was, but in all the time she had been in his house, Sam had only spent sessions with her. Only had sex with her, too.

"Let's go. Jacob's taking care of the suitcases." Pushing off the doorjamb, Sam headed straight for the exit, grabbing his leather jacket. Black, too.

After looking around the almost empty room, Maria grabbed her backpack and headed after Sam. She chose a comfortable black knit suit and sneakers for the trip. Without heels, she looked like a little sister next to a huge, brutal older brother.

All the way to the airport, Maria kept glancing at the aloof Sam. The man plunged headlong into his work. Hysterically typing messages or leafing through complicated charts. Maria wondered exactly where they were going. She'd bought summer clothes, but her excitement didn't fade, nor did the thought that she might need something on the ground.

"Sam," she called softly, watching Jacob, the bulky man who was driving the car. She didn't know how familiar the man was with her boss's predilections. She also liked to call him by his first name. By the way, he demanded it himself when they were in public.

"What?" Sam said calmly.

"Where are we going?" Maria almost whispered.

"New York."

Chapter 38

Trying not to give herself away, Maria quickly ducked her nose into her phone. She flipped through the social media feed in a hysterical manner, ineffectively masking her fear. Despite her roots, the girl had never traveled to her historical homeland.

Only Maria dialed a quick message to Alicia, as the phone flew out of her hands. Or rather, it was taken away.

"You're on the phone too much," Sam tsked unhappily.

He kept his eyes on her. He watched her panic. For a moment, he thought maybe she had a fear of flying. Maria stubbornly refused to look in his direction, which hurt the dominant even more. He missed her attention. Instead of aloofness, he wanted to see her puppy dog gaze directed at him all the way. And that brat was just staring at her phone.

"I was texting my friend."

There was a hint of maturity in her voice. Such boldness didn't go unnoticed. Sam only raised one eyebrow upward, suggesting her place. But apparently, Maria was getting bolder in the presence of a stranger. Reaching her hand forward, she demanded the phone back. Her confident voice made Sam chuckle faintly, but the cock in his trousers began to wake up quickly.

Sassy Maria was turning Sam on. He wanted to squeeze more out of her like a man possessed, to punish her to the fullest and get his share of the high.

"Here you go," Sam tossed the phone in her direction.

The rest of the road was spent in silence.

Maria was a little surprised when their car turned off the main strip and headed for the private jets. She knew Sam was wealthy, but to have his own private jet... Turning away from the window, the girl only grimaced, parodying her Master.

She suddenly wanted to know more about him. Not just his dark side, for in all that time in his house, Maria had seen the other Sam. Caring and calm. Even funny and affectionate in places. The girl remembered yesterday's note again. Her lips curved into a sweet, girlish smile. It was the way love-struck fools smiled. Maria no longer denied that she might be one of them. All that remained was to beg forgiveness and endure the punishment, and she could begin to sink the glacier named Samuel Williams.

Check-in and passport control took less than half an hour. Everyone saluted courteously and smiled sweetly at Mr Williams and his companion. Maria was silent, only smiling discreetly when they addressed her. She answered quickly and to the point.

The aircraft itself was small but very roomy and comfortable. The crew met them at the gangway with smiles. Maria went up to the cabin with undisguised curiosity. Brown leather upholstery and dark wood. Everything in the cabin screamed of luxury and prestige. At the far end were a lavatory and a small private cabin. The doors were closed.

"Are you afraid?" Sam asked with interest as soon as they were seated.

"No," Maria smiled. His question confused her. She didn't seem to be darting from side to side. She was calm and quiet.

"Have you ever flown one of these before?"

"Not on one of these."

As she looked around, Maria didn't keep her eyes on Williams for a second, which was annoying. Sam drummed his fingers on the natural oak tabletop, hoping for some kind of attention. He was hurt by her behavior.

Being in public with her for the first time, he was annoyed that someone was talking to her (so what if it was an officer). He could barely contain himself, catching men's glances in her direction. No, Maria did not reciprocate and did not wag her tail. She looked down at the floor like an obedient slave and followed Sam like a shadow.

Sam was angry at himself for the umpteenth time. At his bad reaction. At the jealousy that had seeped poison into his head and infected every vital organ, including his heart.

He'd never been jealous for anyone. Not even Nina. That night at the club, he'd shared her with Blackwood and Max without the slightest hesitation. But now, the mere thought that one of the men was touching his Maria started a storm of anger and rage, the primal instinct to protect, shield, and hide.

Mine.

"Is everything okay?" A thin voice snapped him out of the deep pit of darkness Sam had thrown himself into. When a warm hand covered what appeared to be a clenched fist, he exhaled loudly.

"Y…yes," the man stammered, a little confused.

Her eyes were the color of his favorite whisky. And in them, he could clearly see worry.

She worried about me, is she? Sam grinned at his own stupid thoughts. With a shake of his head, he went back into his usual state of complete alienation and coldness.

"I just thought you were worried about something. So I asked. I'm sorry." Maria pulled her hand away sharply, her gaze lowered.

She was really scared for Sam. The girl could put her feelings down to inexperience, but she still believed her instincts. In his eyes, she saw nothing but sadness and confusion. Something that dominants never allowed themselves. Something she'd never seen in his gaze.

Sam wanted to say something, but the pilot informed her that they were at the right altitude and that the flight was going fine. That was why Sam loved his plane. He didn't even realize when they took off. Or maybe he was just so deep in his thoughts. Sam also loved his private cabin, the door of which he was now staring intently at.

Quite by accident, his gaze slid towards Maria, who was looking at the fluffy clouds and miniature houses through the porthole like a child. Feeling Sam's gaze on her, she gave him a sweet smile. Again.

There was more warmth in that smile than Sam had seen in his entire life.

Sam remembered all of his actions vaguely. His eyes were a blur, and his trousers were starting to catch fire. He only woke up when he realized he was hovering over a frightened Maria in his cabin. The girl was breathing loudly, staring him straight in the eye. When Sam touched her cheekbone with his knuckles, she trembled.

But it wasn't because of fear. Sam understood her condition, for he could barely contain himself. He wanted her. Everything inside was humming with overflowing excitement and desire.

"No!" Maria burst out as a strong hand slipped under her black jumper. The girl realized from the unhappy growl that she was playing with fire, but she couldn't stop. "They can hear everything," Maria almost whimpered.

A blush flooded her face and neck. The poor girl was struggling with excitement and shame that overwhelmed her. She was calm about the shouting in his apartment, but here, on the small airplane, panic was winning on all fronts.

"I pay them a lot of money to keep quiet," Sam didn't even think about stopping.

His lips were already kissing the bare parts of her breasts, uncovered by her bra. His hands were squeezing her slim waist, leaving red trails behind them, traveling higher and higher. Maria was about to make another argument, but instead of words, a muffled moan escaped her throat as Sam nipped a pink nipple through the thin fabric of the lace bodice with his teeth.

"Master...I mean Sam! Cabin crew can... hear it in there," Maria said in a husky voice, her thoughts already turning to melted butter.

The man was already having fun with her firm peaks, pulling the lacy cloth down under her breasts. Licking the little peas. Biting the skin around them. Kissed the small hollow, moving lower and lower.

Maria was no longer trying to get through to Sam. The girl only whimpered quietly into her fist, trying not to give away their secret. A small puzzle was forming in her mind. Maria had calculated everything ahead of time. Knew that Sam was about to flip her over onto her stomach and take her from behind. He always did. All she had to do was obediently spread her legs and arch her back well. And then maybe he would even let her cum.

But things didn't go according to plan again. As soon as his hot tongue touched her navel, Maria felt something wrong.

"Stand up," Sam ordered hoarsely, pulling down her trousers and shoes. He had already shed his T-shirt and pants. Sam's distracted, languid gaze was frightening. It got under her skin and spread sweetness into every cell. Caressing her without touching. Maria silently watched his actions. Waiting for the order to roll over.

But Sam remained silent. He leaned down to her goosebump-covered flat belly and began teasing the tender skin again with equally tender kisses. Strong hands held Maria's perpetually fidgeting hips. Her tension traveled in waves to Sam. Covered him head to toe with self-loathing. Caused the opposite urge to show a different side of himself. To give her something he'd never done before.

The rough tongue began its slow journey downward. It passed over the neat navel and traveled along the expensive lace of her panties. Two fingers slowly traced along the wet strip. Pulling the fabric aside, Sam abruptly nestled his lips against the wet clit. Started exploring Maria with his tongue. Biting the sensitive clitoris, penetrating her with his tongue, traversing the entire crotch, causing wild convulsions and loud moans from Maria.

"Don't hold back."

Another order echoed in Maria's lust-fogged head. She didn't immediately understand the meaning, but when Sam's tongue replaced his huge cock, Maria clearly deciphered his words. Throwing off her clothing on her own, she crumpled the white sheets, hoping somehow not to fly off the bed.

Sam was pounding into her like his life depended on it. Fully out and into the tight cunt with renewed vigor. He threw his head back and surrendered himself to fate and his own feelings. Fused with her. Healed by her moans and cries. He lost control more and more each time Maria screamed his name, begged him not to stop, and mumbled something else, but he couldn't hear her. While in the air, Sam was flying even higher.

During the entire flight, they didn't leave the cockpit. Maria lost count of how many times they had sex. The semen just flowed down her legs, leaving white stains on the sheets. At some point, the girl just passed out right during the process, collapsing exhaustedly on the hard mattress. But even that didn't stop Sam. He kissed the sleeping Maria for a long time. Couldn't get enough of her. Clung to her with his lips as if she were the source of his strength.

As he continued to tear at her bitten lips, Sam mentally cursed himself. If Maria was an angel, he was the devil who was breaking her wings. Bone by bone.

Chapter 39

New York met Sam and Maria with pouring rain and icy wind. Maria mentally thanked Sam for yesterday's note. The girl wanted to get to the hotel and shower quickly. She slept the rest of the flight, and when Sam woke her up, it turned out that there was no time left for a shower.

Sam had once again pleasantly surprised her. The hotel they were brought to was right in Downtown Manhattan. The receptionist, a nice girl, looked at Maria with interest. She wasn't the only one, though. Everyone who met on their way greeted Sam courteously and looked in her direction in surprise.

"Why is everyone looking at me like that?" Maria couldn't help herself when they were alone in the elevator.

"They're probably not used to seeing me with someone during the day," Sam answered the obvious.

While Maria slept, he had plenty of time to think things over. The problems of their families. The sins of their fathers, or rather, her father. His feelings about it and, most importantly, the reaction of his friends and others to their odd couple.

Yes, Sam was afraid to call himself and the naked girl lying next to him a couple. Just like Maria, he thought a lot about the opinions of others, and in particular, his mother. She would never accept Maria, just as Maria's parents would go everything, but would not allow their daughter to be with an enemy of the family.

Their situation was getting more complicated every day. His anger and reckless actions were getting out of control. And there was no way he could afford that. Not in New York. If he let his guard down, Blackwood and Max would eat him up. They would doubt his ability to run a company in which each of them had invested a large chunk.

In the world of dominance and submission, power was everything. Everyone had to prove their superiority. To do this, it was common to stay with a clear mind and a cold heart. Next to Maria, Sam was beginning to weaken. An inexplicable force was taking all his energy and channeling it in a completely different direction. Beyond the physical attraction, Sam was starting to think about her. About them.

Their suite turned out to be huge. It was the first time Sam had changed from his favorite suite to the presidential suite. Two separate en-suite bedrooms and a huge hall with access to an open balcony were a delight.

"Why two bedrooms?" she asked quietly.

"You want to sleep with me?" Sam arched a surprised eyebrow and grinned faintly. He liked the idea for some reason.

"No, no," the girl blushed, quickly averting her gaze.

Mentally scolding herself, Maria tried to gather her thoughts in a pile, but because of their spontaneous sex in the airplane, the girl's head was still in a pink fog.

Of course not, Sam tsked unhappily. The mood slid to zero in an instant. Sam once again hoped for a miracle that didn't happen. He'd screwed up again.

"It is a very nice place…"

"You talk too much," he said so coldly that Maria twitched involuntarily.

Fear and confusion reappeared in her eyes. When she opened her mouth, she quickly changed her mind and shut up, wrapping her arms around her shoulders. For some reason, she felt like crying. The lump in her throat wanted to burst out with a mass of questions and complaints. But Maria kept silent, realizing how stupid her idea was. She couldn't get through to Sam. He didn't need her love and warmth. Only her body and her submission.

"I'm sorry, Master," Maria lowered her head with guilt, and her voice sounded surprisingly convincing. In fact, the girl was squeezing the maximum out of her acting skills not to give away her suffering and pain.

"Go to your room. We've been invited to dinner tonight. Wear something nice and decent."

Maria only nodded her head at his every command. The thought that now she could be alone made her feel a little better.

"Wait," Sam called to her again when she was almost out the door of her room. "Put this on." The man handed her a square velvet jewelry box.

Disregarding all rules of decorum, Maria simply accepted the box and opened it immediately. A loud "ooh" came out of her faster than Maria realized what was in front of her. An unusually beautiful wide choker studded with Swarovski stones shimmered with all the colors of the rainbow, reflecting the delight in the girl's eyes.

"This is ..."

"..your collar, Maria," Sam finished her sentence for her.

Chapter 40

"Collar?" Maria asked, confused.

"You're not taking it off while we're in New York," Sam ignored her response. "Questions?"

"Not taking it off at all?" Maria was very skeptical of his words.

"You sleep in it, eat in it, shower in it, walk around in it. Twenty-four by seven. Understand, Maria?"

The lower Sam's voice became, the more she shook. His anger-darkened gaze screwed her to the floor. Involuntarily, she wanted to kneel down to relieve herself somehow. But Maria managed to stand on jello legs. With a short nod, she quickly disappeared behind the door of her room.

The rest of the day was spent doing their own things.

Maria laid out her things, glancing at herself in the mirror. The choker sat perfectly, visually lengthening and emphasizing her swan neck. The sparkle of the stones was distracting. The girl adjusted the new accessory every minute. She couldn't get used to it.

Sam talked loudly on the phone. Often swearing and even more often giving out instructions to the people on the other end of the wire. From behind the door, Maria could hear half the conversations. She didn't understand much, but for some reason, she listened to every word.

When Sam answered the next call, she noticed his voice and mood changed. He quickly left the living room, continuing the conversation in his bedroom.

At exactly six-forty-five, Maria was waiting for her Master in the living room. A narrow strapless dress in Bordeaux color covered the girl's body perfectly. Black high-heeled shoes and a small handbag in same color complemented the image. Maria wore only diamond stud earrings and the choker collar. Dark curls fell in a smooth wave on her shoulders and back. The restrained makeup made the already young Maria look younger.

"Ready?"

Sam froze the moment he noticed Maria. Not the slave girl, Maria, but a goddess. A girl of extraordinary beauty. Devouring her with his greedy gaze, Sam involuntarily exulted that it all belonged to him. *Temporarily.*

Putting a collar on her was the best idea he'd had all day. If Blackwood or Woolf saw her without the proper indication, they'd want to taste her. And Sam couldn't allow that.

She belonged to him. And only to him.

"Are you all right? Master?" Maria looked anxiously around herself.

Misinterpreting his behavior, the girl worried that he didn't like the outfit.

"Too gaudy? Is the heel high? Maybe I should have pinned up my hair?" Panic began to take over her mind. Nervously biting her lips, Maria waited for her Master's approval.

"Yes. Let's go. I don't like to be late."

Taking Maria's hand, Sam quickly headed for the exit. Maria had to quicken her steps to keep up with him.

The restaurant was located on the hotel's territory. Light music and dimmed lights blended in seamlessly with the general interior. There were not many people there. Maria immediately determined the level of the guests by their complete indifference to their personalities. Only self-sufficient people behave like this. They are interested in their own lives, not in other people's.

Still following Sam, Maria tried not to glance around, looking every now and then at the massive back of his black shirt.

As always, Sam's perfect look was mesmerizing. The pants sat perfectly on his narrow hips. And the two undone top buttons on his shirt stirred her imagination.

Maria was already beginning to imagine running her fingers under the thin fabric and beginning to explore the perfect abs. At least, that's what she hoped. Today's sex marathon was exhausting, but after a little rest, Maria wanted more.

"Sam!"

A loud male greeting snapped the girl out of her own thoughts. Raising her head, Maria froze like a victim in front of a predator.

Or rather, two.

Two pairs of eyes carnivorously devoured her from the top of her head to the toes of her shoes.

"Maria, these are my friends. David Blackwood and Max Woolf. They're dominants, like me."

Maria looked at Sam and then at the men. The girl was completely lost. The powerful energy of Sam's friends was pressing on the fragile Maria. She felt goosebumps on her exposed skin, and her throat felt dry as if she hadn't had a drink in days.

"You can talk," Sam smiled contentedly.

He noticed the glint in his companions' eyes. Max was watching his slave girl especially avidly. Sam knew Woolf's preferences well. A love of brat girls who eventually became complete submissive masochists.

Too late, friend, I've already cracked that nut, Sam grinned cheekily, glaring at his friend. Tish hummed back at him. After years of friendship, they could communicate without words.

"Good evening," Maria replied in a near whisper, not looking up. She wanted to avoid their gazes as much as possible. It was like she was naked again. But now she was seen not only by Sam but by these two dominants.

"Did Maria have a last name?" Tilting his head to the side, Blackwood waited for her answer. The man grinned playfully with the corners of his lips.

"Maria O'Dell," Maria answered a little more confidently, giving him a restrained smile.

"O'Dell?" Blackwood's face changed.

"Shall we sit down?" Sam demanded confidently.

He was taken aback by Blackwood's behavior. As soon as their gazes met, though, it was hard to breathe in the room. There was no shortage of huge clouds over their heads. Lightning flashed in the eyes of both of them.

"Are you completely sick?" The man snarled angrily at Sam.

"I've got it under control!" Squinting his eyes, Sam mentally growled.

The waiter appeared just in time at the table of the strange party of four and began to represent the dish of the day.

As soon as everyone had ordered, the atmosphere at the table began to change. The men began to discuss work issues from the get-go. Interested in each other's lives and joking.

Maria was no longer paid attention to, which the girl was delighted. She quietly looked at her new acquaintances.

Max, or, as Sam called him, Woolf, caused very contradictory emotions. He looked chic, dark-haired, and brown-eyed; he was attractive. But as soon as Maria met his gaze, she wanted to get out of her seat and run without looking back. Something very unkind flickered in those constantly dark, lustful eyes. He scanned the room, looking for a new victim.

Dressed in a black shirt and jeans, Max himself attracted the gazes of young and silly girls.

The choker around O'Dell's neck no longer seemed so annoying. She was well aware of the rules. A collar on a slave signified belonging to the dominant. No one was allowed to even lay a finger on her unless Sam himself authorized it.

That was comforting.

Unlike Max, David Blackwood looked at least seven or ten years older. Light gray hair was already showing on his neatly cut temples. Sharp cheekbones and a straight nose, a taut body. He looked like an ordinary rich man in the prime of life. But there was a certain mystery about him. And for some reason, Maria did not want to solve it. In the blue, like the ocean, eyes flashed tiredness and strength. Maria was repulsed by his aura. It made her body tingle.

"May I use a powder room? ?" Staring with puppy eyes at her Master, Maria hoped for his approval.

A brief nod and the lack of eye contact hurt the girl. She hoped for at least a brief yes.

In a hurry, she apologized to everyone present and left the restaurant hall. Maria was alone in the restroom. After standing for a good couple of minutes in the huge mirror, she forced herself to return.

It was hard to breathe around them. Her hands itched to wrap around her naked shoulders and pull her knees up to her chest to assume some sort of defensive posture.

"Maria!"

A cold wave washed over the frightened girl.

David Blackwood.

Leaning against the wall, he watched the confused O'Dell with interest. Blue eyes smoothly studied every curve of her body. Shoving his hands into his pants pockets, Blackwood scanned every inch.

Not knowing what to say, Maria stood still. She looked at her interlocutor, hoping that it will ends fast. Blackwood clearly outlined his point on Maria. He knew who she was. He knew why she was with Sam. It didn't take a detective to unravel the contempt and surprise in the man's eyes.

"I apologize for my behavior earlier," Blackwood tilted his head to the side again and smiled sweetly.

That smile made Maria's stomach twist into a tight knot. She didn't believe his apology.

"I understand," the girl smiled naively.

"Yes? And what do you understand, Maria O'Dell?" Blackwood asked coldly. His gaze burned, leaving an unpleasant itch where his eyes looked. Maria held back a muffled groan at her own stupidity.

Why did she even open her mouth!?

"You don't like me. You know who I am. Who my parents are. And, apparently, why I'm here. With Sam," Maria said in one breath. She didn't want to play cat and mouse with such an opponent. She would fail anyway. Maria could only give him a sweet smile and play stupid.

"You think you know everything," Blackwood grinned.

Loudly exhaled, Blackwood tiredly rubbed his face. Maria saw the fatigue. For just a second, she even felt sorry for him.

"Maria," Blackwood began more calmly, "Your and Sam's business... Um, only yours. But what happens then? Have you thought? Can you walk away and live as if none of this ever happened? Like none of this ever happened in your life? Can you forget Sam? Will you get revenge? What will you do?"

With each new question, Maria was getting paler. At the mention of Sam, her chin treacherously trembled. Her hands clenched into fists, and a glassy glint appeared in her eyes.

Noticing this shift in her mood, Blackwood fell silent. He looked at her demeanor and tsked unhappily.

"Too late. Fuck." Lowering his gaze to the floor, Blackwood kept shaking his head negatively. Maria didn't understand him. "Think about what I asked you, Maria. Think hard."

"Can I ask you one question?" Maria asked quietly looking at upset Blackwood.

"You may," the dominant agreed calmly.

"Why is Sam like this? Why does he hate me? My family? Why does he need all of this?"

"It's more than one question," Blackwood looked at her paternally. Maria only lowered her head feeling guilty.

"Do you know what your father did?"

"No," Maria exhaled anxiously. Wide-open eyelids, she waited with bated breath for an answer. What could her father have done? The sweetest man in the world!

"He killed Williams Sr. Sam's father."

Chapter 41

"Took everything from him. Disgraced the William name. Broke it. Stomped him into the ground. A man's already weak heart couldn't take it. He died because of your father's greed. Sam vowed revenge. And as you can see, he succeeded."

After a brief pause, Blackwood continued. He was amused by her reaction. The girl could barely hold back her tears. "Why would he do all this? Show me one person who doesn't want to be rich. Especially when you have such an expensive hobby."

"Expensive hobby?" Maria didn't understand at once. From Blackwood's eloquent look at her choker, the girl instantly blushed. BDSM. He was talking about Sam's kinks. "Club memberships. Toys. Subs. Private rooms. Sam has a session room, doesn't he?" Blackwood grinned predatorily, causing Maria's stomach to cramp again.

"Y…yes."

"This world isn't as cheap as you think," he continued on the subject of dominance and submission. "Have you noticed how people look at you? How do they react? Waiting for you to stumble.

Waiting for you to make a mistake so they can destroy you and take your place. That's what your dad did to…"

"No! My dad is not like that!" Maria shouted fiercely. "He wouldn't hurt a fly. That's not true! You're lying!"

"Yes?" still calmly interrogated Blackwood. His calmness irritated and angered Maria even more. "Ask Sam yourself. See what he says. Actually, no," Blackwood grinned craftily, "Ask your daddy."

"I do not believe you," Maria confidently stood her ground.

"It's your right, girl,"

"I'm not your girl!" Maria gritted her teeth in anger. She wanted to slap him. Only Sam's anger stopped her.

"We all make mistakes," Maria summarized, mumbling and gazing away.

"I agree," Blackwood grinned.

The ringing of a cell phone saved the heated situation. Glancing at the screen, Blackwood exhaled loudly, "Again?"

"Go, Maria, don't keep your Master waiting," it sounded more like an order from Sam's friend, but Maria didn't dare to disobey.

Without waiting for her, Blackwood answered the call.

"Yes. Again?" his voice trembled. "No, do not let her go. Maybe a night behind bars will help her turn on her little brain. No! If I find out anyone's laid a finger on her, I'll kill them all! Including you, Captain."

Maria glanced over her shoulder with interest. She was surprised that even people like Blackwood had their own "mistake."

Chapter 42

"Have you texted her yet?" Max suddenly asked, seeing the girl approaching the table.

Maria returned to her seat as quietly as she had left it. Silently, she sat down on her chair and folded her hands in her lap. She lowered her head and looked at the white tablecloth without interest. Looking for the slightest flaw.

"Not yet. I'll write tomorrow. Blackwood drilled a hole in my head," Sam said grudgingly.

"Nina will be pleased," Max grinned wickedly. "Does she know about her?"

Nodding lewdly toward the surprised Maria, the man unashamedly scanned her face. He smiled when he saw the grimace of pain on her face.

"Well, Blackwood turned out to be right." Shaking his head, Woolf shifted his gaze to a disgruntled Sam.

"Oh," Max clapped his hands together playfully, "And you didn't tell her about your sex friend Nina, did you?"

Swallowing loudly, Maria involuntarily adjusted her collar. All sorts of thoughts popped into her head. But the ugliest of them hurt the most. He hadn't called her "girl" that night when they had sex first time. Sam had been thinking of someone else altogether, holding Maria in his arms. Cradling her body against his, but his thoughts were far away, near Nina.

"Woolf!" Sam growled louder than he should. It was as if he'd been embarrassed in front of a crowd of strangers. But it was Maria who took their place. Sam hadn't planned to tell her about Nina at all. He wanted to talk quietly to his longtime friend and cut all ties except those of friendship. But Max, as usual, ruined everything.

"I was gone for five minutes, and you're already fighting," Blackwood shook his head paternally, sitting down in his seat.

"Sam didn't tell Miss O'Dell about Nina," Max scoffed openly.

"Fucking bastard," Sam jerked toward him but was stopped in time by Blackwood's heavy hand. Patting the enraged dominant on the shoulder, Blackwood glared at him and asked him to sit back down. People in the restaurant began to look at their strange table.

"Maria," Blackwood said quietly to the girl, who was trembling with shock. She could barely hold back her tears, biting her painted lips. "I think you should go back to your room."

Glancing obliquely at her Master, Maria hoped for approval. Another minute with these men, and she'd have to call an ambulance. The savage pain of disappointment crept under her skin, making her want to cry even harder. The woman's resentment clouded her mind, urging her to throw a tantrum and work things out right at the table.

You're a nobody. A doll. Precipitating all her frisky thoughts, Maria remembered the bitter truth.

"Go," Sam ordered, still glaring at Max with an angry glare.

Without saying goodbye, Maria took a quick step toward the exit. She passed the crowded lobby, loudly tapping her heels on the expensive marble. In the elevator, Maria rode by herself. As soon as the doors opened on the desired floor, the girl, covering her mouth with the palm of her hand, rushed to her room.

Swallowing tears of bitterness and resentment, Maria fell on the bed and, neglecting the white sheets, cried loudly. Her chest ached as if someone had poked it with a red-hot poker and left it to smolder. Her heart was rumbling, or rather, what was left of it.

She didn't want to get out of bed. But Maria knew she would anger Sam even more if he saw her like this. She quickly took off her clothes and went to rinse off her makeup in black lace lingerie, taking her phone with her as a habit.

Having finished with water procedures, Maria rested her elbows on the marble countertop. The cold surface cooled her down a little and brought her to her senses. Trying not to think about the unknown and so popular Nina, Maria remembered Blackwood's poisonous words.

Dad was still awake. The time difference played into the girl's hands.

"Hello, my love," the voice of her dearest parent enveloped the tense Maria in a warm blanket. She immediately smiled.

"Hi, Dad. How are you?" said the girl quietly.

"Good, dear. How are you? Where are you now with your wonderful exhibition?"

"In New York," Maria told the truth for the first time in a long time.

"Wow, so far away. Do you even have money?" O'Dell was immediately worried.

"Yes, I do. Dad, can I ask you something?" Nervously biting her lip, Maria looked at her reflection in the mirror. "It's about Sam Williams."

"How do you know this name?" her father's voice changed in an instant. The soft tone was gone. The man on the other end of the wire visibly tensed. Maria felt it too.

"Dad, a lot of people talked about him. And I know how to use the Internet," Maria was a little cowardly. She was afraid to say too much, but she didn't stop. Stubbornly decided to find out the truth. She didn't believe Blackwood's words. Her father was not a murderer.

"He took my company," the man grinned bitterly.

"I heard something else." Withholding the main thing, Maria hoped to get the truth out.

"Maria, I don't know what you're talking about! That arrogant and self-loving asshole took away everything Paul and I had built for so long. Because of him, your mom is in the hospital. I'm under house arrest. And you," his voice trembled, "you've taken a job that's a bit dubious."

"This job is not dubious," the girl tried to calm her father.

"I've made inquiries, Maria," the father raised his voice, "there is no such artist, and there is no exhibition. What did you get into? Did you go to the escort?"

"Calm down, Dad!" she said besiegingly. Her eyes widened from her father's awareness and his words. Shame was a shockwave. Unable to bear the deception any longer, she asked directly, "Did you do the same thing to Sam what he did to us?" Maria said quietly.

"What makes you think so?" he asked in a cold tone.

Maria involuntarily twitched as if from a slap. Her father's voice did not resemble a nice man at all. She was spoken to like this by anyone, but not her parent. She couldn't believe it.

"I heard it."

"Stay out of it, Maria," her father didn't ask, warning all in his tone. The phone in her hands began to shake.

With a trembling voice, Maria dared to ask the main question:

"Is it true that you killed his father?"

"I said stay out of this, Maria!" he shouted fiercely.

Pressing the disconnect button and throwing the phone into the washbasin, Maria settled down on the cold floor. Tears burst out in a new wave. The girl was shaking and feverish. Wrapping her arms around her trembling shoulders, she tried with all her might to at least breathe. Everything else seemed impossible.

Her thoughts were waxing hot. Her body wouldn't listen. It refused to move. Maria realized that she was losing touch with reality. The light in the bathroom began to fade. Everything around her began to swim. The last thing the girl remembered was her father's terrifying scream. The scream of a man trying to forget what he had done.

Chapter 43

"Mr. Williams, I've already done everything I can. It's simple overwork or stress... It's not necessary."

Maria's head buzzed as if she'd been pounded with a metal scoop. The heaviness in her body was a reminder that she was still alive. Maria reluctantly lifted her dense eyelids. The dim nightlight stabbed her eyes. An attempt to cover her face with her hand immediately failed. Her limbs were filled with imaginary lead, refusing to work together. Her throat felt unpleasantly scratchy. The desire to drink a gallon, or better, two gallons, of water did not leave Maria's still hazy thoughts.

On the third attempt, Maria was able to turn over on her side and reach for the water bottle with a trembling hand. Alas, it immediately flew to the floor. Her fingers could not hold anything heavier than a feather.

Quick footsteps came from behind the ajar door. A disheveled, wild-eyed Sam was coming toward her. His rumpled appearance confused Maria. For a second, she thought she saw fear and relief slip into his eyes.

"Water," she wheezed softly. She was afraid of her own voice.

Sam silently picked up the bottle, unscrewed the cap, and gently placed it on Maria's dry lips. Holding her head back with his hand, he watched her movements, her breathing. He tried to catch the slightest sign of pain or nausea.

Having finished the whole bottle, Maria sighed contentedly. The cold liquid, like a life-giving balm, spread over her body. Even the dizziness stopped.

"What happened?"

The weakness in Maria's voice echoed painfully in Sam's chest. Sam sat down on the edge of the bed and gently stroked her thigh, hidden by the blanket and nightie. Frowning her eyebrows, Maria only now realized she was wearing cotton pajamas instead of the lingerie she'd been standing in the bathroom. Questions kept popping into her head. Where did this thing come from? She hadn't brought her comfy pajamas with her, only lewd negligees and silk nighties.

"The doctor told you not to get up. If you need to pee, call me. I've alerted reception to your condition. If you get sick when I'm not in the room."

Sam was monotonous, with a terribly anxious expression on his face, telling Maria the emergency plan.

His speech made her head start to buzz again. For the first time ever, Maria listened to him, hiding how annoyed she was. Only wanting to shout that she was not a little girl and could figure out how to behave in such a situation. But his voice kept buzzing like an annoying fly.

"I got it."

Maria interrupted Sam somewhere in the middle of his boring speech. Rubbing her temple tiredly, she added:

"How many hours did I sleep? How did I end up in bed? Did Blackwood and Max leave already? I must have ruined your evening. I'm sorry," her voice grew quieter with each new word. Embarrassment crusted her already sore head with ice, hurting her whole body.

"Blackwood and Woolf are already gone," Sam grinned sadly. Maria saw a drop of sarcasm in his voice and eyes. What funny thing had she said? The girl once again suppressed her inner protest and the desire to become hysterical.

"What is funny?" Maria couldn't help herself.

"Baby girl," Sam smiled, rubbing his neck. "You haven't regained consciousness for twenty-four hours. I already wanted to take you to the hospital for an examination. We'll definitely go there, but not tonight."

By his soft "Baby girl" rather than the "Maria" she hated, Sam sounded serious. She tried not to look at him, stubbornly studying the nightlight on the bedside table. The shame went nowhere. Guilt crept up to him slowly and settled comfortably.

Maria remembered the phone conversation with her father well. His wild bellowing and avoidance of answering upset her even more. Somehow, Maria didn't blame Sam for all the deadly sins now. She even thought that what she was doing was a drop in the bucket compared to what he had to endure because of what her father had done.

Citing drowsiness, Maria asked Sam for some alone time. Sam reluctantly left her room but left the door open.

"Don't close it," Sam threatened in his trademark domineering voice.

"I'm not supposed to get up," Maria said with a smile on her lips.

"That's right. Good girl," Sam smiled with the corners of his lips, ignoring her tone.

Left alone, Maria pulled the blanket up higher, hoping to hide from all the problems that, for such a short time, had fallen on her head. It had helped as a child, but not now. Maria went back to her conversation with her father again. She remembered every phrase, frowned at the headache, but did not stop thinking.

What would she do in this situation? Follow in Sam's footsteps? Forgive?

Sighing heavily, Maria couldn't hold back the tears. It was too hard for her to realize that her father wasn't who he said he was. That Sam wasn't such a villain anymore. And that the pain of love can sometimes feel good.

"Shh, baby girl" Williams' warm hands gently rolled her over to her other side and pulled her to his stone chest. It felt familiar and secure. Maria whimpered some more and fell into a deep sleep.

Sam kept his arms around her. Protected Maria's fragile body as if she were the world's most precious crystal vase. He held her close to him. Nose against the dark top of her head. Listened to her breathing. He did everything to give her comfort that night.

When a terrified manager with huge eyes flew into the restaurant and a trembling voice tried to explain that Mr. William's companion had been found unconscious in the bathtub, time simply stopped. The last time Sam had experienced something like this was before his father's death. Fear, hopelessness, and a lot of nerves.

Seeing his condition, Blackwood and Woolf were quietly by his side, occasionally calming an angry Sam. The EMTs had convinced the men that hospitalization wasn't necessary, and Sam didn't want to give them Maria. He wanted to be in control here, too, and see her every second. Not wondering how she'd be without him. With Blackwood's help, the doctor showed up on the first call and confirmed the medics' words.

The pale face and dry lips startled Sam every time he cast a brief glance at Maria. Wondering what exactly had happened. Measured his steps across the room. Rushing around like a wounded animal in a cage, and she still wouldn't wake up.

By morning, Sam had calmed down a little. His head and mind had cooled. Thoughts rationalized some of the points on the shelves. Sam began to analyze the whole situation. Assumed that the hysteria and unconsciousness might have been caused by socializing with his friends, but when Sam accidentally discovered Maria's cell phone lying in the sink, everything began to fall into place.

The cracked screen in the top corner confused the man at once. And when the phone displayed an incalculable number of missed calls from her father, Sam tensed. Hacking into the phone had never been a problem for Sam. Luckily for him, Maria's password wasn't difficult.

Hastily sending Jacob all the necessary data, Sam began reading the messages from the man he didn't want to hear in the first place.

"Maria, answer. Maria!"

"Maria, my love, stay out of this!"

"Maria, understand! Sam Williams is a dangerous man."

"My girl, please answer. I didn't mean to scare you. Maria. ANSWER!"

"Maria, please don't get involved with him! He's a dangerous man."

And more than ten other messages of a similar nature. Out of control, Sam deleted all the messages in two clicks. Rage spilled venom all over his body. He wanted to break O'Dell's jaw, or better yet, both his legs. For his father, for his twisted childhood and life, and for Maria.

The call from the security guard brought Sam back from his own little hell.

"Mr. Williams," Jacob's sleepy voice didn't confuse Sam in the slightest. "The recording of the conversation is in your mail."

"Thank you, Jacob. You could have just written a message," Sam said understandingly.

"Yeah, but there's more to it than that. Our guys dug up some very interesting information. I thought I'd call you personally about it."

"Okay, thanks, Jacob."

"Sir, there are two files," the security chief's voice trembled. Frowning, Sam hastily opened the mail.

"I don't understand," Sam said irritably out loud. "Is this information accurate?" Losing the last shreds of composure, Sam quickly got up and closed the door to the sleeping Maria's room.

"Yes, Mr. Williams. I was surprised myself. But IT checked several times. O'Dell was not involved in the machinations in his company. It was Paul who was playing dirty games. Also, Andrew O'Dell was not involved in the collapse of your father's company."

Chapter 44

"Check it again!" Losing control, Sam shouted.

Grabbing the bottle of whiskey, he emptied a third of it in one gulp. He didn't feel the bitterness of the alcohol. Only the pain in his chest and the incipient flames that were burning away the last shreds of common sense.

"The record," Sam remembered, taking a couple more sips.

"You did the same thing to Sam as he did to us?"

"What makes you think that?"

"I heard."

"Stay out of it, Maria."

"Is it true you killed his father?"

"I said stay out of it, Maria!"

Bowing his head and rubbing his neck, Sam listened to the short conversation many times, trying to catch the smallest details to hear something new. But O'Dell Sr.'s behavior surprised him more and more. He was trying to keep Maria safe. But from what? Yes, Sam understood her father's concern; he didn't know exactly who Maria was with right now. There was something in his voice that made Sam wonder. An innocent man was acting guilty. Trying to hide something that wasn't there. Or was there?

In the evening, the doctor stopped by again. After examining Maria and taking her blood pressure, he wrinkled his forehead and mumbled terms unknown to Sam.

"Don't think my question is rude, but is there any chance that your girlfriend is pregnant?" The older man inquired gently.

Sam was involuntarily startled. The doctor's question took him by surprise.

"That's impossible. We're using protection," Sam answered, a little confused.

"Good. It's a standard question," the doctor smiled briefly, seeing Sam's reaction.

"Why isn't she waking up?" With an irritated glance at the door where Maria was sleeping, he shifted his gaze to the calm doctor.

"Maria's body has been under extreme stress. This was how her body decided to deal with it."

"Is that really normal?" Sam raised his voice, pointing a finger in the direction of her bedroom. He was annoyed by the doctor's calmness. It had been almost twenty-four hours, and Maria still hadn't woken up.

"Mr. Williams, I've already done everything I can. It's simple fatigue... It's not necessary."

After escorting his guest out, Sam heard a noise in the bedroom. "Awake!" Sam exulted.

Glancing at the pale girl, his heart shrank unpleasantly to the size of a speck of dust. Again, there arose that strange warmth with which he wanted to envelop Maria. To hold her, to kiss her, to protect her, and to hide her from the whole world and, first of all, from her father. Old man O'Dell's behavior did not leave Sam's mind.

Maria reluctantly ate whatever her Master brought her. She drank her medication by the hour, slept a lot, and obediently lay in bed. On the third day of bed rest, the girl began to whimper and asked Sam to go out to the balcony at least. He reluctantly agreed. He followed her around. Even showered with her, which pleased and infuriated both of them.

The doctor strictly forbade any intimacy until Maria's condition improved. Sessions or plain vanilla sex was out of the question.

Sam often caught Maria's leering eyes. Noticed her licking her lips like a hungry cat. He himself suffered from a nagging hard-on. He could have gone to the club, but something stopped him. Thoughts of submissive subs and hard sessions no longer turned him on like they used to. Sam needed her; the stroppy, perpetually sassy yet malleable Maria. Sam wanted her to the point of trembling in his fingers. Not just her body but her soul. He dreamed of possessing her whole and entirely.

Jacob wasn't happy with the good news. Nothing but the aforementioned could be found on O'Dell. Security dug with their noses but found no new details. About Paul, companion, the security service had collected a rather large and provocative file. It was he who had been organizing scams behind the back of his friend and partner for a long time.

Sam was going to talk to Maria several times, but each time, he kept a cowardly silence.

She's going to leave, he sadly realized the reality and bitterness of the whole situation.

Blackwood had lectured him long and hard about the dangers of having relationships and falling in love with the daughters of enemies. When he heard the word "fall in love," Sam wanted to object, but his friend's gaze stopped him. Made him think. Scared him. He didn't know how to love, and Maria was not the one who would be with him to the end. That's why these relationships and "*love*" were pre-populated.

Max, the asshole he was, only grinned crookedly and laughed like a teenager looking at the confused Sam.

That's how the first week in New York went. Sam never got to meet Nina, though he realized he had to talk to his friend. He wanted to do everything quietly, but Maria had gone rogue again and disrupted all the dominant's plans.

Having sorted out his work, Sam hurried back to the hotel. One of the meetings had been rescheduled, freeing up the rest of the day. Sam had bought a box of delicious eclairs, already imagining how satisfied Maria would lick the sweet cream off her slender fingers or his.

That was something the doctor had not forbidden.

The suite greeted him with silence. After hastily checking all the rooms, Sam began frantically calling the front desk. He was informed that his girlfriend had left no messages. After saying everything he thought about their service, Sam dialed Blackwood's phone. He always knew how to find a needle in a haystack. More than once, he had looked for his.

No sooner had he pressed the call button than the room door opened. Dressed in a black tracksuit, Maria froze in front of him. In her trembling hand, she held a box with a new cell phone.

"Where the fuck have you been?" Without waiting for an explanation, Sam shouted at Maria, who had gone pale with fear.

"I went to…"

"What did I tell you? M?" San said loud and angry.

He was on the edge of punishing Maria right there, right then. Ignoring doctor's advice and his responsibilities.

"Sorry" was the quiet reply. The only word Maria could think of. She was not expecting Sam to be back.

She shuddered when Sam came closer. His gaze was vicious, almost dark from anger. Maria was not sure what to expect, she was not ready to face him. His rage.

"What the fuck is wrong with you? I told you to stay in bed! Why are you so stupid?"

"I am not stupid!" now it was her turn to show Sam her dark side. Maria wanted Sam to hear her. To listen, but he just accused her without the right to explain. "The only stupid here is you!"

Sam grabbed Maria's chin tightly, forcing her to look straight into his eyes. She didn't understand what kind of fire she was playing with. She didn't realize that she was dragging herself down.

"Watch your fucking mouth" Sam growled through his teeth, squeezing his fingers even harder on her chin. "Or I will…" He swallowed hard, realizing that he couldn't.

He wouldn't be able to hurt her.

"Go to your room," Sam said quietly and cleared his throat.

"Sam," Maria tried to speak, but her Master repeated himself more aggressively.

"Go to your fucking room! Now!" He pointed at the door to her suite.

Chapter 45

The earring stubbornly refused to buckle. Losing the last shred of patience, Maria tossed the jewelry back on the dressing table. The collar, studded with stones, was scrunching her skin. The girl looking at Maria in the mirror radiated neither joy nor any other positive emotion.

The ringing of the landline phone tore the girl away from her inner torment.

"Mr. Williams is already in the restaurant with his guest," the sweet voice of the receptionist caused gagging.

He's already downstairs with her.

Maria set about putting on the naughty jewelry again. This time, she succeeded. She hastily freshened her lipstick, took a close look at herself in the large mirror, and walked confidently toward the restaurant.

I'm not losing to that bitch! Maria repeated fiercely to herself.

Pacing through the hall, Maria was catching glances at herself. It was not in vain that she chose the most beautiful dress for this evening. She had to show and prove that she was better than this Nina chick.

The table where the couple had been sitting was in the very center of the hotel's restaurant. Turning his head toward the entrance, Sam saw Maria. He smirked, as he was laughing at her in his mind.

Their eyes met. An unpleasant, burning sensation of jealousy prickled in her chest. She'd never seen Sam so relaxed and calm.

The closer she got, the more clearly she saw Nina. She was just an average blonde. There was nothing special about her, in Maria's opinion. She was petite, with big boobs, and was curiously looking around for Sam's new fling.

Maria quietly said hello to the stranger and, with her eyes downcast, waited to see how long this exorcism would last. Maria had no desire to listen to their conversation at all.

But when the girl heard the cherished "I must break our relationship, Nina," she almost squeaked with joy. He would no longer see her! She wanted to cheer and smile like a fool, but Maria held herself in check.

After their recent fight, she was afraid to show any emotion at all.

"I can't say I'm happy about this news, but I expected this. Although I'm glad you found a worthy replacement for me."

Nina spoke calmly. Maria began to shiver with anger. She was not a "replacement"! Rage and hatred were winning again.

"She has nothing to do with this," Sam answered coldly, not looking at Maria. Not a muscle in his face quivered.

The pain again. Mentally cursing the day she'd decided to leave the room without asking, Maria swallowed her resentment.

Nina said something else, but the girl couldn't hear her. Sam's words were ringing in her head. *She has nothing to do with it,* Maria repeated in her head.

Through the shroud of her own thoughts, Maria heard herself being addressed. The annoying Nina was speaking again. There was no strength left to answer. Throwing in her direction quite an arrogant look, immediately received an angry comment.

"Maria!" Sam growled menacingly, causing the girl to jerk as if she'd been slapped.

"I'm sorry, Master," Maria asked faintly and squeezed her head into her shoulders.

"Dismissed. Go get ready," Sam nodded coldly at his slave.

Trying not to lose face, Maria got up and, without saying goodbye, left the restaurant. Her heart was pounding frantically, painfully crashing into her chest. It was getting harder to breathe with every step. She didn't want to go to the room. Or rather, she didn't want to leave it. Which was exactly what she was overdue to do.

After dinner, they had to go to the BDSM club, *The Kink*. Sam had gone completely off the rails, promising Maria punishment for all her shenanigans. And there were a lot of them. The doctor had given the go-ahead for a full life yesterday, but Sam had decided to wait a day. Not for Maria, but for himself. Intentionally kept her waiting.

When Maria decided to go out to the store to buy a new phone, she never expected Sam to return early. She quietly left the hotel and quickly made her way to the first hardware store she could find. Hastily bought the first phone, and just as quickly, went back to the hotel.

Sam was furious when he saw Maria with a phone in her hands. The girl was so scared she almost fainted again. And when he shouted at her, she completely forgot all the words. She couldn't formulate a single phrase. She stood there gaping open-mouthed like she was drowning.

Sam demanded an explanation, but when Maria was unable to explain, he snapped. Screamed so loud that people could hear him on the first floor. Almost threw her newly purchased cell phone out. Called her stupid. Maria did not like when someone called her names, and Sam was not an exception. She shouted with a claim that he was the stupid one. Maria didn't mean to say it. But the words just came out of her mouth unconsciously.

The look on his face she would never forget. Fire and excitement were replaced by blackness and indifference. Maria shuddered at the coldness that came from Sam.

He hadn't asked her to say it. Maria had ruined it all by herself again. Deceived. Obeyed. Made him worry.

Throwing off her shoes on the run, Maria went straight to the shower. In the morning, she received clear instructions on how and what to do after dinner. Half of the items shocked the girl. Maria's cheeks reddened more than just her cheeks as she reread the entire list several times.

A quick shower. Wash off the makeup. Take off all jewelry except the choker. No underwear. Horrifyingly short black dress, black stockings, and high heels. Hair tied back in a tight, high ponytail.

Maria moved around the room like a snail on cotton legs. Every movement was difficult. Everything fell out of her hands. She almost tore her stockings. She could hardly hold back her tears. The cold chill never left her for a second.

Everything inside shrank to the size of an atom. Strangest of all, in addition to fear, she was buzzing with anticipation and expectation of the unknown. Maria did not leave the hope that after the punishment, there would be encouragement. That's when she could talk to him. At least somehow shake Sam up. Make contact. She hoped like a fool.

For a moment, frozen, thinking about their relationship, or rather about the absence of it, Maria did not notice the huge figure in the doorway.

"Oh!" she shrieked, covering her mouth with her hand.

Sam slid his gaze lazily over Maria's tense body. He couldn't hold back a wry grin, knowing that there was nothing under the short dress and everything that was there belonged to him. And he would remind her of that again tonight. He wasn't even intimidated by the safe word. He knew: Maria won't say it. She wanted what Sam prepared for her. In her eyes, for days now, she'd only asked him to forgive her and, before that, to punish her.

He asked her to obey. He asked her to take care of herself. He was worried like a boy himself, seeing the state she was in. And she ignored all his requests and worries. That's what she'd pay for.

"Ready? Let's go."

Chapter 46

"I thought you weren't coming," Woolf grinned unkindly, licking his lips like a hungry predator at Maria's huddled form.

"I thought I'd stop by."

With his head tilted to the side, Sam slid his hand behind his slave's back.

Max's carnivorous stare sent Sam into a frenzy. It took less than a second for the man to want to break his friend's nose. And that didn't happen very often. It was as if Woolf had invaded his personal space, which had become very important to Sam.

Maria had become his personal space. He'd realized that a long time ago. No matter how much he chased those thoughts away from him, they came back every time he saw her caramel-colored eyes. It was like she was turning off all the evil that had been ingrained in him over the years.

And like a fool, he kept pushing her away. He tried to give her warmth, to protect her. But everything came out so twisted and sharp that both of them suffered. Sam understood perfectly well what Maria tolerated. She tolerated his attacks, his claims, his behavior, and his dominance.

But why? To please in the name of saving her father? Or did she really feel more than hatred and contempt for him? Sam was afraid to know the answer to that question.

Would she stay with him afterward? A bitter chuckle escaped Sam's aching chest. He knew the answer to that question. No one wants to be with a monster. Especially angels like Maria.

Maria. Poor girl, Sam mentally savored her name. Today would be different.

Sam greeted familiar faces briefly. He even exchanged a few words with some old friends. Maria paced quietly behind him. If he hadn't known she was there, he wouldn't have noticed.

Every glance in her direction was annoying and angry for Sam. He couldn't control his emotions. Again. He was powerless against dominants' gazes pointed to Maria. He wanted to hide her from them, from the whole world.

"Room. Now!" Sam snapped. The stiff voice frightened Maria.

"Yes, Master," girl replied fast.

With her head down, Maria walked on steady legs as if on a scaffold. That was partly the case. Punishment awaited her today.

Despite her inner relief, fear knotted her insides tightly. A lump of resentment lodged in her throat. She wanted to say so many things to him. But she was afraid. She kept looking for the right moment, which might never come.

Maria had made her peace with that, too.

His behavior was repulsive, but she was still drawn to him. She fluttered around the burning flames like a silly moth. She knew she would burn, but she couldn't fly away. She came closer and closer. She endured pain and resentment, all for the sake of feelings, without even knowing if they were mutual.

Her mother called such relationships a mess. No specifics. Here Maria could not understand what was between them. Was it a game or the beginning of something much bigger? What was she to him? The daughter of an enemy? A slave? A girl for whom he feels something more?

The bitter thoughts made her want to cry. Maria only quietly walked in the right direction, sniffing her nose.

To the girl's surprise, she liked *The Kink*.

Nothing superfluous. Everything was precise, not shabby, and with style. Good security. A small lounge and bar. A few well-soundproofed rooms and a hall for public sessions. There was also a small courtyard, but Sam didn't take her there.

After a quick tour, he snapped again. And she took offense again. It hadn't happened before. Maria could hate, despise, and wish all the worst but not take offense!

Maria's behavior only strengthened the thoughts about her feelings, which were becoming more and more difficult to hide.

Fully immersed in her thoughts, out of the corner of her eye, Maria noticed a familiar face. David Blackwood, frowning like a cloud, he was walking towards her along the dark corridor. According to the rules, the girl had no right to address him, but for some reason, it became very important for her to talk to him. To speak out. To prove her opinion, which, perhaps, he had nothing to do with but was important to Maria.

"Blackwood, good evening!" Maria called the man confidently.

"Good day, baby girl," still as thoughtfully and aloofly said the dominant.

"Is everything all right? You look… tired." Maria would rather not say what she really saw. Blackwood as drunk. The man was totally wasted.

"Is it really so obvious?" Blackwood rubbed his face tiredly. Maria only now noticed the abnormal pallor. It was as if he had aged ten years, and they hadn't seen each other for just over a week.

"I'm sorry. It's none of my business."

"Do you want to ask me something while your Master did see us?" Tilting his head to the side, he gave the confused Maria a restrained smile.

"Oh yes! You asked me what would happen afterward. Do you remember? At the restaurant," she said quietly.

"I remember."

"So." Resolutely looking straight into his eyes, Maria fell out in one breath: "I do not know. I don't know what's going to happen tomorrow. I don't even know what will happen in the room."

"And?" As if pushing her to the most important thing, Blackwood looked at this fragile but strong girl with interest. She reminded him of *her*. His personal trouble. The one he could not remove from his thoughts. His forbidden desire.

"I love Sam," Maria said confidently, raising her chin. Believing in her words.

"I know," Blackwood grinned contentedly.

"Then you should know that I won't give up on him. I will do everything I can to help and heal his grief. I don't know how yet, but I will not abandon him. Perhaps my decision will bring me pain and bitterness. Maybe we will live happily ever after. I don't know. But I don't want to fool myself anymore. I need him. I feel bad when he's not around. I've even gotten used to this stupid collar," Maria summarized, adjusting her choker.

The clod of innuendo dissolved as soon as she finished her speech. She spoke out. She confessed not only to Blackwood but also to herself.

"So," rubbing two-day stubble, Blackwood looked around, "you want to tame the dominant? Make him yours?"

"I'm not taming anyone. I want feelings. Relationship, not blind submission. And I think he feels something for me, too. And yes, Sam is sweet," Maria repeated stubbornly, "kind, caring, vulnerable, loving, responsible, and passionate. He's alive, even though sometimes he tries to prove otherwise, but I will accept him. On his terms."

"On his terms, yes? That's something new," Blackwood quietly noted.

"Yes, on his terms, but with my conditions," the stubborn Maria did not retreat.

"Go to your room, Maria." Giving the girl a warm look, Blackwood, without saying goodbye, went to the lounge.

"You're not going to say anything to me?" Maria was surprised, looking at his back.

"To you?" Blackwood grinned, turning to her, "No, not to you." A suspicious smile appeared on his face when he walked away.

Sam stood in the company of Harvey Salazar, the club owner, and a couple of other acquaintances. The men were sipping whiskey, discussing the latest news.

"If you let her go, you'll regret it," Blackwood whispered quietly in Sam's ear, appearing from nowhere.

Having patted the shoulder of the confused Sam, he silently, slightly staggering, went to the bar for the next portion of liquor.

Chapter 47

"Blackwood making fates again?" Sam grinned, holding back the storm that had come over him.

"More like ruining his own," Salazar exhaled heavily, looking at his old friend.

Sam only smiled demurely. He didn't answer the suspicious looks of those present. All the more because Wolf was nearby. Max could easily make a scene again, which Sam was trying to avoid.

A very similar conversation flashed before his eyes. The same words Helen had said to him. *Are they conspiring?* Sam thought angrily.

Maria had a way with everyone she met. It was a shame she hadn't gotten along with Nina, but Sam couldn't blame her. Female jealousy was a terrible thing.

"Your little girl is waiting," Woolf said with a sneer. "If you still want to chat, I'd be happy to check on her."

"Woolf, don't you dare to lay a finger on her," Sam stammered, burning him with a glare. His friend's words had struck a nerve again.

After bowing to Sam, Max turned on his heels and strode off in search of another victim.

"Woolf will get his way," Sam muttered angrily.

"You know the rest," Harvey grumbled, watching the slightly tipsy Max out of the corner of his eye.

Sam quickly said goodbye to his acquaintance. He wanted to ask Blackwood what he meant, but he didn't see him at the bar. The man seemed to have vanished.

Frowning like a cloud before a thunderstorm, Sam headed for the room.

His hands itched to touch Maria, to give her what she was afraid of and wanted at the same time.

He couldn't get Blackwood's words out of his head.

Why did he say that?

Had he talked to Maria?

What had she said to him?

What had he said to her?

The questions popped into his head, one after another.

Once at the right door, Sam held his breath. His excitement was growing by the second. He couldn't hold back anymore. He wanted to stomp his foot like a little kid who wasn't getting his favorite candy. And it was all because of Maria. She was doing the unknown to him. She'd gotten him hooked and made Sam addicted.

Standing at the closed door, he realized it. He wanted her, and it was not about revenge. He wanted her for who she was. And not just to possess her like a soulless toy. He wanted all of her. Body and soul. Her submissiveness and her contradictions, her temper, her innocence, and her passion. He wanted it all!

Sam hadn't figured out how to deal with her father yet. Maria must know the truth. It was the truth Sam feared like fire. The fear that Maria would leave was a sore, aching thorn sitting in his heart.

I must fix everything. I must make it right, he decided confidently.

And there, he would solve problems as they came.
But right now, it was just him and her.
Taking a deep breath, he opened the door.

Chapter 48

The dimmed light added a sense of intimacy and a relaxing atmosphere.

Stepping over the threshold, the first thing Sam saw was her. The whole world narrowed down to the size of this small room and the naked girl standing in the middle. Hands at the seams, eyes to the floor. Only a collar, stockings, and shoes showed on the beautiful body Sam already wanted to ruin.

Breathless, Sam almost purred with bliss. Maria did the right thing, taking her dress off. Realized that it had only served as a temporary screen, and now she was giving him a view of all that was most beautiful and sweet.

The heavy saliva made it hard to say a single word. Sam exhaled loudly at the sight of her sharp, erect nipples that he wanted to touch. So loudly that Maria shuddered involuntarily. Her velvet skin was feeling goosebumps, fingers clenched into fists, but she quickly returned to a relaxed state.

Sam had already picked up on her state of mind. Realizing how horny she was, he wanted to get down to business quickly.

"Eyes on me," Sam said huskily.

Her amber-colored eyes met his raging sea of blue. Both of them froze again for a few seconds. It was as if they hadn't seen each other for weeks. And there was only one thing in his and her gaze: desire.

"Take off my shirt," Sam stepped closer.

Maria's trembling fingers grasped the small buttons. Shuddered for no reason. Breathing heavily, she blushed and then turned pale. When the girl reached the last button, Sam stopped her. He took her cold palm with his hot hand, kissed the back of it, looking into her eyes.

"Calm down, baby girl," he said surprisingly gently. The poor thing nearly collapsed to the floor.

Baby girl, her subconscious howled. *Not* Maria. *Just baby girl.*

Sobbing loudly, she nodded nervously. She couldn't control the emotions that were overwhelming her. There was so much she wanted to say to him. She thought that now the formidable Master who had promised her punishment would appear before her. But no. Sam was acting surprisingly strange. Maria was confused. She didn't understand the change in his mood. All she could assume was Blackwood. He was the only one who could influence Sam.

"Thank you, Master," she nodded once more.

"Good girl. Let's go." Pulling Maria by the arm, Sam led her to the bed.

After throwing off everything but his pants, Sam walked slowly back to Maria, who was waiting by the huge bed.

"Do you remember why we're here?" Lifting her head by the chin, Sam asked.

"Yes, Master. I've done something wrong," she exhaled heavily.

"Very badly."

"Very badly, Master," Maria signed his words. Her body shivered with a new batch of shivers.

"Now, Maria, I will punish you. Then, I am going to fuck you hard, do you understand me?"

"Yes, Master," the girl replied, flinching at his calm tone.

Maria was startled by his attitude and calm gaze. No anger or resentment. A relaxed posture, a slight grin, soft movements. She wasn't used to seeing him like this, especially before punishment.

"On the bed. Face up. Put your hands in the handcuffs yourself," Sam ordered confidently, with a slight metallic tang. His gaze was throwing thunderbolts. The man's whole body tensed visibly.

Quickly following Sam's instructions, Maria obediently waited for the next steps. Her heart began to rumble louder and louder, reminding her of herself with her labored breathing. Sweat beaded on her forehead and in the hollow of her chest, betraying her.

Maria involuntarily closed her legs, for it was getting unpleasantly wet. She was turned on by the unknown. She wanted to know and feel Sam's plan. Even if she had to endure pain, it was the thought of pain that turned her on.

Sam quickly locked her thin wrists into the leather bails. Slowly, he slid his gaze over her naked body, stopping at the most prurient places.

"Why am I punishing you, Maria?" Sam asked in a businesslike manner, heading for the dresser with the devices.

"I disobeyed, Master!" Maria said quickly.

"And?"

"You were angry with my behavior, Master."

"And?" Sam glanced at her over his shoulder with a long, irritated look.

"Deceived, made you worry, inconvenienced you. I didn't watch after myself and disobeyed you," Maria began to repeat herself because of the heat of passion.

She mumbled the same thing. She clenched her fists, arching her back as if Sam were already touching her body. She shook her thighs, afraid to reveal her little wet secret.

"That's right, Maria."

Standing with his back to the girl, Sam was having fun. Quite contentedly, he went through the toys for her punishment and smiled like an immature boy on the threshold of his first sex. The back of his neck felt the vibrations coming from her body. Knew how much she wanted it.

"You're a horny slut, baby girl," Sam tilted his head back and savored the thought.

He was getting aroused himself. His cock was pressing against the tight fabric of his boxers and pants. For the first time in his life, Sam wanted to give a damn about the session, the punishment, or BDSM roles in general and just take Maria without all the drama. Sam wanted regular sex. Passionate, maybe rough, but just sex.

"Choose a number between one and ten, Maria," Sam demanded.

The girl was confused. Her head was already a mess. Thoughts were waxing warm in her skull. Her mouth could only produce the usual *yes* or *no*.

Everything else seemed prohibitively complicated. The Master's question finally stalled.

"Hurry up," Sam growled impatiently.

"Four!" Maria exhaled.

A murderous silence ensued. Maria didn't realize whether this number was to her advantage or whether she had just scored herself a direct ticket home through the safe word. The thought of leaving made her chest burn unpleasantly, and all her insides twisted into a tight knot of pain.

Well, what's in there? What did he come up with? When? Biting her lips until they were red, Maria couldn't stop thinking.

"Stop fidgeting."

Sam's voice cut unpleasantly into her ear. By the obvious smirk and the fire in his eyes, Maria realized she had lost.

Sam approached slowly, like a predator, pushing his victim's nerves to the limit. He deliberately tapped the metal nipple clamps and twirled the anal plug between his fingers.

The huge black feather and leather stack confused Maria the most. It was also worrying that there was no blindfold in the Master's hands. If all normal bottom girls feared blindfolding like fire, for Maria, this accessory served as a kind of protection.

"And the blindfold?" Maria asked quietly, hoping Sam had forgotten about it.

"Not today, baby girl. Not today."

Sam's sweet, velvety voice crept under the skin of an already tense Maria. She only sobbed loudly, biting down harder on her lower lip.

Dropping the entire inventory on the bed, Sam touched the unbuckled ankle. Gently ran her fingertips down to her knee and back. Repeated the same with the other leg. Gently removed Maria's shoes.

Sam asked quietly, almost purring: "Spread your legs, Maria, be a good girl today."

Chapter 49

"What?" Maria thought she didn't heard him right.

"Spread your fucking legs," Sam repeated calmly.

His whole look hinted at Maria's total submission. She would rather not contradict him, even though her shame kept blaring like a loud siren about the deluge that was already happening between her legs.

"Maria," Sam called playfully, stroking her knee.

Reluctantly, Maria squeezed her eyes white. Realized: now Sam would see her arousal. Her wet cunt.

Slowly, she drew her knees apart. Exhaled shamefully as the cold air scorched her damp skin. Tucking her toes in, the girl waited for a barb from her Master. Knew his love to phrase her.

At the sight of her wet cunt, Sam couldn't hold back an animalistic, rather loud growl. Again, he wanted to spit on all the rules and take Maria right now. Biting his lips, Sam began to roll the stockings off her slender legs.

The man did everything quickly and silently. Out of the corner of his eye, he saw Maria raise her head occasionally looking at him, nervously swallowed saliva and biting her red, wet lips. She opened her eyes wide, waiting for her fate, which Sam did his best to delay.

"Relax your leg," Sam ordered calmly, fixing Maria's ankle. He didn't touch the other.

Taking a step back from the bed, Sam scrutinized his girl. Businesslike, he checked the tension of her bracelets and ran his fingertip from her neck to her navel. Quite contentedly, he noted her hitched breathing.

"Are you afraid?" Sam asked suddenly, sitting down on the edge of the bed.

"N…no," Maria frowned, though she was more frightened by his behavior than by what he planned to do to her.

"And you?" Maria said nervously.

An unpleasant chill ran down her spine. Sam gave her that strange, puzzled look again. He got to his feet and picked up the nipple clamps.

Maria had never seen one of these before. With rubber drops on the ends, the clamps were connected by a thin chain. For some reason, the girl didn't want to feel them on her.

"You know, Maria," Sam gave her a serious look and began to stroke her erect nipple with one hand, "I've been thinking about how to punish you for a long time."

Sam's movements were smooth, a little painful, the kind that made Maria squirm involuntarily on the sheets. Listening to her Master became harder with each second of intense teasing. With a sharp movement, Sam started on the second nipple and continued his instructive and incomprehensible speech:

"Pain gives you pleasure, and punishment should be, if not painful, at least memorable. Do you understand me?"

"Y…yes," Maria said in a trembling voice. In fact, she didn't understand a word of it.

"Then you and I will play a game. You're going to lose anyway, but I've decided to give you a chance," Sam grinned faintly, not taking his eyes off her.

"Thank you, Master," Maria wheezed. Her body was starting to shake from Sam's aching caress.

"You're welcome, baby girl."

Continuing to gaze into her eyes, Sam leaned down to the firm nipple. Licked, ran the edge of his tongue along the areola. Did the same again with the second one. He gloated mentally as he listened to her quiet moans and shuddered with her.

"Ouch!" A few moans escaped from Maria's lips, along with a couple of meager tears.

A sharp pain pierced her whole body. She arched her back and tried to learn to breathe again and to understand what had happened. She looked down a little absent-mindedly and was horrified. There was a clamp on her right nipple.

"It hurts," Maria said as Sam deliberately pulled on the chain.

"Do you want to hear the terms of the game?" Samuel asked, tilting his head innocently to the side.

"Yes, Master, Please!" Maria shrieked, pulling on the metal chains that held her wristbands together.

"You chose the number four. So now, you have to tell me four reasons why I should forgive you," Sam pulled on the chain again.

Fumbling with her free leg and pulling the other leg up as far as she could, Maria nodded, unable to say anything.

"The usual 'I'm sorry' won't do," Sam warned her.

"Good…oh, Master," Maria stretched out, throwing her head back and writhing in a new wave of pain and arousal.

"Relax," Sam commanded.

Her head and body was still buzzing with aching pain. Maria tried her best to think of four worthy responses, but her brain refused to work.

Meanwhile, Sam wasn't making her life any easier. Leaning over her, he began kissing the free nipple again, pulling the clamp away. The contrast of pain and pleasure made Maria break out in violent moans and uncontrollable convulsions. The last scream was so loud that Sam cringed, still grinning.

"Did you come up with the first reason?"

"Yes!"

"Tell me," Sam asked calmly.

His free hand never stopped teasing her nipple. Sam looked at Maria's face with interest. Enjoyed every emotion she was feeling. Absorbed her pain and pleasure. Saw her total commitment, which was giving him enormous pleasure.

"I promise to take care of my health from now on and not to bother you, Master," Maria said in one breath and froze.

"Good for you, smart girl," Sam purred contentedly.

He took his palm away from the red nipple and touched her open lips. He ran his thumb along her cheekbone, tracing her chin and pulling back her lower lip. Sam swallowed loudly, imagining his next actions and Maria's reaction.

Leaning into her small ear, Sam murmured faintly:

"Breathe."

Maria didn't understand his words right away. But when the second nipple was pierced by a familiar pain, she realized the meaning. She mooed, biting her lips, and gulped for air.

"But I..." Maria was lost in her own words. She refused to understand what was happening. She honestly said the first reason!

"Baby girl, you probably weren't listening well," Samuel whispered, touching her temple with his nose.

"You're going to lose either way," the dominant repeated, pulling the chain tighter.

Chapter 50

Sweat trickled nasty down naked body. Her throat was dry as if the last time Maria had drunk a couple of days ago. Between her legs, there was an unrelenting whine of growing desire that was slowly driving her insane.

After playing with her breasts, Sam picked up the quill. The innocent thing looked menacing in his hands. They had never used feathers before, so Maria didn't know what to expect. Her whole body tensed in anticipation of the inevitable.

"Come up with a second reason?"

Sam ran the tip of the feather along the hollow of her breasts to her neat navel. Drawing a circle, he headed lower. Slowly, he teased the skin, bypassing the thigh, curving down to the buckled leg.

"Y…yes," Maria answered a little uncertainly.

"Are you sure?" Sam grinned, tickling her toes.

"Yes, Master!" Maria giggled nervously. The clamps reminded her of themselves with every wrong and sudden movement. The pain that mixed with pleasure spread throughout her body, gathering between her legs.

"Speak," he said with a calm voice and tickled her tiny foot.

"I... oh!" Maria snapped in another laugh. The tickle was becoming unbearable, preventing her from speaking and formulating thoughts.

"Maria," Sam said, waiting.

"I won't deceive you, Master!"

There was a lingering silence in the room. Maria waited for her verdict. She was afraid Sam wouldn't believe her. But she had really made a decision, first and foremost for herself, to tell him the truth and to confess her feelings. Maria didn't know how or where yet. Right now, she was more concerned with the huge black feather that kept touching her foot.

"Master," Maria squeaked softly, squirming with an unbearable urge to howl.

"Okay, I accept," Sam nodded dryly in her direction.

Pushing the quill aside, he stood up abruptly from the bed. Maria caught the change in his mood at once. She was afraid she'd said too much. Or else, she felt a sudden unpleasant pang in her chest that he didn't believe her.

Maria leaned back against the pillows and closed her eyes. She tried for a second to be somewhere far away in her mind. To calm down. Suppress her inner hysteria.

Staying in a kind of trance, Maria jerked sharply at the unexpected touch on her lips. But instead of a scream, a muffled moan escaped her, muted by the passionate kiss.

Samuel gently licked her mouth with his tongue, biting her lower lip. Didn't give her a second to respite. When he'd had enough, Sam enclosed her face in his huge palms. Locked it and peered intently into her glassy eyes.

"Don't say what you can't do," Sam said bitterly.

"But, I..." she wanted to argue, but Sam squeezed harder.

"I accept your answer, Maria," he interrupted her again, making it clear that he didn't want to talk about it anymore.

Maria didn't know how to respond. The nasty "Maria" was repulsive. But the girl wasn't about to back down. She pressed forward, hoping to explain herself, but Sam's heavy gaze pinned her to the bed. Deprived her of her voice. A hint to behave as a slave should.

"Thank you, Master," she looked away and thanked him grudgingly.

"Ready for the third?" Samuel was in a hurry.

"N…no, Master" she said honestly.

Looking back at the remaining devices, Sam picked up the anal plug. Twirling the metal toy in his hands, Williams moved lower. Pulled Maria's free leg aside. Slowly, he ran the plug along the inside of her thigh, not touching her completely wet labia. All his actions again took on a lazy, sedate character.

Maria's words took him by surprise. He had been expecting anything but this. It was too loud a statement for Maria to make. Even Sam couldn't say such a thing to her. Take the situation with her father. He had so far kept quiet about his lack of involvement not only in his own company's scams but in the Williams' family as well.

Pondering Maria's words, Sam didn't notice as he began to fuck her ass with the plug. From the abundance of Maria's juices, he didn't even need lube. Sam's carefully inserted and withdrew the metal object. With each movement, a loud moan escaped from Maria.

Setting the toy aside, Sam replaced it with three fingers. Those went in like butter. Massaging her from the inside out, Sam himself trembled, feeling overflowing desire.

A drop of sweat quickly ran down Sam's face, hinting at overexcitement. He was indeed on edge. Punishing Maria, yet suffering himself.

"Third reason, Maria," Sam growled.

"I promise to please and trust my Master," Maria moaned, unconsciously thrusting herself onto his fingers.

She wanted so badly to feel Sam inside her. So much that she didn't care where. Mouth, ass, vagina; anywhere to get him inside her. Like her life depended on it.

But Sam was in no hurry. He pushed the plug back into Maria and began to work on her wet folds.

"Ah! Please," Maria whimpered.

She already knew what she was going to say. She was afraid. Shaking like an aspen leaf, not knowing how Sam would react. She tried with all her might not to forget that vital phrase. She kept repeating it to myself.

"Ready for the fourth reason so soon?" Sam was surprised.

"Yes, Master!"

"You sure? You remember you're going to lose, don't you?" Sam smiled sadly.

His hand continued to hold Maria's free leg just above the knee, pulling it to the side due to the slight pain from the tension of the inner muscles. The other never stopped stroking the girl. Slowly and painfully. For Maria had already begun to howl quietly with the desire to cum.

"Yes! I know. But... but I want to say!" confidently answered Maria, looking straight into the eyes of her Master. Throwing him an invisible challenge. And he accepted it.

There was the sound of his fly being unbuttoned. An instant later, a rather violent shriek escaped from Maria. With one thrust, Sam entered her, letting out an equally loud growl.

Covering his eyes and throwing his head back, Sam tried to keep his body from shivering as the pleasure tore mercilessly at every cell. For a moment, he even forgot about Maria's punishment. Wanted to just thrust into her until the girl lost touch with reality.

"Tell me," Sam ordered, still growling, without stopping.

"I... I..." Maria couldn't. Biting her lip, she fought herself. Now, she would have it all or lose it all.

"Baby girl, say it," Williams reminded herself longingly.

Building up the pace, he was losing control. Again, he gave himself over to the feelings that Maria had awakened in him. Strangest of all, he was enjoying it. Sam enjoyed the lack of desire to dominate. He just wanted to keep going and give her pleasure.

"I want to..."

"What?" Sam interrupted her, nearing the finale and sensing how close she was to release.

"I want to..."

"Come on, baby girl."

It was hot and cozy inside her. Sam didn't want to stop, nor did he want to hear the last reason. What Maria had to say didn't matter to him. He wanted to stay with her.

Wanted to and was afraid to. He was in a state of limbo. Next to her, his life had become an eternal purgatory. It brought joy and sadness.

Feeling the first spasm of internal muscles, Sam began to move fiercely, continuing her orgasm and bringing himself to release.

"Sam...," Maria moaned, swallowing the words.

She wasn't going to stop. The orgasm came on suddenly and in full force. Muttering Sam's name, the girl arched up until her vertebrae crunched. Her eyes began to roll up under her eyelids. Gathering the last shreds of consciousness into a fist, the girl screamed: "I want to stay with you! I...I...love...you....."

The last thing Maria remembered was Sam's hot lips on her neck.

Darkness came after that.

Chapter 51

"You just went too harsh on her, Sam."

"Harvey, this isn't the first time! Fuck, we should have gone straight to the hospital."

"Sam, calm down..."

Reluctantly, Maria's eyelids fluttered open, and she tried to direct her unfocused gaze. It took a couple of seconds to realize where she was.

As soon as the angry notes of a familiar voice reached her, the girl remembered. She was at the club. The dark walls and chains hanging from the ceiling confirmed her guess.

"Sam," Maria squeaked faintly. Her throat was sore, her head was buzzing, and her body was aching, reminding her of the recent session.

"Maria, are you okay? Are you hurt? Are you nauseous? Shall I call a doctor?" Sam's frightened voice made the girl feel even better.

"Water," Maria smiled in response.

Sam's reaction was hilarious. The angry and overbearing dominant had been replaced by a caring man.

Her man.

Sam rummaged around the room, looking for the bottle that stood on the table in plain sight. Unscrewing the cap, he spilled half of it on the carpet, cursed softly, and returned to Maria lying on the bed.

"I see you're all right," the strange man in the gray suit said calmly.

"Yes. Thank you, Harvey," Sam thanked the stranger.

"I will leave you both now," stranger gave Maria a weird, but warm look. Saying quick 'goodbye' he left.

"Who's that?" Maria asked huskily as soon as they were alone.

"The owner of the club."

"What was he doing here?" The girl frowned.

"I wanted to call an ambulance," Sam admitted honestly. He couldn't stop staring at Maria's pale face. He tried to catch the slightest change, but she was really coming back to life.

"I'm fine," as if she read his thoughts.

"You need to eat. I'll order food," Sam thought aloud, quickly rising to his feet.

Making a couple of quick calls to the kitchen, Sam ordered steamed fish and vegetables. He also asked for a glass of orange juice and sweets.

He didn't order anything for himself, which seemed odd. Maria furtively watched her Master's abrupt movements. The dizziness and slight nausea passed, and she was able to sit up in bed. With a frown, Sam asked her to lie back down.

"I feel better this way," Maria said stubbornly.

"You need to rest," Sam insisted, not moving closer to her.

Maria felt the tension in the room with every fiber of her being. But she couldn't figure out why it was there or why Sam was staying away from her. Not touching her, looking wistful.

"Is something wrong?" Looking into the man's eyes, Maria asked.

"What do you mean?" seriously interrogated Sam.

"You're holding back. You have not forgiven me?" Maria asked anxiously.

There was an unpleasant, oppressive silence. Maria had other questions she wanted to ask, but she decided to start at a distance.

Sam's whole demeanor expressed detachment and reluctance to talk about the subject. He frowned his eyebrows, clenched his fists, and rubbed the back of his neck. Behaving irrationally and inappropriately for a dominant.

Running her hand through her tangled hair, Maria repeated Sam's gesture. Dropped her hand to her neck and froze. She wasn't wearing a collar. Slow panic crept under her skin.

"Yes," Sam replied sparingly.

"Yes, what?" Maria flinched.

"I forgave you," Sam confirmed his words.

His eyes were looking anywhere but at Maria, which was starting to irritate her even more.

"Then what's the matter?" Maria repeated hysterically.

"I think it's time for us to terminate the contract...."

"Why?" Maria said with just her lips.

The nausea and rumbling in her head returned, making it difficult to think straight. The unpleasant aching pain in her chest was growing with each passing second.

It became harder to breathe with every breath. Maria felt as if she had swallowed a bag of nails, which were digging into all her organs with blunt ends. Tearing apart the girl's body.

"Maria, you need to understand," Sam said, still not looking her in the eye.

"Was it because of what I said? Yes?" she snapped.

There was no strength left to hold in the avalanche of indignation and resentment. She wanted to spill all her worries and thoughts on Sam s as soon as possible. Maria, for a split second, decided that now was the right time to put their relationship on the shelves.

"I was telling the truth! And in case you didn't hear, I said I wanted to stay with you! And that I fucking love you, Sam! Yeah, don't look at me like that. At least I'm not ashamed of my feelings, unlike you!" Maria said angrily, all in one breath.

There was no trace left of the pale girl, who had just woken up.

The girl threw lightning bolts with her eyes and gritted her teeth. With her arms around her bare shoulders, she glared defiantly at Sam. Waiting for his response, for some kind of reaction. Anger, joy, confusion, but Sam only sighed heavily and turned away from her.

Walked to the other end of the room. Maximized the distance between them.

The longer he remained silent, the faster her fuse faded. Hope was dying. With a loud sob, Maria realized she was cold and shivering, almost feverish. Pulling her knees up to her chest and wrapping her arms around them, she turned to Sam again.

"Say something?" Maria almost moaned softly. Tears were streaming down her pale skin in thin paths.

"Are you telling the truth? You are not ashamed of me? Of being with me?" Sam repeated her words with a sneer. "How do you envision it?"

The cold voice hit harder than a slap. Wiping her tears with her hand, Maria looked carefully at her former Master.

"What do you mean?" Her voice became hoarse again.

"A week ago, you didn't want to go out with me, and now you declare your love? Making such a big deal about it? What's wrong with you? Do you even sometimes think with your brain?" Sam chiseled every word and crinkled at every phrase. He was killing himself over and over again, saying it all.

"Don't say that," Maria was embarrassed and hurt. Partly, she knew he was right. But it was different then. Now, she couldn't live without him.

"What's not to say? Have you thought about how we'd live if we decided to be together? What would I tell my mother? What will you tell your father? Have you? I'm not going to hide in back alleys and show up in public with fake prostitutes, and you? Are you ready to tell everyone who you spent almost two months with? Are you ready to tell your father that you fucked the man who practically destroyed him? Are you ready?" Sam shrieked.

It was Maria's turn to be traitorously silent. She honestly wasn't thinking on such a grand scale. She was floating on the turbulent current, sometimes without realizing it.

"Why don't you say anything?" Sam grinned bitterly.

The hot gaze had faded, leaving only gray ash instead of blue sky in his eyes. His slumped shoulders and heavy breathing betrayed his serious condition. He tried not to look at Maria. He was afraid.

For the first time in a long time, he felt so hurt. Hurt by his own words, by the whole situation.

Sam realized that they'd been playing an adult fairy tale. He'd blundered. He'd dragged himself and, worst of all, Maria into a life that was hard to give up.

Brought the poor girl into BDSM, neglecting her. And now he was just letting go, ripping her out of his heart, leaving her alone.

Remembering her reaction to the whipping, Sam gritted his teeth in an unpleasant grind, realizing that she could find another dominant. After all, he was the one who had given her the drug. He was the one who had told her who she really was.

"I heard you," Maria forced herself out. "Is it over?" she said in a low voice.

"Yes," Sam exhaled painfully, covering his face with his hands.

The girl was visibly shaking. Her gaze became blank and detached. It was as if she mirrored his condition. Faded as quickly as Sam had.

It even seemed to Maria that she was no longer alive. Nothing hurt, no aching wrists, no buzzing in her head. Nothing. Maria suddenly smiled hysterically.

She thought that was what zombies did. Soulless, dead creatures that could wander the earth for years.

So would she. She would leave Sam and live without a heart and soul, for her Master would have them forever.

When she could resist the urge to cry, Maria proudly got out of bed and slowly made her way to the bathroom. She planned to drown out her hysterics with the sound of the water.

As soon as the door closed behind her, Sam slammed her fist into the wall with a wild roar. And again. And again.

Punching the poor wall until he saw the red marks on the expensive wallpaper.

Sam was sick to his stomach. Torn apart by his own stupidity and anger, again at himself.

He knew he couldn't do that to her. It wasn't Maria's fault, not anyone's. These Shakespearean games had gone too far. Panic made it hard to concentrate.

All his attention was drawn to the bathroom door. Maria had only just left the room, and Sam was already freaking out.

His adrenaline began to drop, bringing all his other senses back into working order. Only panic and anger persisted. Sam was angry, as usual, at himself, and Maria was suffering, as always.

Cold, clammy panic enveloped every cell, making his hands shake like an old man's.

You've ruined everything again, the dominant inside Sam roared.

He didn't want to let go of Maria. Neither he nor his dominant.

The quiet chuckle turned into a hysterical cackle. Tilting his head back, Sam couldn't stop the laughter. For a moment, tears rolled from his eyes; it all seemed so utterly absurd.

He wouldn't let go because he couldn't. Even if he let her go now, he'd start looking for her in twenty-four hours, maybe even sooner.

If someone had told Sam a couple of months ago that his obsession, pain, and love would be the daughter of the enemy, he would have laughed hysterically in that person's face. But now he didn't feel like laughing anymore.

Moving on instinct and feeling alone, blocking and overriding all thought and logic, Sam rushed to the bathroom. He opened the door hysterically, it nearly flew off its hinges.

He squeezed his eyes shut, getting used to the bright light, but he saw her right away. His Maria, baby girl, Maria. Frightened, trembling, and confused. Completely naked, she huddled in the corner of the shower stall. Crossed her arms over her chest in a defensive posture. She clenched her thighs, but even from this distance, Sam could see her knees shaking.

Slowly, with the grace of a tiger, Sam approached the glass door.

Without taking his eyes off his girl, he quickly threw off his clothes and stepped in. Hot jets of water scorched his skin, but Sam didn't feel them. All he saw and felt was Maria's fear. Again, he had frightened her. Gritting his teeth, Sam held back his urge to nuzzle into the plump lips. To press her fragile body against the cold tile so that her bones crunched and a low whimper escaped from her throat.

"What are you..." Maria said quietly, almost in a whisper, frightened out of her wits.

"Shh-shh-shh-shh," Sam stopped her with a thumb on her lower lip. "Don't be afraid." As if reading her thoughts, he slowly touched his lips to her trembling lips.

Maria had never had such a tender kiss before. Afraid to interrupt the unearthly pleasure, she rose on her toes. She put her arms around Sam's broad shoulders and moaned softly into his mouth.

She didn't understand what was going on, and she didn't want to understand. She was fine with the here and now. And even if it was a goodbye kiss, the thought of which was destroying her, Maria wanted to drink every last drop of it. To squeeze out everything she could to remember forever the taste of his lips, the heat of his touch to engrave those seconds of happiness on her scarred heart.

Sam pulled away, though. He scrutinized the pale face. He was glad when he saw the slight blush on her cheeks and the painfully familiar gleam in her eyes. He was not mistaken. He realized how much she wanted him. Made a final decision for himself, looking into those bottomless eyes the color of his favorite whiskey.

"Listen to me," Sam said seriously, taking her face in his hot hands. He was scared shitless to look away, even for a moment. Catching her micro-emotions like the air of salvation. "I don't know how, but we'll be together. I cannot live without you, Maria O'Dell. You won, damn it," Sam grinned, "You tamed the dominant."

"But you said it was over," Maria frowned.

She was afraid to hear that hated "yes" again, but Sam only silently touched her forehead with his lips. Slowly, she traced a path of kisses down to her red ear. Without releasing her from his arms, Williams whispered softly:

"I'm an idiot. Just don't tell anyone. Especially Blackwood and Woolf."

"But..."

"No buts," Sam insisted sternly, looking into her tear-stained eyes again.

"I'm not letting you go. I can't. I'll figure it out. I'll figure something out. Just trust me, Maria. Please believe me. Say you do, baby girl."

Sam pressed himself tighter and tighter into her naked body. He wanted to be one with her. His rock-hard cock pressed against the girl's belly.

The hot water seemed even hotter from the heat of the situation. Sam mentally prayed and begged all the gods in existence to give him another chance with her. He didn't give up his fragile hope.

"What about Dad?" Maria asked in a trembling voice.

"I'll fix it," Sam nodded briefly. Too short.

He tensed at the mere thought of lying. Now, he had to tell her the truth about her father's non-involvement in the scams and in the collapse of his family, but Sam couldn't. He was afraid of Maria's reaction. Didn't want to ruin the moment. He wanted to hear her agree to stay, to be with him, and to do what everyone feared. They were afraid of him.

"Okay," the man barely heard over the sound of the water and the loud pounding of his own heart.

"Yeah?" Sam smiled like a child, hugging an already stiff Maria. There was a joy and relief in Sam's voice that he had never felt before. Once again, she had made him experience feelings he had never felt before.

"Yes," Maria repeated with her eyes closed, and she smiled.

Unable to hold back any longer, Sam pounced on her tortured lips. He kissed long and sweet. Until his whole body trembled, until the sweet cramps under his knees, the burning heat between his legs.

Maria had only to obey to surrender to this viciously wild beast. To accept all the warmth and affection that he kept deep inside him and now shared without regret.

Sam didn't let Maria out of his embrace until morning. There were no sessions or punishments. He simply loved and took care of Maria.

Giving her unearthly pleasure and soaring to heaven with her.

Chapter 52

"Thank you, Charlotte."

Unable to see who Sam was talking to, Maria tried to gaze at the figure behind the door with interest.

"What are you doing?" Sam grinned in surprise when he saw his baby girl wrapped in a sheet and standing on her toes. From the side, she looked like a cute little squirrel.

"Who were you talking to?"

"Jealous?" Sam decided to make a joke.

"Yes," Maria furrowed her eyebrows.

Her answer took the man by surprise. He wanted to laugh and cheer.

Everything seemed to have turned upside down in just one night, and he loved the change. Maria was no longer frightened, nor did she squeeze her head into her shoulders when she gazed at Sam.

She looked at him with a slight challenge, which only made Samuel admire her.

"I was talking to Charlotte."

"Who's that?"

"The secretary. She works here. Nice girl, Salazar's right hand." Sam shrugged. But when he looked into Maria's squinting eyes, he realized he'd said something stupid. "She brought your clothes."

"What do you mean?" Maria's already big eyes widened. "I have clothes!"

"Baby girl, you're not leaving the room in that dress," Sam summarized calmly, pointing to a black piece of cloth that was lying on the chair.

"I don't like people going through my things," she muttered, pulling on jeans and a loose sweater. Much to Maria's surprise, the admin girl had taken care of fresh underwear and shoes. Everything matched perfectly in style.

"If Salazar trusts Charlotte, so do I," Sam explained calmly.

They didn't speak about the subject again. Sam silently took Maria's hand and led her out. On the way out, they met only a couple of cleaning ladies and, to Maria's surprise, Max Woolf.

He was not fresh and already drunk at ten in the morning. With a predatory grin, he headed straight for Sam.

"Sam, my friend! You still here?"

"We were just leaving, Woolf."

"Oh, really? I was going to offer you the chance to stretch one obedient girl," Woolf grinned contentedly. Throwing a humiliating, contemptuous glance at Maria, Woolf tsked unhappily.

"I said no," Sam answered him rudely.

He had to put Maria behind his back. Sam was afraid of the eloquent Woolf.

Max knew and had a lot of interesting things to say. Things Sam wasn't ashamed of, but he didn't want to drag Maria into it. Knew how badly she'd react. Even pissed off at the sweet and ever-quiet Charlotte.

"I see." Having quickly lost interest in the couple, Woolf abruptly shifted his gaze to his new victim. Maria didn't know how she felt that he was preparing for a throw, like a silent leopard in the bushes.

"Hey, blondie!" Max shouted loudly, heading for the bar. "Be kind and serve me a drink," Max grinned predatorily, putting a double meaning into his phrase and bypassing Maria.

"My name is Charlotte. And I am not your servant! Stop drinking!"

"It's not for you to decide, blondie. Fucking bitch," Woolf snapped. Maria felt shivers all over her body from his commanding tone.

"Let's go," Sam pulled her along.

"Why is he like that?" Maria asked with interest.

"Who? Woolf?"

"Yeah."

"Sometimes life breaks people too much and then throws them away like garbage," Sam answered cryptically.

Maria did not ask any more questions. They drove to the hotel in silence.

Williams did not let go of her hand, and Maria only smiled furtively out the window with happiness. Now, she could touch him and not be afraid. She dreamed like a fool about evenings and walks together. She wanted to shower only with him.

Maria hoped it would always be like yesterday.

"Are you hungry?" Sam asked, stroking her hand with his thumb. The innocent gesture made her cheeks flame.

"No," Maria shook her head, panting with desire. She couldn't believe it was possible to want a man so much. To the point of shivering, to the crunching of her knuckles, to the dizziness, but she wanted to.

"What do you want?" Sam leaned toward her.

A storm was brewing in his eyes again. Maria could feel his arousal on some new level. She was shaking herself. She didn't answer, only sighed loudly, confirming her condition.

"You, damn it," the girl giggled.

As soon as the couple crossed the threshold of their suite, Sam pounced furiously on Maria's lips. She only squeaked softly, a little startled by his sweet dominance.

"*Mine*," Maria couldn't stop repeating, surrendering herself to Sam's thrusts.

"*Mine*," Sam savored the sweetness of her lips.

Sam grabbed the edge of Maria's sweatshirt, but the phone ringing instantly ruined all plans.

"I need to answer this," Sam whispered.

"Uh-huh," Maria mumbled, continuing to cover her man's neck and chin with small kisses.

"Three minutes," Sam asked her, though he didn't want to let her out of his embrace.

Maria let Sam go with understanding. She went to look for her cell phone. It was on the bedside table, where the girl had left it yesterday.

Grabbing the device, she returned to the living room. Sam was hiding behind the door of his room, still absorbed in the conversation.

Maria wanted to share the news with Alicia to the point of trembling in her fingers. She didn't even care that her friend would poke fun and joke at her.

Settling down on the comfortable couch, Maria began to type a long, detailed message as Sam's open laptop came into view.

Maria wanted to continue typing but suddenly noticed a painfully familiar surname among the string of e-mails.

O'Dell.

The girl's hand reached for the computer. Quickly clicking the mouse, she opened the letter. She read it even faster.

Her heart beat painfully against her chest, wanting to fly out and collapse at her feet. She couldn't believe her eyes, denied the very existence of this information. Deep inside, Maria was glad her father had nothing to do with the Williams' collapse or the scams in his own company. But that wasn't what was tearing her apart.

Eight days.

Sam had received and read this information eight days ago.

Her mouth was dry and unpleasantly scratchy. Nausea was coming up her dry throat. The room began to fade.

Maria felt as if she had drunk a lot of alcohol. She seemed to be thinking, but her thoughts were clumped together into one sticky lump of questions.

He knew. He knew! A howling siren grew inside Maria. It drowned out all other feelings, leaving only bitterness, resentment, and anger on the surface.

"Baby girl," a familiar and already so hateful voice brought the girl out of her trance.

Sam looked at the pale Maria with bewilderment. She was standing at the window, resting one hand on the cold glass and holding her side with the other.

The confusion in her eyes changed in a second to anger as he returned to the living room. Sam was startled by the grimace of pain on her beautiful face.

As soon as Sam took one step in her direction, Maria snapped into a yell:

"Stay back! Don't you fucking dare!" Maria howled like a wounded animal.

"Baby girl, what's wrong?"

Sam was not going to stop, but when he took another step, Maria rushed to the dresser, where she saw a vase of flowers. Grabbing the heavy object, the girl swung it toward Sam. That's when he stopped.

"I. Said. *DON'T*. Come over," Maria hissed wildcat-like. Despite her aggressive posture, the girl's eyes ran fearfully from Sam to the laptop and back again.

Unwillingly clenching his fists, Sam slowly walked over to the computer. His face contorted into a sad grin as soon as he looked at the screen.

An e-mail from Jacob.

"Fuck."

"You knew. You knew all along," Maria babbled like a madwoman. The puzzles were slowly coming together in her head.

"Baby girl, listen." Keeping his voice calm, Sam made another attempt to move closer to her.

The bitterness of hir own lies spread under hir skin. Paralyzed every cell, but Sam held on. He wanted to scream, beg for forgiveness, promise anything she wanted, just so he wouldn't have to see her pain.

"Don't call me that! Did you take it back?"

"What?" Sam asked again. Maria's question caught him off guard.

"Did you take my father's statement from the police?" Maria hissed, holding the vase in her hands.

"No," he shook his head guiltily.

"Why?" swallowing the first tears, she was on the edge of madness.

"Why?" Sam asked himself the same question.

Was he unsure of what he was doing? Or was he simply afraid of losing the object of his revenge? After all, if O'Dell was not guilty, then who was?

With a shame and bitterness Sam realized his own worthlessness. The one that Maria now saw in him.

"Maria, baby girl, you need to understand it's too complicated."

Taking another step in her direction, Sam deftly dodged a crystal vase flying at his head. It shattered into millions of pieces, just like Maria's heart.

"You're selfish! You're a bloody lunatic and a scoundrel. I thought you'd changed. I believed you. I fucking fell in love with you! And you stomped me into the mud. You watched me suffer and smiled. Are you having fun now, too? Yes? Answer me!" Maria was getting quieter and quieter with each word. It was like she was withering away. The life was slowly draining out of her, robbing her of her voice.

"I didn't realize it was so important," Sam bowed his head guiltily.

"You... what?" Maria squinted her eyes and, the next second, burst into hysterical laughter. "You!" She jabbed her finger at him. "Devoted your whole life to destroying your family's abuser, and when it turned out he wasn't guilty, you just decided it didn't 'matter'?" Maria imitated quotation marks in the air.

Clenching his fists convulsively, Sam couldn't find the right words. There was a crushing wave of anger and disappointment coming from Maria. Disappointment in him. In them.

"Stop," Sam asked calmly, stepping toward the unarmed Maria. He tried with all his might to keep his whole body from trembling, to appear as cold and commanding as ever. But it was becoming impossible around Maria. Especially now.

"Don't come near," Maria said as calm as before and put her hands in front of her for the sake of convincing. "It's over. It's no longer impossible to fix. I don't trust you. You screwed up. You were supposed to keep me safe, and you failed. Don't you ever come near me again. Do you hear me? I don't want to see you anymore. It hurts. It hurts a lot because I thought you were different." Maria grinned, adding quietly, "I'm a fool. God, what an idiot I am."

Sam's stony, unwavering face frowned with every word she said. He was breathing raggedly, his gaze becoming frantic in places. Frightening.

Maria didn't look at him anymore, destroying him in her own way, ignoring him. And there was something to look at.

Maria expected anything but what Sam said when she finished pouring out her soul to him:

"I'll have the jet ready."

"No need. I have money for a ticket home."

Sam didn't hear her. He pulled his cell phone out of his pocket and quickly dialed the number he needed.

The pain in his chest was increasing with every second. Maria found it hard to breathe. It hurt to think. She couldn't believe it could end like this.

"The plane will be ready in five hours."

"That's good."

They did not speak again. Maria went silently to her room. There was no point in packing her things. They didn't belong to her. Throwing her passport into her old backpack, she sat down on the bed. The room was warm, but she was freezing. She wrapped her shivering arms around herself and furtively glanced at the ajar door. Foolishly, she hoped that he would come in. Say something. He'd promised. But no one came.

Maria was unable to control her emotions, and she suddenly felt sick. She barely had time to run to the bathroom before she felt sick to her stomach. Her hands were shaking, her teeth chattering unpleasantly from the painful spasms in her stomach.

By the time she rinsed her mouth and washed her face with cold water, the room deafened her with a murderous silence. Maria knew she was alone.

Sam had left.

Chapter 53

Blackwood watched his friend tense and pale as death in silence. Sam hadn't left the walls of *The Kink* for the third day. The other dominants were avoiding him, and the sabots weren't even turning toward the creepy Sam.

The first day Maria left, Sam got drunk. He silently arrived at the club and went straight to a vacant room. The staff swapped empty bottles for new ones until Salazar himself showed up.

The old dominant refused to provide Sam with booze or favors unless he went to shower and sleep. Reluctantly, Sam agreed. He slept for ten hours and, changing the entourage of the room to the main hall, proceeded to pour whiskey on his mute misery.

Woolf, out of an old friendship, was pulling Sam drinks and light snacks to keep him from getting alcohol poisoning. Sam couldn't taste or smell anything.

The world around him blended into a homogeneous gray mass. Time had no meaning. He seemed to have slept for a few hours these days. Or not. Samuel didn't give himself credit for any of it. Eyes black with inner despair stared ceaselessly at one point. Three-day stubble lent sternness to an already sullen dominance.

"Maybe you'll finally tell me what happened?" Blackwood rubbed his neck tiredly.

"You're the all-knowing and all-seeing one. So you tell me what's wrong," Sam grumbled without raising his head.

Dressed in a black T-shirt and jeans of the same color, Williams seemed even bigger and scarier, like a bear that had wandered into a stone jungle.

"She's gone," Blackwood grinned like a serpent. Blackwood didn't mean to offend Williams; the chuckle came out of his mouth, for he had been in a similar situation. They silently shared the same pain.

"He reminds me of someone," Woolf laughed, landing on a nearby chair with another bottle of whiskey in his hands. He glanced at Blackwood with a sneer and began pouring the amber liquid into glasses.

Sam flinched every time he saw anything remotely resembling the color of her eyes. He'd seen them everywhere. Dreamed about them for three days. Stalked him like an obsession and a curse. Hearing the girl's ringing laughter, Sam involuntarily turned his head, like a paranoid man looking for Maria with his eyes. Became twitchy and aggressive.

"Shut your mouth, Max," Blackwood growled. "You've already made a mess of things."

"Did I?" Max squinted unhappily, leaning closer to Blackwood. He tensed as if preparing for an attack. Throughout his appearance, he radiated aggression.

"Having fun?" Salazar's voice rumbled over the heads of the trio like thunder in the midst of an already gloomy day.

Woolf pulled back sharply, leaning on the back of the chair. Blackwood straightened like a delinquent schoolboy, and only Sam didn't move. He sat like a statue, hypnotizing the liquid in his glass.

"We're talking," Woolf grumbled.

"How long has he been sitting here?" the owner of *The Kink* asked.

Salazar watched Sam carefully. Blackwood nodded briefly, confirming the words of the club owner. He didn't look any better himself. Harvey gazed at him with anger. He couldn't forgive Blackwood for what he had done.

"What a mess you guys have made," Salazar said with a shake of his head and a brief smile.

"Yeah," Max sneered.

"And you shut your mouth!" Salazar snapped at him, which he rarely did. "If I see you near, you know who again, I'll take away your membership not only in my club. I'll make it so that they'll never sell you a fucking ruler in the store again! I'll shut down the entire BDSM community in America for you, understand?"

Sam looked up with interest. It wasn't often that anyone saw Salazar angry, and when he did, it was to his own detriment. Now, Woolf could barely contain himself. He knew the danger of contradicting the owner of the club. Especially Salazar did not throw words into the wind. If he had threatened, he'd do it.

"So, maybe you can finally stop squeezing your tits like women and remember who you are?" Salazar turned to Blackwood and Sam again.

Max was no longer interested in the old dominant. He was not used to repeating himself twice and hoped that Woolf would switch his attention to more available candidates.

All the more that the man understood perfectly well the interest of the impudent man in her. He himself saw a long-forgotten grief in his assistant Charlotte.

"Harvey, don't make it even worse..."

"Shut up, Sam," Salazar growled. He'd realized even then how badly Sam was in trouble.

When the dominant burst into his office and, almost threateningly, demanded an ambulance, Salazar was shocked. He had to spend a good hour explaining to Sam that the girl had just passed out, probably from pleasure rather than pain. Sam's frantic eyes Salazar would not forget for a long time. Nor the guilty look in his eyes. The same one he'd gotten today.

It wasn't often that Salazar meddled in other people's lives, but he'd had his eye on these three for a long time. And, as if by agreement, they'd each screwed up almost a week apart. And now they were sitting in front of the director's office like delinquent kids, snot on their fists. Salazar's pissed off.

His club was no place for anonymous losers and snotty-nosed pussies.

"It's like you're fucking conspiring. First of all, keep your faces straight, or I'd like to put collars on you and give them to Lilith. She'll beat the shit out of everyone. She'll fuck you in the ass too, so you won't whine."

At the mention of Lilith, Blackwood, Sam, and even Woolf involuntarily shuddered. Salazar, did not hold back, put the sour men in their place. He reminded them that they were dominants, not inferiors.

"Didn't you learn to take responsibility for your actions? Even if it would tear your heart apart. If you screwed up, son," Salazar turned to Sam, "Then fix it!"

"I cannot."

"Don't you dare say you can't! What, your pride doesn't allow you to do that?" skeptically sneered the owner of the club. "Where was your pride when you mixed your slave with shit? You made this mess, and now you don't want to clean it up?"

"Maria! Her name is Maria!" Sam glared angrily at Salazar.

Sam grimaced as if he'd been kicked in the stomach. The bitter truth poured over the man like ice water. Sobering. Salazar didn't choose his words. He spoke as he was. So that Sam would realize how badly he was in his own mess.

The shame of what he'd done was quickly creeping under his skin. It had been there before, but it sat deep, in places Sam didn't want to look.

Salazar calmly opened all the locks and wiped out the cockroaches that were stubbornly preventing Sam from thinking straight and, more importantly, acting.

There in the room, he'd just let her go. Didn't even try to fight, even though he'd promised to fix everything before. Fooled her. Again.

Salazar was right about one thing: mistakes must be corrected. Emptying the contents of the cut glass, Sam exhaled loudly.

"Back to life?" Salazar grinned.

"Yeah, sorry about it," Sam stammered, not even sure where to start apologizing.

"What are you gonna do?" Woolf asked with interest. He crossed his arms over his chest and pretended to look at his fried, though all his attention was occupied by one blond girl, whom he watched with his peripheral vision.

"I need to go back to London," Sam replied thoughtfully.

The gears in his head were already starting to work. The man had a long and painstaking job ahead of him if he was going to get Maria back and mend his relationship with her father. The latter still seemed impossible, but Sam decided to try his luck. One more time.

"And?

"There's a couple of things I need to take care of. And talk to someone," Sam said confidently, imagining the severity of the conversation with O'Dell.

He still regretted what he had done. He blamed himself for Maria's suffering, for his insecurity and passivity. At that moment in the hotel, he was confused. He nullified everything. He ran away like a girl.

The next morning, radiating his former confidence and strength, Sam stopped the car at the low fence behind the O'Dell country house.

Chapter 54

"Hello, how may I help you?" asked women voice in the speaker with an English accent.

"Good afternoon, my name is Samuel Williams. I've come to talk to Andrew O'Dell."

The sunglasses did not save Sam from the scorching rays. His shirt clung unpleasantly to his sweaty back. Gritting his teeth, Sam waited patiently for O'Dell to open the gate. The possibility that he would be sent away was not off the table.

The intercom was silent for about ten minutes. Tense, Sam was about to press the bell again when the lock clicked.

"Come in," a woman's voice answered.

The neat yard, with many flowers and overgrown blossoms, gave a clear indication of the financial side of the house's inhabitants. Heading quickly toward the front door, Sam tried to quiet the trembling in his hands. He was overwhelmed by two emotions, oddly enough: fear and joy.

Sam was afraid, and he wanted to see his baby girl. He wanted to touch her delicate fingers and take her in his arms and kiss her until he had squeezed all the air out of her. He was well aware that more than one object would fly in his direction tonight.

Accepting his fate as a bastard, Sam proudly went to his knees, kissing her feet and begging for forgiveness.

"Mr. Williams," a short woman greeted him with an emotionless face, "Mr. O'Dell is waiting for you in the living room."

A simple interior. Pastel colors. There was not much furniture. The O'Dell's house was not characterized by luxury or wealth. Everything was surprisingly restrained but very cozy. Staying in the territory of the former enemy, Sam noted that he felt comfortable.

There was no pressure from the walls. He didn't want to turn around and wait for a knife in the back. And the most amazing thing was the wonderful aroma of cinnamon coming from the kitchen. Swallowing involuntarily, Sam remembered that he hadn't eaten breakfast. That rarely happened to him.

"Mr. O'Dell," the woman hesitated, not knowing what to say next. Apparently, she knew exactly who had come to see O'Dell.

"Thank you, Luisa. You can go now."

The gray-haired man did not hurry to approach the guest. O'Dell stood at the window and looked at something with interest. A light-colored tennis shirt and gray pants gave the man simplicity.

When Andrew O'Dell turned to face Sam, he was surprised to see the same gray beard. Unwittingly noting that Maria's father now looked like Santa Claus, Sam smiled with the corners of his lips.

"What do you want?" O'Dell began. The cute uncle's entourage fell away as soon as he looked at Sam. His eyes were filled with anger and rage. Sam couldn't blame him for that.

"I've solved the problems with the police," Sam got right to the point. "All your assets and accounts will be available within a couple of days."

"I know," the man grinned, bowing his head. "So, what made you change your mind? Who?" Andrew said the last one faintly, with a touch of venom in his voice.

"Is she here?" Sam asked for some reason, thus causing a wave of aggression in the owner of the house.

Andrew looked at Sam with angry black eyes. The man's face stretched, his lips compressed into a thin line.

Sam noticed at once how nervously Maria's father played with his knuckles. In a second, there was nothing good left on Andrew's face. Only hate and rage.

Exhaling loudly, Sam saw himself in him. His pain and the same rage. Quickly, he realized he had to break the cycle.

"I don't know what she told you."

"Nothing," Andrew gritted his teeth. A red wreath pulsed defiantly on the exposed part of the man's neck. A couple of drops of sweat appeared on his forehead.

"I came to apologize," Diplomatically putting his palms up at chest level, Sam took one step towards Andrew.

"You slept with her?" Holding himself back, the man growled.

Like Sam, he started walking toward him. Searing him with his gaze. In Andrew's mind, he had begged all the gods to help him not snap and kill the boy right in the living room of his house. And Andrew was close. Not for money. Not for revenge. For Maria. His favorite girl. His only blood. For the fact that she wasn't with her mom and dad anymore.

"I, we, well," Sam stammered. Clenching his teeth, he hesitated to answer. He looked away, making a huge mistake.

The heavy fist hit the target. With a loud clack of his jaw, Sam slumped to the floor. Before Sam could realize it, Andrew, a nice-looking old man, began to deliver very sharp and painful blows to Sam's face.

Sam didn't try to stop him. Didn't even put his hands out for defense. Took each new attack as punishment for everything he had done to this family. Andrew O'Dell, his wife, and his daughter.

"Andrew, stop it!"

A ringing, hysterical female voice deafened the whole house. Sam's heart suddenly clenched with pain. A different but painfully familiar voice kept screaming. Begged him to stop, but Andrew didn't hear, having lost contact with the world around him.

"Andrew!" almost crying, howled Lena. And then Andrew stopped.

Heavily down near the bloodstained Sam, Andrew swore loudly, looking at his fist and the guest's face. The old man began to shake. His face, crimson from anger and high pressure, was distorted with a grimace of grief and guilt.

"I'm sorry," Andrew apologized without looking at Sam.

"Andrew! Look at your hands. Luisa, get the first aid kit." Lena looked in horror at her husband and the blond stranger.

Both looked like kids from the street. "Who is this young man?" she whispered to her husband.

"Sam Williams himself," Andrew said tiredly. His fist was sore from unaccustomed use. Heart rumbled like an old tractor, struggling to cope with the adrenaline.

"Sam?" Lena asked in surprise.

Sam nodded briefly and immediately paid for it with a pain in his cheekbone. He realized from whom Maria had adopted her beauty and manner of surprise. The same dark hair that shimmered golden in the sun, huge eyes with a scattering of wrinkles that did not age the woman.

Lena looked at the stranger with interest. She wrinkled at the sight of blood that kept pouring from his nose. She tsked unhappily, realizing that his lip and eyebrow needed to be urgently reanimated.

"Can I see Maria? Please," Sam asked, ignoring the aching pain.

"No," Andrew objected firmly.

"Ms. O'Dell," Sam spoke again, still wrinkling his nose a little. "I understand your distrust and hatred. I deserve it. All my life, believing in your involvement in my father's death, I wished the same fate for your family. Hate. Fostered anger and despised you. But everything changed when I met your daughter. She came to me. And I…" Sam stammered. He tried to find the words so as not to anger Andrew even more. "I fell in love."

"Oh..." Lena involuntarily shuddered. Noticing how both men turned in her direction, she covered her mouth with her hand.

"Your Maria…she's... she's unusual. Bright, stubborn, absent-minded, gentle, vulnerable. I didn't realize how I fell in love. I knew you weren't responsible for my father's death. I knew, and I didn't tell her. I kept it a secret. I was afraid she'd leave, and I made it worse. I know she hates me, but I just want to talk to her. Explain. I'm not happy without her. I can't be without your daughter. She's become the meaning of my worthless life." Bowing his head guiltily, Sam grinned. It took him to lose one person to find another and lose her again.

"She cried so much," Andrew rubbed his eyes tiredly. He shrank from Sam's speech, for he had kept a terrible secret.

A secret that still made his hands shake and his chest ache.

Sam's words had wounded him to the very soul. Andrew bitterly realized that it was he who had caused his daughter's separation from Sam. If he had told everything at once, it could have been avoided. But Andrew had chickened out. He kept silent, pushing Maria away when she needed his help.

Glancing at the wrinkled Sam, the man lowered his head guiltily. He would remain silent even now. Andrew O'Dell had made a promise, and he couldn't break it. Not now.

"Please, I need to talk to her!" Sam didn't back down.

"It's impossible," Lena reminded herself.

All this time, the woman quietly stood aside and listened. Observed both of them. She immediately caught the change in her husband's face. She saw Sam's puppy eyes. She watched and drew conclusions.

"Why?" Sam asked. His hands clenched into fists at the thought that something might have happened to her. He wouldn't forgive himself.

"She's gone."

"Where?" Sam raised his voice in a burst of emotion.

"We don't know," Andrew replied tiredly. "We don't know where she is now."

Chapter 55

It had been two for two, but his jaw never ceased to remind him of Andrew's heavy blow. Sam held no grudge against the old man. In truth, he felt better when he came face to face with Andrew.

Sam had closed a couple of gestalts, but not all of them. The most important one still kept the man from breathing at full strength.

He was having disturbing dreams. Milk chocolate-colored eyes everywhere. Sam even grabbed the elbow of a girl, similar to Maria. He had to apologiz, but he couldn't stop the sudden impulse. He began to rave about finding her.

Jacob, his trusty security guard, was combing London nonstop. He had to send his men to the airport to keep an eye on the departure lists. Maria O'Dell's name was on the radar of the city's most nimble trackers.

In a terrible state of mind, Sam struggled to keep up with his duties.

Postponing appointments and turning down all Helen's invitations. She called incessantly, offering the best girls in town. The most submissive and willing to go to the end to please their masters.

Sam cringed at the thought of being touched by someone other than Maria. So, he had to threaten the dominatrix with violence if she disturbed his peace one more time.

Another phone call sent Sam into a fit of aggression. For some reason, he thought it was Helen again.

"Mr. Williams?"

"What?!" Sam almost roared like a wild animal answering the phone.

"Oh!" the female voice on the other end squeaked softly. "I'm sorry, it's Dr. Perkins," the woman whispered quietly.

"Who?" Sam asked a little less fervently.

"Your personal gynecologist for, uh, your, uh, your mistress."

"Good afternoon, doctor," the man interrupted her, realizing how uncomfortable she felt talking about her work.

"I'm here for the test results. I can't reach Maria, I don't have her e-mail, and I need to schedule her prenatal vitamins and an ultrasound."

"What's that for?" Sam rubbed the bridge of his nose. He didn't understand a word he had just been told.

"The HCG confirmed the pregnancy, and by my count, it's week four. Mr. Williams, first of all, I congratulate you, and secondly, I'm sorry to ruin such an important moment for your family. Maria wanted to surprise you, but it's very important that she get to her appointment as soon as possible. She has toxicity too early. She needs to eat right and...."

Dr. Perkins went on and on, but Sam wasn't listening. Or rather, he didn't hear her. His heart was pounding against his chest so hard it hurt in places.

Pregnant.

Sam automatically dropped the call and threw the phone against the wall. The third one since Maria had left. He wanted to howl like a wolf and bang his head against the wall. Sam frantically remembered what he'd done to her at the club, how he hadn't let her out of bed all night. And it was slowly burning a huge hole of guilt in him.

What if he'd hurt her or the baby? And how much stress had she been under?

The fainting spells, the constant pallor, the poor appetite. Sam had written it all off to...anything but the damn pregnancy!

Questions began to clutter his already aching head. Grabbing the landline, he dialed the clinic. He wanted answers. Maria had been using protection. He'd seen the reports, the tests himself. How could this have happened?

A slightly aggressive Dr. Perkins explained what had happened to Sam. The doctor told him that Maria showed up with tear-stained eyes and ten positive pregnancy tests. It took the doctor a long time to calm the shaking girl.

The explanation was as simple as stress.

Perkins had explained to Maria that any contraceptive was not 100 percent effective. The girl mentioned a little stress, which only made Sam growl unhappily.

"She'll be here soon," Sam replied briefly and hung up. He was cowardly and angry. At that moment, he wanted to find that brat and give her a good whipping. And he didn't care if Maria hated him.

That thought passed quickly, replaced by fear. What if she decided to get rid of the baby? Sam broke out in a cold sweat.

No! She wouldn't. She wouldn't!

Acting on bare instincts, the man dialed another number quickly with trembling hands.

"The house of the O'Dells, how can I help you?" He recognized the governess's voice at once.

"May I speak to Miss O'Dell?" Trying to keep his breathing calm, Sam asked.

"Who's asking?"

"Sam Williams," Sam introduced himself after a moment's hesitation.

"Miss O'Dell is busy right now."

"It's very important! It's about Maria."

A heavy sigh and the sound of footsteps pleased Sam. Apparently, the magic name "Maria" had worked on Luisa.

"Hello," Lena answered, a little confused.

"Good afternoon, Miss O'Dell."

"Good afternoon. Excuse me, who am I talking to?" The woman never ceased to be surprised.

"This is Sam."

"What do you want?"

The woman got straight to the point. Unlike her husband, she had a way of keeping an icy calm. The confusion in her voice evaporated, replaced by a note of displeasure, even arrogance.

"I need to talk to about Maria. It's very important."

"We've already told you," Lena began her familiar rant. But Sam wasn't going to back down.

"You know where she is. You're very close."

"We haven't spoken in a while. She didn't call while I was at the clinic..."

"I know she was on the phone with your governess. I know she was looking for money to pay for treatment at St. John's. She didn't talk to you because you asked her to. I saw how worried she was," Sam said in one breath.

"Maria didn't know I was at St. John's. Luisa didn't tell her. Neither did I."

Sam felt like he was underwater. It was hard to breathe. He had to undo the top button of his shirt for some imaginary freedom.

"You," Lena continued calmly, grinning into the receiver, "are the patron. You paid for my treatment."

"I was trying to help," Sam confirmed her hunch without even trying to interrupt. He was tired of lying. It's what took Maria and his baby away from him.

"Why do you want to talk to my daughter, Mr. Williams?" Lena asked prosaically. Sam could have sworn she was examining her manicure, and he wouldn't have been wrong.

"You know why," Sam went all in. Something he was good at, and he knew how to negotiate.

"Let's say I do. So why do you want to talk to her?" Like a lioness, Lena was not going to back down. Defended her beloved daughter as best she could.

"I want that baby! It is our baby," Sam snapped.

The silence on the phone spurred him on even more. She knew! Another woman in her place would have started screaming or deny, but Lena gave herself away with her silence.

"I know you hate me. You have every right to. But I wouldn't forgive myself if anything happened to Maria or the baby! The doctor said she was not answering her phone. She needs to get an ultrasound and start taking some vitamins!"

"Prenatal," Lena said quietly.

"Please." With excitement, Sam rose from his chair. The cord of the phone did not allow him to move far away from the table, and he wanted to rush around like a caged animal.

"She's at her friend, Alicia's," the woman breathed heavily.

"Thank you," Sam breathed in time with her and closed his eyes. Now he knew where she was. His girl. His Maria. He'd gnaw at the ground, but he'd fix everything. That was for sure now.

"And another thing, Sam," Lena's voice changed. It became tense. She was almost whispering. Sam had to strain his ear.

"My husband knows nothing. I hope it will stay that way."

"Of course. You have my word," Sam replied without hesitation.

Chapter 56

At last, he saw her. It seemed to Sam that in the time they had not seen each other, Maria had become even paler, even thinner, even more petite.

Clenching the steering wheel to an unpleasant grip, he furtively watched Maria striding through the London night.

Why the fuck is she walking the streets so late? Sam couldn't stop freaking out. In her position, one must take care of oneself.

The neighborhood where Alicia lived wasn't the worst, but it wasn't the best either. The apartment was a fifteen-minute walk to the bus stop and the subway. The streetlights were burning every other day. And Sam didn't want to talk about the dark park that lined the road home. He just clenched his teeth and wolf-watched to make sure that not a single living soul got near his girl!

Sam rushed to the right address as soon as Lena told him where Alicia lived. After four hours of waiting, Sam saw a familiar figure. Hair pulled back into a high, sloppy ponytail. A baggy black sweater and fucking leggings.

I'll kill every man who looks at her! Sam raged mentally, imagining the London perverts staring at his girl.

When Maria was almost to the right door, he got out of the car, quickly ran across the road, and began to approach leisurely.

"Maria!"

The keys fell to the dirty asphalt with a clinking sound. She recognized that voice. Her body recognized it. A warm wave traveled from the top of her head along her vertebrae lingered at the bottom of her stomach, where his child was already, and slipped into her heels.

Shaking her head, Maria quickly dispersed the butterflies that were beginning their dance in her still flat stomach. Too many questions lodged in her. Half of them had already been answered. The rest she was afraid to ask.

The resentment didn't go away. It hadn't subsided. Every day, it grew weeds in her body and soul. It completely took over her consciousness and prevented her from thinking rationally.

In addition, Maria was constantly crying and cranky. Hormones were prancing with such force that even her best friend began to be late at work.

Maria could not accept the idea that she was pregnant. She would never forget that night. Alicia returned from the supermarket, bringing her favorite potato salad. As soon as the lid on the container opened, Maria stormed out of the kitchen.

She barely made it to the bathroom, and there she almost spits out her stomach. That's when Alicia made her friend take the test. That minute turned out to be the longest of her life.

Maria only twirled her finger at her temple and laughed when Alicia said her thoughts aloud. But when she saw the two stripes, she stopped laughing.

Shock, panic, denial. Maria raided every test her friend had. She even wanted to go to the pharmacy at night for more accurate ones, but Alicia was able to convince her that eight positive tests were definitely a pregnancy.

Maria answered Alicia's questions with difficulty. She sat in the small kitchen and stared at one point. She frantically remembered the contraindications and the doctor's words. In the morning, she ran to the clinic. Tearfully, she had begged Dr. Perkins not to say anything to Sam. The thought that he would find out made her feel scared.

Then, out of desperation, Maria called her mother. Her father had practically kicked her out of the house. Wanted to know where and with whom she was all this time, but Maria was silent as a partisan. That's when he told her to either stay, tell the truth, or leave with her secrets. Maria chose to leave.

Mom took the news surprisingly calmly. She suggested not to tell Maria's father until they had decided what to do with the child. Her mother's words angered the girl.

"I'm not going to get rid of the baby!" Maria flared up. Tears flowed at the mere thought that something might happen to the baby.

Sighing heavily, Lena admitted that she and her father knew where and with whom Maria had been living for two months. And the news about the baby could have completely shattered the father.

Maria was completely confused. She barely made it to the bench near the clinic. She sat and roared into her mother's voice over the phone. She had no strength left to lie to her family.

Respectfully omitting the moments of their intimate relationship and BDSM, Maria told her mother everything about how she herself came to Sam. How she hated him, but in time, fell in love, how he deceived her to keep her.

Maria refused all her mother's requests to return. She was afraid of shame and her father's anger. Even though she didn't want the money, Lena still persuaded her daughter.

"Not for myself, but for the baby," Maria was convincing herself.

She tried not to think about Sam. Forgot for a couple of minutes and again plunged headlong into self-destruction. She cried, blamed herself and him for weakness, for deceit, for powerlessness. She repressed the frequent urge to call or even write. Even asked Alicia to hide her phone at night because that's when it got the worst.

This morning, going to an interview in a small cafe, Maria decided to forget about Sam and to cut him out of her life. It had been a week, and he still hadn't shown up. However, he could have easily found her. Rubbing her flat stomach, the girl chuckled bitterly at her inherent naiveté.

He can have any girl in London and even England, Maria couldn't stop thinking about her own stupidity.

The nice receptionist promised to call back. Despite the sullen Alicia, who muttered non-stop about the fact that pregnant women need to rest and not stand on their feet for eight hours, Maria was glad that she could become financially independent.

And then all her plans fell apart the second a familiar voice said her name. She was afraid to turn around. For some reason, she had a feeling Sam would be angry. Maybe even yell. She knew who he was, didn't she? A dominant.

"What are you doing here?"

Still half-turning toward him, Maria folded her arms across her chest. She didn't want to look at him. One look from him and all her confidence would be gone. Catching a glimpse of a bunch of keys, Maria began to hypnotize them. Just so she wouldn't have to look at him.

"We need to talk." Sam said firmly.

"We've already talked. I've said everything, just like you," Maria blurted out with resentment.

"Don't decide for me," Sam asked quietly.

He was having a hard time keeping his temper in check. His fingertips tingled with the urge to rake her into his arms. To throw her on his shoulder and carry her away from this rough neighborhood. He would have if he hadn't known she was pregnant.

"I have to go," Maria squeaked softly.

His phrase didn't make the best impression on the girl. Her eyes began to sting unpleasantly. She wanted to cry from resentment, hormones, and anger.

"Baby girl..."

"No!" the girl shrieked, stomping her foot for more confidence. "Don't come near me. We don't need anything from you! Go away."

"We?" Sam pretended. He wanted to smile, but he refrained. She'd left the baby. Sam felt an inexplicable warmth inside him. His cheekbones curled with the urge to grin like a fool.

"Me. Only me," Maria faltered. Her eyes darted around, looking for something. It was as if someone had written the answer to Sam's question on the walls of old houses. But it wasn't there. "You heard what I said."

"You said 'we'," Sam insisted. Even dared to take a step closer. They were now separated by a measly half a meter. He could already reach Maria with his hand. It was getting harder and harder to restrain himself.

"Don't mince words!"

Picking up the keys from the asphalt, Maria rushed to the door. It was as if the key was not getting into the keyhole on purpose. Her hands were shaking.

"Ouch!" Maria tried to pull away, but a hot palm covered her cold one.

"Why are you dressed like this? Where is your jacket?" A hot voice scorched her temple.

Maria's leg was nearly cramped with excitement. Sam was using a forbidden technique. And it was working. Maria bit her lip to keep from groaning in frustration. No matter how angry she was at him, no matter how much she hated him, her body betrayed at the mere touch of Sam.

"I'm not cold."

"You," Sam emphasized the first word and placed his other hand on her stomach, "should not be cold, much less sick."

Chapter 57

"I don't understand you," Maria gathered the last shreds of her courage into a fist and tried to push Sam away.

"Baby girl, I know everything." Giving her a supposed victory, Sam pulled away.

He had to hide his hands in the pockets of his pants to keep them loose. He wanted to. She was driving him crazy. No makeup, a little confused, with the look of an angry cat. His groin tingled with arousal. Sam wanted to scream, to berate himself. He should be having a normal conversation, and he was already thinking about how and where he was going to kiss and fuck her.

"Perkins, you bitch," Maria muttered resentfully, averting her gaze.

"She's worried, and so am I. You need to call her."

"No," Maria insisted. She even put her palm forward. No, she wasn't embarrassed to talk to Dr. Perkins, but she couldn't afford the service at that clinic.

"She's a good specialist. I'll pay for it," Sam read her mind.

"You know what, Sam? Fuck off!" the girl said with anger.

Maria began to shiver. She wanted to claw at his smug face and scratch it bloody. How could she love such a man? He didn't hear her. He continued to bend his way and ignore her wishes.

"Baby girl," Sam grabbed the edge of her sleeve. "I'm sorry."

"What exactly are you apologizing for?" Maria frowned but didn't pull her hand away.

"Everything. I talked to your father," Sam grinned faintly, rubbing his cheekbone. "He is a strong man for his age."

It was only now that Maria noticed the bruises on his face. Involuntarily, she rose on her toes and touched with her fingers the place where Andrew had bruised his face.

"Did my father do it?" Maria whispered.

"Yes," Sam grimaced.

Maria's gentle touch was breaking down the last barrier. Breaking the already fragile dam of the feelings Sam was hiding. With a loud growl, he backed away from the girl himself. Couldn't afford such a luxury as a kiss.

"There's nothing wrong with him if that's what you're interested in."

"Mom didn't say anything," Maria said thoughtfully.

"Maria, please. Come home. Or do you want me to buy you an apartment? Or a house? In the downtown. Only where it's not noisy, so you can walk with a stroller. And I'll buy you a car. I'll get you into the best clinic. I'll provide for you and the baby. I want this baby, baby girl. Do you hear me? I'll do everything for you. Just, please, let me take you away from here."

"I can't go home," Maria shrugged her shoulder.

"Let's go to my place, then? Please," Sam begged with a tremor in his voice.

"No," Maria quietly declined his invitation.

"Why can't you go home?" Sam decided to ask.

"Dad doesn't know about us."

"He knows," Sam interrupted.

"What?" exhaled, dumbfounded Maria.

"This bruise proves it. He knows everything, Maria, except for the pregnancy. But we don't have to tell him yet. We'll figure something out."

Sighing heavily, Maria looked around. Alicia tolerated all her psychos and antics, but the girl realized that she was disturbing her friend. Sam's words had struck a nerve. She really missed her family. Even the perpetually grumpy Luisa.

Giving Sam a skeptical look, Maria didn't want to acknowledge another of his victories. Things were once again happening the way he wanted them to. As usual, on his terms. But the sense of responsibility for the little life in her made her stifle her selfishness and pride.

She really would be better off at home. And Sam? She'd deal with him later.

"Okay," Maria agreed briefly.

They drove to the O'Dells house in silence. Maria had a chocolate bar and tried not to look in Sam's direction. The conversation was tiring her. She felt drowsy. Alicia hadn't responded to the message. But Maria knew that her friend would be happy when she found out that Maria had returned home.

As soon as the car pulled up to the familiar gate, all the girl's confidence vanished.

"I'm not going," Maria clung to the seat. Like a little girl, she frowned and looked at the surprised Sam frowningly.

"Maria, you need to."

"I said I'm not going!" she almost cried.

Looking at his former, very submissive slave, Sam wondered to himself. Before, he would have growled, ordered, and crushed her with the aura of a dominant, but now it was as if he had been replaced. He eyed Maria with interest, wondering how he could lure her out of the car without shouting and threats. He had no thoughts of ordering her out. He wanted to negotiate with her, to persuade her.

"You're tired, and you need to rest. Your feet must be swollen," Sam tilted his head to the side.

With a loud sigh, Maria opened the door. The demon was right again. She was really tired from today's walk and wanted to throw her legs up on the pillow.

Maria walked along the narrow path to the house and tried to come up with a hasty greeting speech. No sooner had she thought of half of it than the door opened. Maria's heart fell into the heels and came back in that second. On the threshold stood her father. Frowning like a cloud, Andrew slowly shifted his gaze from his daughter to Williams.

"Come in," Andrew said tiredly, rubbing the back of his neck.

Maria glanced at Sam unhappily, to which he only briefly shrugged his shoulders. She didn't like the fact that her father had called Sam into the house.

Luisa, who was always clucking, began showering Maria with greetings, hugs, and kisses on the cheeks. At Maria's attempt to go to the kitchen for water, the governess sent the girl straight to the living room and ran to get a glass.

"Your father is waiting for you."

Maria was even more alarmed. Sam, as if he were already at home, calmly walked into the living room, where the same frowning man was waiting for him.

"My baby!" Lena's voice gave Maria strength. The woman hugged her daughter tightly and looked at the pale Maria with wet eyes.

They entered the living room together.

"Have a seat, Sam," Andrew addressed the guest.

Maria tensely watched that picture. The more her father remained silent, the more her insides twisted into a tight knot, and her heart rumbled so that it became hard to breathe.

"I do understand that I am the elephant in the room and in this house. Maria's here, and that's all that matters," Sam replied succinctly, keeping his head down.

"You're not an elephant, boy," Andrew grinned.

The man stood at a small bar with his back to everyone else. Maria realized from the distinctive clatter that he was pouring alcohol into glasses.

"Here," Andrew held out his hand with a faceted flute to Sam.

With incomprehension, Sam accepted the drink. He still looked at the owner of the house and at Maria and her mother with confusion.

"I'm driving," he tried to explain.

"I'm not forcing you to drink," Andrew grinned kindly, "but you may need a couple of sips when you hear what I have to say."

Sam didn't like Andrew's tone. Though the old man spoke calmly and quite friendly, there was something cold about him. His eyes gave him away. Tired, with a touch of pain as if he'd been carrying a heavy load on his shoulders all his life. And for some reason, Sam knew right away this wasn't about Maria or his company.

"I knew your father," Andrew sat down in the chair opposite and began his story.

The more Andrew spoke, the paler Sam became. He drained the glass of whiskey in two gulps. His chest ached unbearably, and his brain refused to accept what he had heard.

"I promised your father I'd take that secret to my grave. Williams was an ambitious, risk-taking man. He went to extremes, and fortune almost always. He had no equal in business. I honestly envied your father. He worked hard and tried to be just as successful. But when he reached the top, for some reason, he decided to try his luck at gambling."

"I didn't know," Sam said quietly. With his head bowed, he listened attentively to Andrew. Did he believe him? Sam had no good reason to question his words.

"Your father blew it all in less than six months. That's when he came to me. Offered me a good deal. Knew I was the only one who could buy a business in a state of bankruptcy. He was already bankrupt. But for his family's sake, I took the gamble. I wanted to help a friend," Andrew grinned bitterly. It was as if he were reliving those memories. "But on one condition," he grinned again, "no games. With the money I paid him, Williams could have started a new business. But he lied to me. Showed me fake documents while he went to underground casinos. My business went uphill, and I began to disappear more at work, less time to devote to family and friends,"

He looked with guilt at his wife Lena, who, faintly snorted, rolling her eyes. "When I found out about your father's death, I could not believe it. I tried to find you and your mother, but, again, stupid work took all my time and energy. And my, God forgive me, partner Paul assured me that he had arranged financial assistance for the Williams family. I believed him. I always did. I trusted him about plenty of things."

On one hand, Sam wanted to throw an empty glass at Maria's father. On the other, he wanted to hug an old man.

Sam was tearing up inside. It wasn't every day he was told that his father had just let things slide. He'd practically driven himself into his own grave.

It was only now that Sam remembered his father's tired and sometimes mad look on his way home from work.

"Thank you," Sam said in a hoarse voice.

Andrew's story had knocked all the ground out from under his feet and the air out of his lungs. Staggering, Sam rose to his feet and silently headed for the exit. It was as if the life had been sucked out of him. He urgently needed to be alone to think and accept the bitter truth.

"Shouldn't we call a cab?" Lena shook her head in worry.

She didn't like the look of Sam, and she wasn't going to let him drive in his condition.

"Yeah, I guess so," Sam agreed. Rubbing his face tiredly, he leaned against the doorjamb. "Thank you."

Watching Sam, Maria could hardly hold back her tears. She stared at her sweet dominant's back and didn't know what to do.

Anger and resentment prevented her from lifting her skinny ass and hugging Sam, who was broken from the grief of the truth. But guilt and affection screamed to spit on her pride and step up.

She didn't have time to finish her thought. Andrew had made up his own mind for the two of them. After scanning the distraught Maria with his gaze, he turned to Sam without a drop of sarcasm:

"I realize this may be a bit of a bad time, but Sam, are you going to take Maria as your wife, or will my grandson be born out of wedlock?"

Chapter 58

The empty apartment greeted Sam with silence, as always. Every day, he found it harder and harder to come back here. There were days when Sam spent the night at work or went straight to the gym on the second floor of the building. Pulled weight until his knees shook and went to bed exhausted.

Rosita tried her best to give Sam a home life and color, but every time, she failed. The man had become a robot. He worked, ate, exercised, slept, and so on.

Sam's not-so-little body had turned into a pile of muscle. He even had to buy new shirts because the old ones did not fit or were simply torn on the shoulders.

The meaning of Sam's life was reduced to one capricious and painfully desirable brat girl.

He texted Maria every day, inquired how she was feeling, and sent flowers, gifts. Ordered the most expensive and healthy sweets when she wanted something special.

He made his peace with Maria blacklisting him a couple of times a week, then deleting him and being the first to write that she was hungry again.

Dr. Perkins ran all the necessary tests and ultrasounds. Prescribed the best vitamins and personally monitored the baby mama's condition. Sam spared no expense, but he demanded more. That's where his dominant side kicked in.

Perkins feared Sam's meticulous nature. She always answered at the first beep and sent all the test results to him and then to Maria.

After Andrew asked about marriage, Maria snapped. She yelled and roared, cursing everyone who got under her arm. Even Lena could not calm her daughter. As it turned out, the woman told her father about her daughter's delicate situation as soon she ended her conversation with Sam. Otherwise, the reason for Sam's call, she could not have explained.

Surprisingly, Andrew took the news of the pregnancy calmly. Only his hands were shaking, but his wife politely poured her husband a hundred grams of sedative.

Maria flatly refused to talk. Her father's words and pressure from Sam led to a terrible hysteria and a sea of tears. The girl threatened to leave if Sam didn't leave the house. Screamed that she hated him and forbade him to see the child. And she cried. She cried nonstop.

Sam took her threats and cries calmly. He shook Andrew's hand, quietly hinting that they would definitely return to the conversation about marriage. The man nodded understandingly and hugged Sam firmly, live Sam's father did.

Three months had passed since that day. Maria refused to see him.

In the first few days, she didn't respond to messages, but eventually, she gave in. It started with a short "OK." Then she answered a question about how she was feeling. The only thing that annoyed Sam was her aloofness and the separation between "Maria" and "the baby."

Her messages always began with "baby is fine," "baby is hungry." She didn't talk about herself, which caused a wave of resentment. Sam hinted to her that he was interested in her too, but the girl immediately shut up and sent Sam to the blacklist.

Sam could spend hours looking at articles about pregnancy. Like any father, he wanted to know the sex of the baby. Unlike others, he wanted a girl. A little princess he would spoil. Even started looking at a house in the suburbs near the O'Dells.

Alas, Sam's fervor faded each time. Maria did not make contact. Lena sighed heavily, not happy with her daughter's state of mind. With each passing day, hope for a reunion vanished.

Sam was in agony, unwilling to accept the fact that they wouldn't be together. But with each passing day, reality painfully confirmed his hunch: Maria didn't want to be with him.

Since Sam no longer went to the BDSM clubs, he spent his weekends at work and at the gym. Barely dragging his feet, Sam made his way to the shower, thinking about his long-awaited sleep.

He liked to sleep. Sometimes, he dreamed of his baby girl, Maria. Tied with silk ribbons to the headboard of the bed, she gladly accepted the blows of the stack. Trembling at the touch of an ice cube to the red stripes on her skin. Begged to be fucked, spreading her legs.

In the morning, from such dreams, Sam had to take long cold showers or simply jerk off like a schoolboy in puberty.

During one of the lonely evenings, Sam's phone started to ring faintly.

Pulling his home pants over his naked body, Sam quickly grabbed his gadget.

"Are you home? We need to talk! I'm downstairs! Why won't your concierge let me through!" There was so much anger in that text.

The next second, the phone rang.

"Mr. Williams, you have a visitor. Claims to be…"

"Let me in!" Maria growled. He had a sudden urge to wring the neck of that smug turkey.

His palms were sweaty. He hadn't been this nervous in a long time.

She's here! She's here.

Quickly throwing on a T-shirt, Sam hurried into the hallway. Somewhere in the living room, Sam stopped abruptly. Reread the message again. She was angry or upset.

Sam's heart twitched painfully. Cold sweat ran down his spine. His first thought was that something had happened to the baby. That was what Sam feared the most.

Perkins assured him the pregnancy was going smoothly, but he couldn't stop worrying. Blamed all the things he did to her in bed and himself for the stress Maria had endured. Their last session.

There was a soft knock on the door. Quickly covering the remaining distance, Sam opened the door with a deep exhale.

He'd wanted to see her for long three months, and now he stood there like a fool, not knowing what to say. The eyes with the color of his favorite whiskey stared back at him with the same apprehension.

Slowly, he glanced down at the painfully familiar face, noting at once, the healthy color and the slightly flushed cheeks.

She looks good, Sam thought with relief.

"Hi," Maria said quietly.

"Hi," Sam frowned.

Chapter 59

He was both pleased and worried by her appearance. It was immediately clear from her appearance that Maria was in a hurry.

Disheveled hair, a wide sweater, and leggings. It was as if she hadn't changed her clothes since they had seen each other the last time. Looking at Maria, Sam didn't immediately notice the small box in her hands.

Without saying a word, Sam let Maria into the apartment. He closed the door and watched her carefully. He could touch the tension emanating from her with his hand. The joy was evaporating by the second. And then there was that strange box in Maria's hands.

"Have a seat," Sam suggested once they were in the living room.

"I don't want to," Maria mumbled.

With all his composure in his fist, Sam tried to ignore her whims. It worked much better on the phone than it did in real life. The desire to dominate hadn't gone away.

"Is something wrong?" Sam asked gently, bowing his head. He tried to look into her eyes, which Maria stubbornly averted.

"Am I interrupting?" Maria snapped at him. "Are you alone? Torn away from the session with a new toy?" She asked him with a sizzling look.

Sam's mouth dropped open in surprise. He didn't know what to do first: reprimand the wretch or laugh. Still mindful of her condition, Sam made a serious expression and dismissed her speculation.

She is pregnant, it's all hormones. He tried to calm down himself.

Maria only hummed and took a seat on the couch. She held the box in her hands as if it were her most precious treasure.

"I'm very glad to see you. And I am alone," Sam said sincerely. "Has something happened?"

"Why does something have to happen for me to come?" Maria replied with frustration.

"No, I am just asking. You haven't visited me too often for the past few months."

Unable to think of a decent answer so as not to upset Maria, Sam shifted his gaze to the box.

"What is it?" Sam asked softly.

With a pale look, Maria was visibly nervous. She was biting her lips and frowning her nose. Sam didn't rush her. Waited for her to answer. He was dying to place Maria on his lap. To hold her. And kiss her pink cheek. But he remained titanically calm.

"Cake."

"Cake?" the man was stunned.

"Yes, cake." she repeated herself.

"Baby girl," Sam said softly, almost purring, "please don't be offended, but it's very hard for me to get one word out of you at a time. Can you explain why you came to me almost at midnight with the cake?"

On the verge of another tantrum, Maria turned away abruptly and covered her mouth with her palm. She was crying again.

The girl herself was tired of crying all the time, but she couldn't stop these impulses. Maria cried when she was happy and when she was sad. When she was angry and when she forgave. In other words, all the time.

"Mom and Dad went to a party, and the courier got mixed up the dates and brought a cake," Maria said, holding back her tears. "I had a blood test, and Perkins said it was already possible to know the sex of the baby. Mom ordered a cake. This one." Maria finished, sobbing and gazed at the box.

Sam didn't get her words right away, but then he remembered watching happy couples cutting cakes and finding out the sex of the baby. Maria's words began to make sense.

"Do you want to find out together?" Sam asked calmly, though he wanted to cheer and shout with joy. His lips trembled treacherously, and Sam tried not to smile.

"The courier messed up. He was supposed to bring it tomorrow morning," Maria repeated hysterically. Tears in thin streaks began to flow down the girl's face.

Sam had no strength left to control himself and play the gentleman. With a slight onslaught, he took the box away, set it back on the table, and pressed the whimpering Maria against his stone chest. Kissing the top of her head and temple, whispering how much he missed her.

"We could wait until tomorrow and find out together," Sam suggested breathlessly when Maria calmed down and sniffled softly in his arms.

"Okay," Maria sniffed her nose amusedly.

A small victory. From the bliss and joy that overflowed, Sam, covering his eyelids, stepped out in relief.

"I am going to go home," Maria hissed.

"Maria, it's late," Sam frowned.

"Don't tell me what to do!" Maria hissed, jumping up from the couch.

This time, Sam had to count to twenty. The man mentally sympathized with Lena and Andrew. They had mentioned that it was hard with Maria, but now he realized that it was just a disaster.

"Baby girl, it's night outside. I won't let you go. It's a 40-minute drive home. Stay with me tonight, and tomorrow, we'll go to your parents' house and find out the sex of the baby."

Maria was tripping on her tippy-toes, trying to decide. She folded her hands behind her back and lowered her head, pondering his words. Sam saw a different implication in that pose. The cock in his pants twitched, reminding him of its existence.

Take it easy. The important thing is to breathe, Sam exhaled heavily, angry with himself.

"Okay, I will stay," Maria agreed.

She looked at Sam furtively, as if he were an enemy, and kept pressing her lips into a thin line, as if she wanted to say something, but stopped herself.

Rosita kept her room clean. All the things Sam had bought before the trip to New York had been left behind. He often went to the dressing room and remembered how chic Maria looked in her clothes.

Maria's aloofness frustrated Sam. He asked a hundred times if she needed anything. He brought a glass of water at room temperature. He made sure that there was food in the refrigerator in case Maria suddenly got hungry and put the cake there.

"Good night," Maria said dryly, hinting that it was time for Sam to leave.

As soon as Sam reluctantly left her room, Maria flopped down on the bed and cried in silence.

Corroborating herself for her impulsive impulse to come. For the hit-and-run, Sam wasn't alone. And that was what she feared most of all.

Maria could not and had no right to order or give ultimatums about his preferences. In truth, the girl herself missed their sessions.

At first, Maria denied her attraction, but over time, she realized there was still a hunger. And only one person could take it away.

During all three months, Maria scrolled over and over again the time spent with Williams. Didn't separate the good from the bad. She just remembered every day, every minute spent together.

One evening, when Mom and Dad went out to dinner, Maria snapped.

Biting her palm like a thief, she slipped her hand under the elastic band of her home shorts and began to touch herself. At first, she slowly drew out patterns, hitting her clit, increasing the speed. Covering her eyelids, she imagined only one man. His hands, his lips, his velvet voice that made her cum.

Since that night, she hadn't been able to stop. Every time she brought herself to orgasm, she felt she hadn't had enough, like a broken clock with one piece missing.

Had she forgiven Sam?

Maria thought about it a lot. But every time he wrote or sent gifts, Maria struck a pose. Anyone else would have hung around her lover's neck by now, but not her. An inner block prevented her. Too strongly lodged resentment.

However, love does not go anywhere. Muted until better times.

Even her father began to side with Sam when he once again pleased his daughter with sweets, flowers, and a basket of various trinkets and goodies.

"Not in words, but indeed," Maria teased her father. The more her family pushed Maria toward Sam, the more she drifted away. It was as if she were being forced again, not asked, though she missed him.

The cake was the last straw. Not only was the girl's interest piqued, but her parents had left for the party. After sitting alone with the box, Maria went to see him. She didn't think. She just did what she wanted.

Suddenly, she was dying to see him. But once again, she ruined it with complaints and tears.

The water treatment brought Maria to her senses. As always, red eyes from tears immediately gave her away. During these three months of pregnancy, Maria had forgotten how to get into character.

All emotions were displayed on her face in a huge ticker. It was annoying. Parents immediately began to annoy her with questions and tried to calm her down. Maria only got even more annoyed by this.

In the closet, there was nothing but a silk red nightie. Her tummy was just beginning to show, so the garment fit her as if she were wearing it. Climbing into bed, Maria looked around once more.

Memories came flooding back about how she had first come in here. How she had stripped and flaunted naked around the house. How she had cried. How Sam had punished her repeatedly right on this bed, how he'd fondled her and had sex with her.

The latter made the girl's cheeks redden. Not just her cheeks, though. A chill ran through her entire body. A warm wave arose in the heart area and traveled along her spine, thickening just below her belly.

"Shit," Maria moaned in a voice of arousal.

It's true what they say: women do inexplicable things when they're pregnant.

Some want shawarma at five in the morning, and some want to have sex. And now Maria quickly threw back the blanket, jumped to her feet, and quickly, before all her courage was gone, headed for the Sam's bedroom.

Chapter 60

The door to Sam's room appeared to be open. Stepping on her toes, Maria carefully peeked inside. What she saw made the heat between her legs increase.

Sam was sprawled out on his huge bed. He had thrown off his shirt and was lying in just his pants. Maria immediately noted the change in him. He had gotten bigger than the last time she saw him naked. His shoulders were even broader, and the reliefs even clearer.

Poor girl almost choked on saliva, studying the naked torso of the father of her future child.

"Maria? Something happened? Do you need food? Water?" Sam looked at the girl with worry.

Jumping up from the bed, he was beside her in two steps. Sam frantically scrutinized her face, wanted to touch her, but stopped. Afraid of scaring her off.

"No."

"Are you hungry? Water? Tea? Can I give you juice?" he kept asking.

"No," the girl laughed. Sam's hyper-parenting was adorable. For a second, Maria was glad that she lived with parents who were more cooperative than he was. "Can I come in?" she asked, needing to tilt her head back to see him.

And there was plenty to see. His eyes, blue as the sky, darkened with lust. Clearing his throat, Sam tried to speak calmly, but the playful cheekbones and the hurricane in his gaze gave him away.

"You want to sleep here?" Sam wheezed.

"Yes," Maria smiled with the corners of her lips.

"Baby girl, I don't mind, it's just..."

"Perkins said it was okay," Maria interrupted him.

It was as if she'd caught the same disease as he had: desire. She was treacherously trembling. She looked away first when Sam raised one eyebrow in incomprehension at her words.

"Sex," she added faintly.

Maria clearly heard Samuel exhale. Loud and labored as if the nose had been removed from his face.

"Are you sure?" Sam squinted his eyes and tilted his head to the side.

"If you want to know, call and find out," Maria shrugged and invited herself in. Without a shadow of embarrassment, the girl climbed onto the bed and covered herself with a blanket.

Stunned by her behavior, Sam grabbed the phone from the bedside table, to which Maria snorted defiantly.

"I'll whip your ass for sure! Later." Sam raged, covering his eyes.

Despite her insolence, Sam's was aroused beyond belief. This was something he'd never expected from Maria. It was as if she'd read his mind. Staring at the ceiling alone, Sam envisioned this night differently.

Dr. Perkins answered on the third dial tone. Sam could immediately hear the displeasure in the woman's voice, but the mention of good compensation cheered her up. Maria had not been deceived. The doctor confirmed every word and, in addition, told him about the most suitable positions.

"Are you convinced?" Maria asked mockingly, which she immediately regretted.

Pushing the phone back on the nightstand, Sam was close too quickly.

Maria did not have time to draw air into her lungs, but the next second, her mouth was captive to his lips. Sam was afraid of himself. He was like an addict getting to that long-awaited dose.

Balancing on the edge of a feral animal and affectionate boy, Sam walked on thin ice. Cradled a trembling Maria, keeping his wits about him. Biting desirous lips, mindful of her hypersensitivity.

Maria willingly responded to his lustful desires. She herself arched like a cat, wrapping her arms around his massive neck. She purred into his mouth.

"Take it off," Sam ordered, breaking the kiss. Sitting back on his heels, he waited for Maria to recover from her mini-marathon.

The dominant in him had awakened again. Seeing his baby girl before him, Sam wanted to seduce her to the point of pain in his fingertips.

Maria stared intently at her dominant. She trembled at his imperious and pressing gaze. Her fingers clutched at the silk sheets.

She did not understand her own condition. She froze at a simple "take it off." She listened to herself. Everything was burning inside. She wanted to spread her legs and invite Sam in.

Then why wasn't she moving?

There was no desire to be outraged; instead, her entire body became one bare wire that shorted out wherever Sam looked.

I want him so bad, the girl admitted to herself.

Resting her head back on the pillows, Maria slowly took hold of the hem of her nightie. She took her time pulling it upward.

The higher the fabric rose, the more clearly Maria understood herself. Her desires. She was not embarrassed to obey Sam. She only now realized that she had missed it. She missed the orders, the ass slaps, his intimidating tone, and most importantly, him.

It was Sam who had shown Maria that the pain and desire can work together. He showed her a new world of pleasure.

Sam couldn't take his gaze off the slightly bulging tummy that was causing delight in his chest. He touched the velvet skin with trembling fingers. Barely touching, traced a circle. He stared mesmerized at the naked Maria. She giggled softly when his hand touched her navel.

"It tickles," Maria explained quickly, seeing Sam's frown.

"Is he in there?"

"Or she," she smiled.

Without changing his expression, Sam leaned down to her tummy. He began to kiss every inch of it slowly. Maria's quiet giggles were quickly replaced by languid sighs and moans.

The frantic pounding of her heart prevented her from thinking straight. Sam gave himself over completely to his emotions. Getting high on his girl's trembling and her moans. He began to slowly lower himself, which caused another muffled moan from Maria's lips.

This was exactly what she had been missing, his tongue. Maria cried, wriggling and bucking. She arched her back, wanting to get to the finale as quickly as possible.

At the moment when the butterflies began to flutter in front of her eyes and in her stomach, Maria moaned, "Permission to cum, Master."

"You may, baby girl," followed immediately.

She had not experienced such a powerful orgasm for a long time. Stars flashed before her eyes, and her body turned to hot wax.

Trying to catch her breath, Maria smiled stupidly. The inner pregnant woman had gotten what she had been dreaming about for three months.

"Maria," Sam called softly, taking the almost asleep girl into his arms. "You didn't have to ask. We're not..." Sam stopped talking abruptly.

"But I wanted to," Maria said seriously and then added with annoyance, "Or don't you want a slave like me?"

Sam had to pull away. He wanted to get a closer look at her face. He didn't want her?

He'd been busting his ass for over three months for her, and that brat dared to say those words. The dominant in the man began to boil with resentment, but Sam was quick to put him down.

"Don't joke around like that."

"I'm not joking," Maria jabbed at his shoulder.

"Fuck, baby girl," Sam growled. He was starting to chicken out again.

Her words went straight to his heart and accelerated the blood in his veins to incredible speeds. "I need you so bad. I was dying to see you all these times," Sam put his hand on her bulging belly. "It was so painful without you. I've been going crazy. I need you. Our baby. And it's not about BDSM. Do you want me to give it up? I love you without all that stuff. I love you, not slave Maria. But the real you. I love you, baby girl."

"You love me?" Maria sobbed. Tears came treacherously as usual. Hormones were doing what they wanted, and Maria couldn't control it.

At this moment, she didn't want to. It was the first time Sam had ever said those words out loud. She guessed it, knew it deep down, but he'd never said "*love*" to her.

"Yes," Sam smiled. Saying words of love felt good. It made him want to say "I love you" every day. Even Maria's tears didn't scare him.

"Honestly?" she childishly asked.

"Honestly," Sam did not stop smiling.

"Sam," Maria called quietly.

"What?"

"You were joking about the BDSM, weren't you? We are not stopping doing that!" Maria said gently, and she heard a quiet laugh.

Epilogue

"Andrew, cut it already," Lena hurried the man.

With shaking hands, O'Dell Sr. cut a piece from the cake completely covered with white mastic.

"Boy!" squealed Maria as soon as her father carelessly cut off a big piece. The blue colored knife almost fell out of his hands.

"Boy," Lena repeated, almost crying, clapping her hands.

"Are you sure you want to be part of our family?" Andrew mockingly addressed Samuel.

The O'Dells did not hide their joy when Maria showed up on the doorstep with Sam. Before that, they were nervous when they did not find their pregnant daughter at home. The worried father immediately realized to call Sam. Everything was quickly resolved, but Maria still got a light pinch on the nose from the Master.

"Absolutely," Samuel replied, smiling.

Such a pun was a novelty for him. The man mentally prepared his mother to meet the O'Dells. After their conversation with Maria, Sam immediately indicated his intentions to get married. Her parents didn't object, but Maria, as usual, stood up.

"I need time to think," the girl frowned her forehead.

"Baby girl," Sam's short glance put everything in its place. Maria squeaked quietly, biting her tongue. Sam had made a joke about BDSM, and Maria knew he would definitely add her statement to the list of punishments.

The tea party turned into an early dinner on the veranda. Maria's mom was so excited, pondering in her voice which room would make the best nursery. Andrew was quietly pouring whiskey for Sam, and Maria was watching this buffoonery with amusement.

"Are you happy?" Maria glowed with happiness.

"Yes," Sam answered thoughtfully.

"Then what's the matter?"

"I'm thinking."

"About what?" Maria kept up.

Leaning close to her ear so that no one in the room could hear their conversation, Sam answered quietly, savoring each word: "I was imagining putting you in chains and whipping you for every tantrum. I'll listen to your sweet cries and enjoy it. Then I'll make you suck my cock naked, with your hands tied and your ass red. And if you have any strength left, I'll fuck you the rest of the night. Oh yes, of course, with an anal plug in your sweet ass."

Maria's ears reddened at the words of her almost-husband. She was wet just by his words. Sam knew the ways .to make his baby girl blush. Her ass was already starting to itch. Biting her lip, Maria looked carefully into Sam's eyes. He wasn't joking, which made the girl shiver even more.

"Honey, are you cold?" Lena asked with worry.

"It's windy," Maria wheezed in a trembling voice.

"Do you regret getting involved with a dominant?" Sam whispered just as quietly into her red ear. The man was having fun watching Maria puffing like a steam engine.

"No," she lifted her chin defiantly. "I am okay with that; it's on your terms. I accepted it."

"On my terms," Sam smiled and hugged his beloved future wife and bratty slave.

Acknowledgment

Wow, we did it! When I started my journey as a writer, I doubted that I would end up here, on the pages of my first published book. I did not know that I had such a wonderful people around me. Big thank you to my family and my husband! He is my number one fan, and I love him so much for all the support and help with our two-year-old daredevil. Thank you to my all my friends, especially to Alla, Anna L., Abigail, and Sharon. You, ladies, are my rock. We had a great time giggling while talking about all kinky stuff. Thank you to my trainer Ayhan for all the crazy ideas I was telling you during every gym session. I made you blush a few times. Thank you to my therapist Olga for pushing me into this journey, I owe you a big one. Jet River, my friend, my fellow author, thank you for your patience and believing in me. Thank you to my friend Pierre for eagerly waiting for a book to be published. Thank you, Amy and Jay, for the great job you did, for all your help and teamwork. We did great!

Thank you to all the readers and people who helped me to make it real!

Coming Fall 2024

Not one but two stories about men that will make your heart beat faster.

David Blackwood and Max Woolf are so different, but they both want something that they can't have.

Forbidden desire

About author

Anastasia Hill is an author with a massive love to morally gray and dark romance. Happy ending is something that you always find in Anastasiia's books (almost always). Her favorite tropes: from enemies to lovers, age gap, BDSM, and a lot of spice. Anastasia lives in Toronto with her husband and their son.

TikTok: @ana.hill.author
Instagram: @ana.hill.author
Website: anastasiahillauthor.com